D0434852

Crazy Dangerous

Also by Andrew Klavan

The Homelanders Series

The Last Thing I Remember

The Long Way Home

The Truth of the Matter

The Final Hour

Crazy Dangerous

Andrew Klavan

THOMAS NELSON
Since 1798

NASHVILLE DALLAS MEXICO CITY RIO DE JANEIRO

Published in Nashville, Tennessee, by Thomas Nelson. Thomas Nelson is a registered trademark of Thomas Nelson, Inc.

Thomas Nelson, Inc., titles may be purchased in bulk for educational, business, fund-raising, or sales promotional use. For information, please e-mail SpecialMarkets@ThomasNelson.com.

Library of Congress Cataloging-in-Publication Data

Klavan, Andrew.
Crazy dangerous / Andrew Klavan.
p. cm.
Summary: Sam Hopkins fights back when he sees bullies harrassing Jennifer, an eccentric schoolmate who, he learns, is having terrifying hallucinations about demons, death, and destruction which may just come true unless Sam can stop them.
ISBN 978-1-59554-793-4 (hardback)
[1. Conduct of life—Fiction. 2. Schizophrenia—Fiction. 3. Mental illness—Fiction. 4. Prophecies—Fiction. 5. Bullies—Fiction.] I. Klavan, Andrew. II. Title.
PZ7.K67823Cr 2012
[Fic]—dc23 2012001221

Printed in the United States of America

12 13 14 15 16 17 QG 6 5 4 3 2

This book is for Ellen Treacy.

You see that dead guy by the side of the road? Yeah, the one lying in a pool of his own blood with his face all messed up and his clothes all torn and dirty. That's me. Sam Hopkins. And okay, I'm not really dead, or at least not completely. I've just been beaten up. A lot. Badly. Which I guess is a little bit better than dead . . . although when I think about how I'm going to have to explain this to my parents—frankly, dead doesn't seem like such a bad alternative.

Anyway, you're probably wondering how I got myself into a situation like this. You probably want to hear about Jennifer and the demons and how I played chicken with a freight train and—oh yeah—the weird murder and how I found out about it—you're definitely going to want to hear all about that.

But first, I have to tell you about the stupidest thing I ever did . . .

PART ONE

DRAGNET

WHISPERS CAME AT HER OUT OF THE DARK.

Death.

We are death.

We are angels of death.

We will destroy them.

We will destroy them all.

The whispers came from every corner. They crawled up the sides of her bed, skittered over her blankets, over her skin. Like cockroaches. First one, then another, then a swarm of them, covering her.

We are angels of evil.

Angels of death.

We will teach them to be afraid.

Jennifer gasped and sat up quickly, staring into the shadows, searching the shadows of her room, her lifelong room, her girl-room, suddenly strange to her now in the dark. So many eyes staring back at her. Stuffed animals—friends all her childhood long—her teddy bear, her crocodile, her baby giraffe. Glass eyes, black glass eyes, staring back. The posters on the wall: her favorite singer, her favorite band. Paper eyes, flat eyes, staring. Her calendar. Disney princesses. Their bright smiles suddenly different, suddenly knowing and mocking and wicked. Eyes staring at her from the shadows.

And the whispers everywhere:

We are angels of evil, angels of death.

We pledge in blood to kill them all.

Who was it? Who was there? Her heart beat hard as she scanned the room, searching. No one. Just her computer, the dull screen, watching her out of the shadows. Her stereo. Stary-oh! Scary-oh! Circular speakers like eyes, staring.

Jennifer grabbed her pillow, held it in her arms for comfort, held it in front of her as if it could protect her.

But the whispers kept coming. They skittered up the wall. Roaches swarming darkly up the wall and over the ceiling where they could drop down on top of her and scramble over her skin, get tangled and crawly in her long brown hair.

They will see our power.

They will be afraid.

Afraid of us.

Because we are angels of death.

Terrified, Jennifer slid quickly off the bed and stood in her pajamas, still clutching her pillow in front of her. Her breath trembled out of her as she turned and searched the shadows. Teddy bear, princesses, scary-stary-oh all watching her.

Yet no one was there. Everything was motionless, still.

We pledge in blood to destroy them . . .

She dropped the pillow. Clapped her hands over her ears. Stop! Stop!

She wanted to cry out. Should she? Should she call for her mother? She so, so wanted to. She could feel the cry wanting to explode inside her. But she didn't. She knew what would happen if she did. If she cried out, her mom would come. Tired. Frowning and narrow-eyed. Needing her sleep so she could go to work in the morning. She would come in and turn on the light . . .

And there would be nothing. Nothing but the stuffed animals and the princesses and the scary-oh, no longer staring, pretending not to stare.

"There's nothing," Mom would say, impatient, annoyed. "It was just a nightmare. Go back to sleep. For heaven's sake, you're sixteen years old!"

That's what would happen. Jennifer knew. It had happened before. Then her mother would turn out the lights again, flicking the switch with an angry snap. Jennifer would hear her heavy, weary, long-suffering footsteps returning down the hall to her room. She would hear her bedroom door close. *Snap.*

And then it would all start again. The whispers. The staring. It would all come back and there'd be no chance of calling for Mom this time. Jennifer would be totally helpless.

She tried to swallow now but couldn't. She was too scared, her throat was too dry. She looked around for an idea, a way out, a way to escape. She saw the door. Ajar. When is a door not a door? When it's a jar—right? She could see the lighter dark of the hallway. Her mom kept the bathroom light on so she could find her way there in the night. The glow bled out into the hall a little, and the lighter dark was a thin line where the edge of the door parted from the jamb.

Oh, I'm in a jam, all right, Jennifer thought frantically. *But at least the door is a jar.*

Mark, she thought.

Her brother, Mark. She could go down the hall. Knock softly on his door so it wouldn't wake her mother. Mark would help her. Mark would protect her. He always protected her. He was strong where she was weak, brave where she was frightened. Mark was her hero—and he was here—oh! When kids made fun of her at school, he stopped them. Whenever anyone picked on her or called her crazy or pushed her or tipped over her lunch tray, Mark grabbed them by the shirtfront, pinned them to the wall, and made them apologize. Whoever was whispering would be afraid of Mark. Whatever was hiding in the room, watching her . . . Mark would make it leave her alone and go away.

She held her breath for courage and darted quickly through the staring, whispering shadows to the partly opened door. She was afraid—so afraid—afraid that any moment some whispering shadow-thing would rush at her out of a corner, would grab her and drag her forever into its world of whispering darkness. But she kept moving, as quickly as she could, toward the thin line of light.

She made it. Opened the door. The moment she stepped into the hall, the whispers ceased. It was quiet. The whole house was suddenly hugely, darkly silent. She could hear the silence of it, settling, ticking, waiting.

She breathed out: Oh.

Her brother's room was down at the end of the hall. Far away, it seemed. His lights were out. His door was shut. He must be sleeping.

But Jennifer started down the hall. Through the dark silence—so silent she could hear the brushing-together of her cotton pajama legs. Stepping slowly down the hall.

But the hall—the hall was different! The hall had changed. She turned her head this way and that. The usual wallpaper was gone. The yellow paisley wallpaper . . . She saw drawings on the walls now. Horrible drawings. Dark, violent, horrible images spray-painted and slashed onto the walls. And the walls themselves were different. Not like they were during the day. The walls were rough, splintery broken. And beneath her feet she felt . . . not the carpet of her own home but packed dirt with pebbles that bit into the flesh of her bare feet . . .

She was halfway to her brother's door, near the stairway—the stare-way—when without warning, they started again:

They will be afraid.

Afraid of us.

Because we are angels of evil.

Jennifer gave a little cry of fright—no, no, no, stop—and stumbled around, turning this way and that trying to find out who—who—who was whispering?

And there! Something! A shadow. Yes. Hunkering, moving. A terrible shadow-thing, with the whispers dancing around it like worshippers at a primitive shrine.

We will kill them all.

Kill them all.

In a sudden moment of courage and determination, Jennifer reached out for the light switch. She would turn on the lights. She would catch it. She would face it. It was a thing of darkness. It couldn't stand the light.

Her fingers felt the wall. Not her wall. Not the wall at home. The rough, splintery wall splashed with hideous drawings and signs.

But there. There it was: the switch. The light switch. She flipped it up.

Light, blessed light, flared through the room. Jennifer braced herself and looked—looked down the hall—her heart beating hard.

No one.

No one was there. Nothing. The hallway was empty. And it was her hallway. The old familiar yellow paisley wallpaper. The carpet. The bathroom door with the light on. Her mother's door. Her brother's.

Her house. Just her ordinary house. Everything the same.

She stood there a long moment as relief started to creep through her. Maybe Mom was right. Maybe it was all a dream.

Then—from directly behind her—from inches behind her—a single voice—deep, gruff, clear, commanding:

Jennifer!

She cried out, spun around, and the thing stood towering above her, eyes red, flaring, fangs bared, dripping, lowering toward her, closer, closer!

Jennifer could not even scream.

Under the Bridge

I was running when the thugs attacked me.

I ran a lot, almost every day after school. It was part of my secret plan to get in shape and try out for the track team. Which was a *secret* plan because I was never much of an athlete, and the track team was the most important team in school, and I didn't want anyone to laugh at me for thinking I could make the grade.

So almost every day, without mentioning it to anyone, I would go home and change into my running clothes. I would ride my bike out of town, then set the bike down among the trees and take off on foot along one of the empty country trails.

This particular day was in early March. I was pounding my way over the McAdams Trail, which goes up a steep hill through the woods and then comes out for a long, steady stretch along a ridge. It's a nice run with a great view of my hometown below. You can see the houses clustered in the light-green valley and the brick towers of the town hall and the column of the Civil War monument and the river sparkling reddish in the afternoon sun. I could even make out the steeple of my dad's church as I ran along above it.

The cold of winter was still holding on. The trees were still bare, their branches stretching naked into the pale-blue sky. But as I ran along, I caught an occasional whiff of spring drifting through the air. The last snow had melted. The ground that had been ice-hard all winter long felt softer now under my sneakers.

Up ahead of me, at the end of the ridge, there was a railroad bridge. Very old, very narrow—just one thin track supported by concrete pylons. The bridge stretched from the crest of the hill, over the river, to the edge of another hill on the far side. Then the train tracks took a long looping curve around the far ridge over the valley before they ran out of sight behind the surrounding hills. It was an old line, but the freights still used it. They'd go whistling past above the town two and three times a day.

Usually, when I reached the cluster of trees just before the bridge, I would turn down and follow the trail along the descending slope of the hill, heading back for home. That was my plan for today. Only I never made it.

I had just come into the trees. I was running along under the lacework of tangled winter branches. I was feeling good, feeling strong, my legs pushing hard, my wind easy. I was enjoying the touch of spring in the air. And I was thinking about getting on the track team. I was thinking: *Hey, I might do this.* Thinking: *I might really be able to do this.*

Then suddenly, I fell. For no reason I could tell at first, I pitched forward, just lost my footing and went flying through the air. I came down hard on the earth. I was going so fast that I knew I couldn't catch myself on my hands—I'd have broken my wrists. Instead, I twisted as I fell and took the worst of the impact on my shoulder. It was a good, solid jar too. I felt it right up through my forehead, a lancing pain. My momentum carried me along the dirt path a few inches, the stones tearing at my clothes.

When I finally came to rest, I lay where I was for a second, dazed. Thinking: *What just happened?*

Then I looked up—and I knew.

Jeff Winger was standing above me. Seventeen, wiry, narrow rat-like face with floppy sandy-brown hair falling down over his pimply forehead. Black hoodie and sweatpants too low on his waist. Quick, darting weasel eyes that seemed to be looking in every direction for trouble. A thug.

And he wasn't alone. Ed Polanski and Harry Macintyre were also there. They were also thugs. Ed P. was a big lumbering thug with short-cropped blond hair and a face like a potato. Harry Mac was a muscular thug with bulging shoulders and a broad chest.

They must've been hanging back in the thick bushes

behind the trees, hidden from my view as I ran past. I figured one of them—Harry Mac, judging by his forward position—had seen me coming and tripped me as I ran along.

Now Jeff Winger looked down on me where I lay. He grinned over at his two friends.

"Somebody fell down," he said.

Ed P. laughed.

Harry Mac said, "Awww. Poor baby."

Painfully, I sat up. I brushed the dirt off my face, also painfully. I spit the grit out from between my teeth. I rolled my shoulder, testing to see if it still worked. It hurt when I moved it, but at least it was operational.

I looked up at the thugs laughing down at me. "That's funny," I said to them. "You're real funny guys."

Now let me get something straight right up front. I am not a tough guy. In fact, I'm not a very good fighter at all. I'm a little under average height and not very big across. I'm not particularly strong, and I never learned to box or anything like that. Every time I'd ever been in a fight, I got beaten up pretty badly. So probably? In a situation like this? I should have tried to be a little bit more polite. It would've been the smart thing to do, if you see what I mean.

But here's the problem: I hate being pushed around. Really. I hate it. Like, a lot. Something happens inside me when someone tries to bully me—when someone shoves me or hits me or anything like that. Everything just goes red inside. I can't think anymore. I go nuts. I can't help it. And I fight back—whether I intend to or not—and even if it means I get my head ripped off. Which, in my limited experience, is exactly what happens.

Now, I could already feel the anger building in me as I climbed to my feet. I dusted myself off. I saw Jeff watching me, still grinning. That made the anger even worse.

"I guess you want to be more careful next time," Jeff said. His thug friends laughed as if this were really hilarious, as if he were a professional comedian or something. "Running around here can be kind of dangerous."

Again, this would have been an excellent time for me to keep my mouth shut. But somehow I just couldn't. "Okay," I said. "You tripped me and I fell. Ho ho ho. That's very funny. If you're, like, seven years old . . ."

Harry Mac didn't appreciate that remark. "Hey!" he said, and he pushed me in the shoulder—hard. I knocked his hand away because—well, just because, that's why. Because I don't like being pushed around. That made Harry Mac even angrier—so angry, he cocked his fist as if he were about to drive it into my face. Which I guess he was.

But to my surprise, Jeff stopped him. He slapped Harry Mac lightly on the shoulder. Harry Mac hesitated. Jeff gave him a negative shake of the head. Harry Mac lowered his fist, backed off me with a look that said: *You got lucky this time.* Which was true.

Jeff looked me over, up and down. "I see you in school, don't I?" he said. "Hopkins, is that it?"

I slowly drew my eyes away from Harry Mac and turned them on Jeff. "That's right. Sam Hopkins," I told him.

Jeff nodded. "And you know who we are, right?"

I nodded back. Everyone in school knew Jeff Winger and his thug buddies.

"Okay, good," Jeff went on in what sounded like a reasonable voice. "Because here's the deal, Sam. This isn't a good place for you, okay? This isn't where you want to do your running anymore."

Some part of my mind was telling me to just keep quiet and nod and smile a lot and get myself out of this. Any one of these guys could've pounded me into the earth. All three of them could pretty much kick me around like a soccer ball at will. But the part of my mind that understood that was somehow not getting through to the part of my mind that

Just.

Didn't.

Like.

Getting.

Pushed.

Around.

So instead of keeping quiet, I said, "What do you mean, it's not a good place? It's a great place. I like running here."

Jeff laughed. It was not a friendly laugh. He took a

casual step toward me—casual, but threatening. He went on smiling and he shook his head as if I had misunderstood him. "No, no, Sam, I don't think so. I don't think you *do* like running here. Not anymore, anyway."

"Oh yeah?" I said—and, okay, it wasn't exactly a brilliant comeback, but it was all I could think of under the circumstances.

And of course Jeff answered, "Yeah. In the future, Sam, I think maybe you ought to run someplace else. Anyplace else. This isn't your place anymore. This is our place. It's our place and we don't want you here."

Through the red haze of my anger, I began to understand what was going on. My eyes moved back over the trees and the bushes around us. It was a dark, lonesome spot up here. You could sit in the underbrush and no one would ever see you or find out what you were up to. So I guess Jeff and his pals were up to stuff they shouldn't have been up to, and they didn't want me or anyone else to see.

"Okay," I said. "Okay, I get it."

"Good," said Jeff.

"Sure. You guys want to be left alone. And that's fine with me. Really. I don't want to bother you. I don't want to bother anyone. I don't care what you're doing here. I don't know what it is and I don't want to know. And I'm sure not gonna report you to anyone or anything. I just want to go for my run, that's all, okay?"

"Sure," said Jeff with another laugh. "Sure, you can go

for your run. You can go for your run anytime you want. Just not here, Sam. This is not your place, I'm telling you. This is our place now."

Just so I'm sure you have the picture here. Them: three big tough guys. Me: one little guy, not tough. Place: middle of nowhere. Raise your hand if you know what the smart thing to do would have been. Right. I should have smiled and said, "Okay, Jeff, sorry to intrude," and shut up and run off on my way just as fast as my legs would carry me.

Instead, I said: "Forget it, Jeff. This is where I run. I like it. I'm not getting chased off. No way."

Jeff gave what sounded like a grunt of surprise. He looked over his shoulder at his buddies. He looked back at me.

Then, so fast I had no time to react, he grabbed hold of the front of my sweatshirt. While he was at it, he grabbed a handful of my chest as well. He dragged me toward him.

"Listen . . . ," he started to say.

I punched him in the face.

I didn't mean to. Okay, I did mean to. Of course I meant to. It's not the sort of thing you do to someone by accident. What I'm trying to say is: I didn't plan it. I just got so angry when he grabbed hold of me that I sort of automatically let fly.

My fist cracked into Jeff's cheek, right under his eye. I didn't connect very hard, but it was hard enough, a good solid, stinging jab. And, of course, Jeff wasn't expecting it—not at all. He was so startled, he actually let go of me and staggered back a step. He grabbed his cheek and just stood there, stunned.

They were *all* stunned. Jeff and Ed P. and Harry Mac. They all just stood there for that long second, staring, as if they couldn't believe what had happened. Which they probably couldn't.

And you know what? I couldn't believe it either. I was stunned too, totally taken by surprise. I just stood there, staring at Jeff and the others.

Then—out of nowhere it seemed—there came a loud, high shriek. It pierced the air, deafening. I didn't know what it was at first, but whatever it was, it sort of jolted me awake. My brain started working again.

And my brain said to me: *Uh, Sam? Run for your life!*

Which is exactly what I did.

A Game of Chicken

Harry Mac made a grab at me, but too late, he missed. I took off along the ridge. Jeff and Ed P. and Harry Mac charged after me. When I looked back, I could tell by the expressions on their faces that they were determined to catch me and take their revenge. They were gaining on me too. Especially Harry Mac. He was a muscleman, like I said, and a lot of times guys like that aren't flexible enough to move well or run fast. But just my luck, Harry Mac was plenty flexible, and it turned out he could run like the wind. He *was* running like the wind, in fact, his thick, powerful legs pistoning under him, driving him after me, leaving his two thug pals behind and quickly closing the gap between us.

Then I heard it again: that high-pitched shriek—the sound that had brought me back to my senses. I glanced across the valley as I ran and I saw what it was. It was the whistle of a freight train. I could see the train winding out from behind the hills, heading for the far end of the railway bridge.

Which gave me an idea. And I think it's safe to say it was the craziest idea I had ever had. It's possible it was the craziest idea *anyone* had ever had. But what can I tell you? I was totally panicked. I knew if Jeff and his pals caught me, they would break me into little bits and then break the bits into even littler bits. I saw only one chance to escape them and, crazy as it was, I took the chance without really thinking.

I ran for the bridge. Moving off the McAdams Trail onto the gravelly dirt along the ridge. Dodging through the sparse and scraggly trees. Running as fast as I could.

I glanced back over my shoulder as I ran. Harry Mac was closing in on me fast. I had to go up a steep little incline to reach the end of the bridge and that slowed me down, and Harry Mac got even closer.

Now I stepped onto the bridge, onto the tracks, and started running over them. The world dropped away on either side of me. Suddenly I was high, high up in the air with no escape route, Jeff and his pals behind me, the train coming up ahead of me, nothing but sky to my left and right. I kept to the center of the tracks, between the rails, between the edges of the bridge. My feet flew over old brown wooden ties that were strung close together with only small strips of grass and gravel between them.

As I ran, I looked up ahead. I could see the train. It sent out another piercing whistle as it steamed along the ridge over the Sawnee, heading for the bridge's far side. My idea was this: If I could run across the bridge fast enough, I would get to the other end before the train reached it. Jeff and his friends wouldn't follow me because they couldn't possibly be ridiculous enough to run across a single-track bridge with a freight train about to cut off their only exit.

You can see what I mean when I say I hadn't quite thought this idea all the way through. For instance, if I thought Jeff and his thug pals were too smart to run across the bridge with the train coming—well, then, shouldn't *I* have been too smart to do it also? Just to save you the trouble of looking up the answer, it's: Yes! Of course yes! What I was doing was absolutely insane! But with everything happening so quickly, and with the whole panic thing going on and my fear of Jeff and Ed P. and Harry Mac, I just wasn't being very smart, that's all.

So I continued running as fast as I could, down the center of the train tracks, over the bridge.

It wasn't easy running over those wooden ties. I had to be careful not to catch my foot in one of the gaps, where I could've twisted or even broken my ankle, running as fast as I was. Also, some of those wooden ties felt kind of soft and rotten under my feet, as if they could break at any time. I didn't know what would happen then. If one of them broke and I plunged through, would I just land on the gravel underneath? Or would I keep on falling down and down into the river below?

Even in my panicked state, it was beginning to occur to me: this was a dumb plan. A really, really dumb plan.

I was about to stop. I was about to turn around and run back. Then, amazingly, I felt fingers snag the collar of my sweatshirt. Startled, I whipped a look over my shoulder.

You gotta be kidding me! I thought.

But no, there was Harry Mac, his face red and twisted with effort, running after me, closing on me, reaching out with one hand to grab hold of my shirt.

He'd followed me out onto the bridge. How crazy could anyone be? Didn't he see there was a train coming? What was he, some kind of idiot?

I faced forward and put on some extra speed, fueled by fear. I felt Harry Mac's fingers lose their hold on my shirt and slip away. I looked ahead and there was the train, snaking around the curve to head for the end of the bridge. Once it got there, there would be no way to get out of its path.

I glanced back one more time. Now, even Harry Mac had figured out this was the craziest thing ever. He had stopped on the bridge. He was standing in the middle of the train tracks, breathless, staring after me, shaking his head.

Just before I faced forward, I saw him turn away. I saw him start jogging back toward where Jeff and Ed P. were standing in safety at the bridge entrance. They had stopped where they were. They had not come after me. They weren't complete idiots after all.

I wish I could say the same about myself. Even then, I might have had time to turn around. I might have headed back toward where Jeff and his thug pals were standing and gotten off the tracks before the train came. Why didn't I do it? What was the worst that could've happened to me? Jeff and his friends would've picked me up by my ankles and driven my head into the ground and left me there buried up to my neck with my feet dangling in the air. That wouldn't have been so bad, really—at least not when you compared it to getting flattened by that oncoming freight.

But I just couldn't think that clearly. All I could think about was getting away from Jeff—and beating that train to the end of the bridge. So I kept running, watching as the train got closer and closer and closer to the other side.

Now I was about two-thirds of the way over. The freight engine was chugging hard across the last stretch of the ridge, winding around the bend toward the bridge entrance. Right at that moment, I liked my chances. I thought I had a good shot of getting all the way across before the train cut me off.

I gave it everything I had, pouring all my strength and effort into my legs. With the fading blue of the afternoon sky all around me, I felt as if I were suspended in midair, running desperately through the middle of nothingness. I caught wild glimpses of the hills up ahead and the town below. But mostly I saw that train. Closer and closer to the bridge. Fully around the bend now so that the front of the engine was pointed straight at me, barreling straight toward me.

The whistle pierced the air again, so loud it hurt my ears. I raced headlong toward the front of the engine. Yes, I truly believed I was going to make the exit before the freight got there and blocked it off.

Then I stepped on a rotten tie, and the wood snapped. My foot went crashing through, my ankle twisting. I stumbled forward, trying to keep on my feet. I couldn't. I fell, putting out my hands to brace myself. My palm smacked the rough wood of the railroad ties, and I felt the burning pain as my skin was pierced by splinters. I screamed and hugged my wounded hand to my chest.

But there was no time to worry about it now. I scrambled to my feet. With horror, I saw that the freight was less than a hundred yards away from the end of the bridge. I cried out and ran straight toward it—there was no other choice. If I turned and tried to run back now, the thing would just plow right over me.

The freight whistle screamed again as if in anguish at what was about to happen. I screamed too, just from the effort of running—and, oh yeah, from terror. The thing was fifty yards away.

I reached the end of the bridge. The freight reached it at the same moment. The front of the locomotive loomed, gigantic and deadly. There were maybe ten yards separating us now.

I hurled myself through that gap.

The scream of the freight whistle filled the air, filled my mind, filled everything, and my own scream filled everything too, as I hit the ground and tumbled over the gravelly slope.

Lying on my back, I looked up and saw the great monster of a train flashing over me, the giant cars flashing and flashing past me, rumbling out onto the bridge, the whole long beast going on and on and on it seemed forever.

I lay on the ground, staring up at the massive, murderous wheels. I was okay. I had played a game of chicken with a freight train and survived.

Pretty stupid, yes?

But it was still not the stupidest thing I ever did.

3

The Red Camaro

It was long, long moments before I could catch my breath, before I could stop shaking, before I could slowly climb to my feet and look around me.

When I did, I gazed back across the bridge. The long freight filled it now end to end. As my eyes rose to the far hill, I expected to see Jeff and his fellow thugs standing there, watching me. Maybe shaking their heads. Maybe muttering, "Curses, foiled again!" Or something like that.

But to my surprise, they weren't there at all! They weren't anywhere in sight. They had vanished. They were totally gone.

I panned my gaze over the ridge, searching for them. Nothing. Not a sign. Just hillside and trees. Just the sky through the lacework of winter branches. Just the freight train now moving off across the hillside, to disappear on the downward slope into the next valley over.

I stared, my mouth open, my breath still coming fast. My mind ratcheted into overdrive, trying to figure it out. Jeff and Ed P. and Harry Mac—they'd been there a moment ago and now they were gone as if they had never existed. As if I'd imagined them or dreamed them. But I knew I hadn't.

And then my mouth clapped shut.

And I thought: *Oh no.*

It wasn't easy to start running again, but I did it. At least it was downhill this time—steeply downhill. I plunged down the slope, taking long strides over the rough ground. My ankle ached. My lungs burned. My hand throbbed with pain because of the splinters still buried in my flesh. I ignored all of it and just ran.

I'll tell you why. There's a road up beyond the McAdams Trail. Right up there beyond the trees and the bushes where Harry Mac had tripped me. It's an old road of broken asphalt and gravel that leads to several other roads, dirt roads, that go into several wilderness areas where there are farms and abandoned farms and campgrounds and other stuff like that.

I felt pretty sure that Jeff and Ed P. and Harry Mac hadn't hiked to the spot where I had found them. They didn't strike me as the healthy, happy hiking types, if you see what I mean. No, they had probably driven up the old broken road and parked nearby and walked into the trees to sit and smoke and drink beer or whatever it was they'd been doing that I wasn't supposed to see. So that meant they probably had a car up there, maybe the hot red Camaro Jeff was always driving to school, the one that had the muffler modified so you could hear it roaring three counties over. And if they had a car up there, well, then they could get in that car and drive it down the hill, couldn't they? Down the hill to the road below. Which was where I had to go now. It was the only way I could get back to my bike from here. In other words, if they got to their car fast enough—if they drove fast enough—they could still catch me on the road.

So I ran down the hill.

It was so steep, I must have stumbled a dozen times on my way. I nearly fell down half a dozen. As I reached the denser trees by the roadside, I had to dodge between their trunks, leap over their roots, and push my way through the underbrush that tore at my sweatclothes and my hands. But I kept on going, fast as I could. And at last I spilled out onto the road at the bottom of the hill: County Road 64.

I had to stop there. I was gasping for breath. I leaned forward, my hands on my knees, trying to recover. I turned my head and looked up the road. It was two narrow lanes of pavement winding through pine trees and out of sight. I turned and looked the other way. It was the same: two narrow lanes, pines on either side. Not a car to be seen. No one coming from either direction.

I knew where I was. About three-quarters of a mile from the edge of town, maybe half a mile from where I'd left my bike. If I could jog it, I ought to be able to get home before dark.

I took a look at my hand. The sight made my heart sink. My palm was red and swollen. There were black marks on it where the splinters from the railroad ties had buried themselves deep. Even worse, there were two or three big old chunks of wood in there, one end protruding out of the flesh, the other visible under the skin. I knew I ought to hurry and get out of there fast, but somehow I just couldn't bring myself to leave those big splinters in there. I grabbed the end of one of them and drew it out, grunting with the pain. I grabbed hold of another, then another. Lines of blood began streaming down over my hand.

By now I'd recovered my breath and was ready to start running again. But before I could, I heard an engine.

There was no mistaking that sound, that aggressive unmuffled roar. That was Jeff's red Camaro, coming after me.

There was nowhere to go, nowhere to hide. I couldn't get back up that hill into the woods. So I just took off, away from the direction of the noise, toward town, toward home.

I ran as fast as I could, but I was flagging now, really low on energy. The engine quickly got louder behind me. I glanced over my shoulder.

Yeah, there it was. A flash of sunlight on its silver fender. Then another flash, and I saw the fire-engine red of its hood.

I tried to put on some speed, but I was practically staggering now. What was the use anyway? Even at my fastest, I couldn't outrun a car. Behind me, the red Camaro gave a guttural roar of acceleration. In another moment, the sound dropped to a guttural hum and the car was right beside me.

I turned to it. Harry Mac's face was grinning at me through the passenger window.

In pure panic I tried to get away, to dash into the woods to escape. It was no good. I got about two steps up the dirt slope and fell—collapsed, really. I slid back down over the bed of fallen pine needles and dropped onto the road's sandy shoulder. I knelt there, panting, exhausted.

The Camaro stopped. The doors opened. Harry Mac and Ed P. got out. One of them grabbed me under one arm, the other grabbed me under the other. They hauled me over to the car. They hurled me into the backseat. They got in, one on either side of me. They shut the doors.

Jeff was at the wheel. He hit the gas. The Camaro roared and took off again. Jeff gave the wheel a hard twist and the car pulled a great big Huey, turning full around. Then it headed back in the direction from which it had come—only with me inside now.

If you have never been in the backseat of a Camaro, let

me tell you: the legroom is nil, zero. I had to bend my legs so much, my knees were practically in my teeth. Also, there are only really two places to sit back there, one on the left and one on the right, and I was sitting in the middle. The lumbering Ed P. was pressed against one shoulder, and the enormous Harry Mac was pressed against the other. There was no room to move, so all I could do was sort of press my arms close to my sides and make myself small. Oh, and by the way? Ed P. and Harry Mac smelled like old socks.

I was nervous. All right, I was scared. I didn't know where we were going or what they would do to me once we got there. Whatever it was, I didn't think it was going to be too good.

I heard Jeff snicker. He looked up at me in the rear-view mirror as he drove along the winding forest road. I could see his weaselly eyes reflected in the narrow strip of glass. "We got you now, don't we?" he said slowly. "We do got you, sure enough."

"You got me, all right," I said. "So what are you gonna do with me?"

"Why do you ask?" said Jeff, and this time, all three of them snickered. "You're not scared, are you?"

"Oh no," I said. "Why would I be scared of a nice bunch of guys like you?"

I could tell by the reflection of Jeff's eyes that he was smiling. "That's funny," he said. "You're funny even now. I like that. You're a tough little punk, aren't you?"

I shook my head. "Not very tough, no."

"Oh yeah, you are. You punch me in the face like that? With three of us standing there? You run across that bridge, right into that train like that? You're a tough little punk, all right, no mistake."

"All right," I said. "I'm a tough little punk." I hate to admit it, but I actually felt a little proud that Jeff had said that.

And he went on too. "Really," he said—kind of earnestly, as if he were trying to convince me of this very important point. "Running into that train? I don't think I ever saw anything like that before. That impressed me. It *really* impressed me."

I shrugged, trying to hide the fact that I appreciated the compliment. "I'm happy I could bring a little entertainment into your shabby life," I told him as sarcastically as I could.

At that, Jeff let out a real laugh, a big laugh. "See, that's what I mean," he said, talking to me through the rearview, glancing back and forth between the rearview and the windshield as he drove. "Saying stuff like that? When we've got you like we do? That's tough. I like that. It impresses me."

I shrugged again. I wondered if Jeff being impressed meant he wasn't going to kill me.

I fell silent for a while and Jeff fell silent too. He drove the growling Camaro along the winding road until we reached a turnoff hidden in the trees. He turned there, and we started heading over broken gravel back up the hill, back to where we'd been before.

I looked out the side window, past the hulking—not to mention smelly—shape of Ed P. Outside, I saw that we were in deserted territory again. Empty, rolling hills. A spreading dark oak tree with a flat, dark lake underneath it. The sky.

Not much to see—and no way to escape. I looked away and tried to forget my fear by picking a few more splinters out of my bleeding hand.

After a while Jeff started talking again. "I'm gonna tell you something," he said. "Normally, if a guy does what you did, if a guy hits me like that, I gotta do something about it, I can't just let something like that go unanswered. You see what I mean?"

I sighed. "Yeah. I see what you mean."

"Normally? A guy does something like that to me, I gotta do something back to him, only a hundred times worse, enough times over to put him in the hospital. You can understand that, right?"

I didn't answer. I felt my stomach drop. Getting put in the hospital didn't sound like a happy end to my day.

"But I don't know," Jeff went on. "What you did. The way you were. The things you say. The way you ran right into that train . . ." He gave a kind of thoughtful sniff as he guided the car around another turn. Now we were bouncing and bounding over a dirt road, past trees, hills, more deserted territory. "I *like* you, Sam," Jeff said then.

I couldn't keep the surprise off my face. Jeff was the kind of guy people feared. The kind of guy people treated politely. It was odd to have him tell me he liked me.

"I'm serious," he said. "You're just the sort of guy I like to have around me. You're the sort of guy I want on my team, if you see what I'm saying. Really, I can use a tough guy like you."

I didn't know how to answer. No one had ever said they wanted me on their team in anything.

The car came to a stop. I tried to look out past Jeff's head, out through the windshield, but I couldn't see much. Then the doors opened and everyone got out. Harry Mac grabbed me by the arm and dragged me out too.

The Camaro was parked in a sandy spot, a sort of driveway. There was an old barn in front of us. Brown, unpainted, the clapboards rotten and splintering. Around us was . . . well, nothing. A hilltop. Trees in the distance. No other building or person in sight. Not even a sheep.

Jeff came around and stood in front of me. I looked up at him—up, because he was taller than me by about a head.

His rat-like face broke into a grin. "I mean it," he said. "I like you, Sam."

Then he punched me in the stomach—hard. Really hard. I gasped and lost my breath and bent over. Then I sank to my knees and gasped some more.

"That was for hitting me," Jeff said, standing over me. "I can't just let that pass. You understand, right?"

"Sure," I managed to gasp after a second. "Sure, what's not to understand?"

Then Jeff reached down and grabbed me by the shirt collar. He hoisted me roughly to my feet. He slapped me twice in the face. It stung like fire and made me so angry I wanted to strangle him. But I managed to control myself because I didn't want to die. Through tear-filled eyes I squinted at his blurred, grinning face.

"Now that we got that out of the way," Jeff said, "I think you and me are gonna be friends. What do you think about that? You want to be friends with me, Sam?"

I gasped a few more times before I got my breath back. Then I thought about it. I thought: *Well, why not? Friends with Jeff Winger. That could actually be kind of interesting.*

So after a second or two, I said, "Okay. Sure."

And *that* was the stupidest thing I ever did.

Preacher's Kid

Here's what you have to understand: I'm a PK, a preacher's kid. My dad, Matthew Hopkins, is the rector of East Valley Church, which is on Washington Street, which is in our town, which is Sawnee, which is a small place of about seven thousand people in upstate New York. And see, when you're sixteen and your dad is a preacher—and you live in a small town so everybody knows who he is and who you are—there's a lot of pressure on you. It's not that anyone expects you to be perfect or anything. You don't have to be brilliant. You don't have to be an athlete. You don't have to get great grades in school. All you have to do is—well, nothing. Or nothing wrong, that is. You can never, ever do anything wrong. Ever. Other kids can get into trouble, get sent to the principal's office, get a little wild sometimes. But not you, not the PK. See, people like to gossip about the preacher. Since he's always reminding them to be moral and good, they get kind of a thrill out of it when they find out his life isn't perfect. And if you—the preacher's kid—get in trouble, everyone will start whispering to one another: *Did you hear about the preacher's kid? Tsk, tsk, tsk, Reverend Matt's boy has really gone off the rails* . . . It makes your father look bad. It makes your mother upset and angry. And it makes you feel like the worst person on earth. Trust me on this.

So, on the one hand, there's all this pressure to be good. But then, on the other hand, you don't want to be *too* good. You don't want to be so good you can't be . . . well, ordinary. One of the guys. You don't want the other kids to feel like they have to fall silent whenever you walk by or stop telling the joke they were telling or say "Excuse me" to you after they curse or something as if you were their maiden aunt and had never heard a bad word before.

It can be a problem. Like, with girls, for instance. I can't help noticing that a lot of the girls in school are very polite to me. I mean, *very* polite. Extra polite. *Too* polite. Like I'm their best friend's little sister or something. Like I'm their mother's good china and they want to be careful not to break me. Now and then, for instance, I'll be looking at a girl . . . Okay, specifically I'll be looking at Zoe Miller. Because I have what is technically called "a major thing" for Zoe Miller. Because Zoe Miller happens to be insanely cute and nice. She's got this short black hair and these big green eyes and this pug nose with freckles on it and this smile that makes you feel like she really means it. And the thing is, when she's with most people, she's really funny too. Not funny like a circus clown or anything, but just kind of good-natured and teasing and easygoing and comical. People are always laughing when she's around. She's fun to be with, that's what I'm trying to say.

So anyway, I'll be looking at Zoe when she's talking to—let's say, for instance—Mark Sales. Mark Sales, the star runner on our track team. Mark Sales, who set a new school record in the 3,000-meter steeplechase of eleven minutes and five seconds. Mark Sales, who's seventeen and nearly six feet tall and whose teeth practically flash and sparkle when he smiles, so that girls wait until he walks by and then clutch their books and look up to heaven with their mouths open as if some sort of miracle has occurred just because he said hello to them. And don't get me wrong: Mark is a great guy, a really nice guy—but somehow that only makes the whole situation worse . . .

So, as I was saying, I'll be looking at Zoe when she's talking to Mark Sales. And Zoe will be all relaxed and easygoing and joking around like she usually is. And Mark and his track-star pals, Nathan Deutsch and Justin Philips, will all be laughing around her with their sparkly teeth. It'll just be cute Zoe and the Big Men on Campus standing around the school hallway having a blast. Right?

Then I walk by.

And I say, "Hey, guys."

And suddenly everyone stops laughing. Everyone kind of clears his or her throat and they all glance at one another. It's as if I'd caught them doing something really embarrassing.

And then Mark says, "Hey, Sam." In this sort of formal way.

And Nathan and Justin mutter, "Hey." Because they're not as good at pretending to be relaxed as Mark is.

And then finally Zoe smiles at me, but it's not her supergreat smile that she gives to everyone else. It's this ever-so-polite smile. And she says, "Oh, hello, Sam. It's nice to see you," in such a polite, formal, inoffensive, and not-joking way that I really would prefer it if she just took out a gun and shot me dead on the spot.

That's what I'm talking about. Being a preacher's kid. It can be a problem.

So you might be wondering: What has this got to do with Jeff Winger? With me saying I would be friends with Jeff Winger?

Well, okay, since you ask, here's the answer: whatever else you could say about him, Jeff Winger was *not* a preacher's kid. Jeff Winger didn't have a father at all as far as anyone could tell, and he only lived with his mother when he could find her. As a result, Jeff didn't have to worry about being a good guy all the time. Good guy? He was a full-blown juvenile delinquent! He had once been arrested for stealing a car. He had once been arrested for driving under the influence—under the influence of what, I'm not entirely sure, but it must've been pretty influential because he piled his cousin's pickup fender-first into a lamppost. What else? Oh yeah, Jeff had been suspended from school twice or maybe three times for various reasons: fighting, smoking, carrying a weapon—a knife, I think it was. And one time he had shown up for first period with his face a mass of purple bruises—the rumor was he had taken part in a knock-down, drag-out brawl at the Shamrock, a nasty bar over in Ondaga, one town over.

So that was Jeff Winger. And again, the big question: Why would I have any reason to want to be friends with a thug like that?

Well, for one thing, I couldn't help noticing that girls didn't fall silent around Jeff. They didn't treat Jeff like their best friend's little sister. Not at all. Girls loved Jeff. Okay, not all girls. Not—just to be completely accurate—any of the girls I was particularly interested in knowing. But still, they were girls, which is no small thing, and they just loved him. No kidding.

One day I remember I was sitting in algebra class. And unfortunately, at Sawnee High School, algebra is taught by Mr. Gray, who is every inch as exciting as his name suggests. You know the sound a lawn mower makes when someone's cutting the grass about halfway down the block? Like: *uuuuuuuuhhhhhhhhh*? That's how Mr. Gray talks.

So anyway, Mr. Gray was droning on in that *uuuuuu-hhhhh* voice about how some imaginary guy named John Smith took a job and received a three percent raise in salary every four years—which, by the way, sounded like a pretty crummy job to me. And the numbers and letters Mr. Gray was scrawling on the whiteboard were beginning to blur in front of my eyes into a single hazy shadow. And after a while I sort of turned and glanced out the window, hoping there might be an alien invasion or nuclear war or *something* distracting out there to keep me awake. And instead, far across the track field, I saw Jeff out by the bleachers with Wendy Inge. And to put it bluntly, Wendy Inge was hanging from his lips like a cigarette.

Now, again, let me emphasize: Wendy Inge is not a girl I really want to know very well. In fact, she's not someone I even want to stand very close to. All I'm saying is: she was a girl and she wasn't being superpolite or formal or saying, "Oh, hello, Jeff," like he was her maiden aunt. Nobody ever mistook Jeff for anybody's maiden aunt.

So sometimes I couldn't help thinking: *Hey, if I could learn to be just a little more like Jeff, then maybe people wouldn't expect me to be so* nice *all the time. Maybe people would feel more relaxed around me. Maybe they could clown around with me like they do with everyone else. Maybe Zoe would laugh with me the way she laughs with Mark Sales.*

And that's why, when Jeff Winger asked me if I wanted to be one of his friends—that's why I said, "Sure. Okay."

Because I was thinking: *Hey, maybe this is my chance. Maybe this is exactly what I need in my life. Maybe I can learn something important from these guys.*

Like I said: stupid. Very.

A Couple of Cars

Here is what happened when we went into the barn—me, I mean, and Jeff and Ed P. and Harry Mac.

Jeff led the way. Ed P. and Harry Mac followed. For another minute or so, I couldn't do much but stand there by the Camaro, gripping my stomach and trying not to throw up. I was in pretty bad shape at this point. My gut hurt from Jeff punching me, my face hurt from Jeff slapping me, my hand hurt from having splinters in it, my shoulder hurt from falling on it when Harry Mac tripped me, and my lungs ached from running so hard. Plus I had a whole bunch of other assorted cuts and bruises to show for my afternoon's adventures.

More than that, my brain was kind of swirling. I knew it was not a good idea to be hanging around with these guys. But for the reasons I've already explained, I was kind

of—I don't know—curious about what was going to happen next. It was interesting. It was exciting. It was just the sort of thing a preacher's kid wouldn't do.

So after another moment of recuperating and catching my breath, I straightened up and followed the three of them over the sandy driveway to the barn.

Jeff was unlocking a padlock that held the barn's big door closed. Then Ed P. took hold of the door and sort of walked it open. Inside, it was dark and shadowy.

"Get her going," said Jeff to Ed P.

Ed P. squatted down just inside the door. I could see him yanking at something—the way you yank on the cord of a lawn mower or a motorboat. After a couple of yanks, I heard a gas engine rumble to life. I guessed what it was: a portable generator. Sure enough, a moment later some lights flickered on inside the barn.

Jeff turned to me and grinned and made a grand gesture, sweeping his hand toward the barn as if to say: *Enter a world of enchantment.*

Which I did.

The first things I noticed inside the barn—the first things anyone would have noticed—were two cars. Very, very nice cars. Luxury cars, like something some of the richer people in town might have driven. One was a great big black Audi, brand-new. The other was smaller, a cool, sleek silver Mercedes, also new. The barn was lit by these hooded lamps held up on tall silver poles, and the bulbs were directed at the cars so that the cars were sort of spotlighted as if they were on display.

"Whoa!" I said. I moved around the two cars, staring at them. I don't mind saying I was impressed. My dad drives a Volkswagen Passat. It's about five years old and kind of rattles when it gets up past fifty miles an hour. My mom drives a clunky minivan that I think dates back to cowboy-and-Indian days. I have a learner's permit and I get to drive the Passat sometimes, but mostly I still get around on a bike. Staring at the Audi and the Mercedes in the barn, I was mesmerized. I forgot all my aches and pains as I imagined what it would be like to sit behind the wheel of one of these babies, to drive one of them through town with everybody standing back to admire me.

The rest of the barn was mostly clutter and dust. A hard-packed earth floor. Tangled extension cords. There was also a small sitting area in one shadowy corner. There were a bunch of old office chairs there—swivel chairs with torn upholstery—plus an old sofa that looked like someone had rescued it from a garbage dump. There was a small cooler too, a big white Styrofoam box with a blue Styrofoam lid on it.

Jeff plunked down on one of the chairs. He sprawled in it like a drunken king on his throne. He swiveled back and forth. Finally, he leaned back and pried the top off the cooler so that it slipped over and stood slanted, leaning against the cooler's side. He reached into the box and pulled out a can of beer. He tossed it to me—so quick, I caught it kind of automatically. I held on to it for a second and then tossed it away again to Harry Mac.

Jeff laughed at me. "You're not gonna tell me you don't drink, are you?"

"No," I said. "I'm gonna let you guess."

Everyone stopped moving. Harry Mac and Ed P. looked at Jeff to see if he was going to get angry at me for being a wise guy. But after a second, Jeff laughed.

"S'what I'm talking about," he said to Harry Mac, pointing at me. "He's a tough little punk. I like that."

Now that they knew what they were supposed to think, Harry Mac and Ed P. nodded in appreciation of my tough little punkitude. Jeff tossed Ed P. a can of beer and took one for himself. The barn popped and hissed as they tore open their tabs.

"So," said Jeff, kicking back in his chair. "What do you think, punk?" He was indicating the cars now. "They're nice, aren't they?"

I looked the two cars over some more. I nodded. "They're nice, all right," I said.

"Which one you like best?" Jeff asked me.

I moved around in front of them, examined their fenders.

"I guess if I had to choose one, I'd take the Audi," I said. "It has this feeling about it like . . ." I couldn't think of the right word.

"Money," Jeff said, nodding at it. "It feels like money. It's a money car."

I nodded too. He was right. That's what it was. It was the sort of big limo-like car people drove when they had a lot of money.

"Get in," said Jeff.

I looked at him, uncertain, excited. Did he mean it?

He lifted his chin at the car. "Go ahead. Get in the car. See what it feels like."

I shrugged. *Why not?* I thought. I went over to the Audi and tugged on the handle. The door didn't open.

I glanced over at Jeff.

"It's locked," I said.

"Is it?" said Jeff—though I was pretty sure he already knew it was. He gestured at Harry Mac with his beer can. "Sam says the car is locked, Harry."

"Oh yeah?" Harry Mac answered dully. Harry said everything dully. He had the kind of voice where, the minute you heard it, you knew he had the same insight and intelligence and sensitivity as a clump of dirt. "That's too bad."

"Well, don't just stand there, man," Jeff Winger said to him. "Teach our new friend Sam how you get into a car when it's locked."

Harry Mac slowly understood and slowly smiled. He walked over to the Audi—no, he *swaggered* over to the Audi—swaggered like he felt like a big man because Jeff had given him this important task. He was wearing a black hoodie. He reached inside its pocket and pulled out a tool: something sort of like a Leatherman, one of those tools with multiple blades and extensions. He held it up to me.

"Know what we call this?" he said.

I shook my head.

"We call it Buster," said Harry Mac. "Know why?"

I shook my head again.

"Because it busts into things. Watch."

I watched. Harry Mac unfolded a long thin blade from the Buster. He worked it smoothly through the edge of the Audi's window. A moment later, the door clicked open.

"Cool, huh?" said Jeff from his chair.

I nodded. Because I had to admit: it was pretty cool. It was just the kind of thing I wanted to see. The kind of not-too-good thing a preacher's kid never does see.

"Now watch this," said Harry Mac.

I leaned in at the door and watched as Harry Mac lay down on the front seat and reached under the steering wheel. Using another of Buster's extensions, he worked behind the dashboard panel for a moment. Then suddenly, with a thrilling roar, the Audi's engine started.

Harry Mac sat up and held up the Buster for me to examine. "Easy-peasy, right?" he said.

Jeff laughed with delight. "You should see the look on your face, punk." Then he gestured with the beer can at Harry. "Shut it off," he said.

Harry Mac used the Buster to turn the engine off. He got out and shut the car door. It let out a tone as it locked.

"Now you do it," said Jeff.

Startled, I turned to him. "Me?" I said.

"Sure. Show him how to pop the door, Harry."

It didn't take long. In just a few minutes, Harry taught me how to use the Buster's blade to unlock the Audi. I got in the car and sat behind the wheel. Oh, man, it was nice! A nice feeling. Soft, soft leather seats. This great, fresh, sweet smell like it was brand-new, straight from the factory. And with the built-in GPS monitor and the elaborate radio and temperature controls, the dashboard looked like something you'd see in the cockpit of a jet.

I ran my fingers over the smooth surface of the steering wheel. It was easy to imagine sailing down the highway in this beauty. Not likely to happen in real life. When I got my driver's license, I'd be lucky if I would occasionally get to borrow the Passat like my older brother sometimes did. Pretty doubtful I would ever get to drive something like this.

"Now show him how to start it," said Jeff.

Harry Mac showed me how to use the Buster again. When I made the Audi roar to life on my own, I laughed out loud. It was an incredibly exciting feeling to have that big machine smoothly humming around me. It made me feel powerful, like now I could get into any car I wanted anytime.

Jeff got out of his chair. He carried his beer over to the open door of the car. He looked in at me with his weaselly eyes. He pointed his chin at the Buster I was still holding in one hand.

"There's a lot more that thing can do, punk. Wanna see?"

I looked up at him. The car hummed around me. Everything felt exciting, dangerous, different from anything I'd done before.

I thought to myself: *Hey, what's the harm? It's not like I'm stealing anything. The cars are already here.*

"Sure," I said out loud. "Show me."

6

My Life as a Thug

I went back to the barn the next day. And the day after that. And the day after. I stopped running. I stopped training for track. I biked up the hill to the barn and hung out with Jeff and Harry Mac and Ed P. instead.

They taught me how to break into different kinds of cars and how to start them all without a key. They taught me how to disable a steering-wheel lock so I could drive the cars once I started them. They even let me drive the Audi a couple of times—just around the driveway and a few hundred yards along the empty dirt road. Still, it was cool. It was a lot of fun.

They showed me other stuff too. How to pick different dead bolts and padlocks and knob locks. They even showed me a way to disable a computerized keypad if it was the right kind. All of this using that little Buster device with the various tools inside it.

How did it feel to be doing stuff like this? It was exciting. It made me feel like I wasn't such an innocent and goody-goody preacher's kid anymore. When I went to school during the day and Jeff said hi to me in the hall or Harry Mac nodded at me or Ed P. slapped hands with me as he went by, I thought I saw the other kids look at me differently. I felt I was into something they couldn't get into, that I knew something now they didn't know. Something secret. Something dangerous. Something forbidden.

And I told myself: *Hey, it's just fooling around. It's not like I'm really breaking into anybody's car. It's not like I'm really stealing anything. I'm not really doing anything wrong at all.*

But yeah, I knew that wasn't true. I knew the cars in that barn didn't belong to Jeff. I knew the stuff that Jeff and his friends were doing was wrong—not to mention illegal. I knew I shouldn't be hanging out with a thug like him. And I knew that every day I did hang out with him made it harder for me to tell him I was going to stop.

But I knew I had to stop. Jeff kept telling me that I was almost ready to go on a "job." And I had a pretty good idea what a job was. And I knew once I went out with Jeff and his crew, once I really did steal something, it was going to be even harder for me to make things right.

Now during this time, I didn't talk to my parents very

much. In fact, I kind of avoided them. Which was easier than you might think. See, my family lived in the East Valley Church rectory, which was sort of diagonally behind the church, on Maple Street. It was a big, rambling house with a lot of different doors—so many doors that I could always come in and get to my room without anyone seeing me. Plus my parents—and my older brother—were always kind of busy—usually too busy to notice whether I was around or not.

My brother, John, for instance, was usually busy working out which college he was going to go to. I knew this because whenever I knocked on his door, he would shout out, "Leave me alone. I'm working out which college I'm going to go to." This was a hard choice because practically every college in America wanted him. John was always hardworking, always had his face in books or was practicing his soccer skills or whatever. But now I barely ever saw the guy anymore.

My mom was busy with—well, like, a million different mom-type things. If being a preacher's kid was tough, I guess being a preacher's wife was no picnic either. She called herself the church's unpaid music director, plus she ran a bunch of committees and charities and was always going off somewhere in dirty jeans and a sweatshirt to rebuild a house or paint a children's center or serve meals to the homeless or something. Plus she served meals to the *homed* too—meaning us—and kept the house nice and did the laundry and stuff like that. So yeah, she was busy.

And my dad, of course, was busy with all the stuff he did, like meeting with church people and visiting sick people and burying dead people and marrying people in love and writing sermons and studying to write sermons and giving sermons and other stuff like that.

And listen, my dad and mom and brother were all nice people—they really were. Just busy, that's all. Which, as I've said, made it easy for me to come home at the end of the day and go to my room and do my homework and whatnot without talking to anyone at all.

Finally one evening, the last evening before all the trouble started, I was hanging out in the barn with Jeff and the guys. Jeff was sitting in his swivel-chair throne, kind of kicked back with a beer in his hand. Ed P. was lying across the front seat of one of the cars, with his legs hanging out the door. He was doing something with the dashboard radio, I'm not sure what. Anyway, it wasn't the same car as before. It was a big blue BMW. The Audi was gone, I don't know where.

Harry Mac was lying stretched out on the sofa, reading *Sports Illustrated.*

And I was sitting in one of the swivel chairs, examining one of these Buster things, pulling the different blades and tools out, looking them over, pushing them back in.

All of a sudden Jeff said, "You can keep that one if you want."

Startled, I looked up at him. "What?"

"Sure. The Buster. Keep it. It's yours."

"Oh no, I don't wanna . . ."

"Keep it. I'm telling you," said Jeff. "It's a present. You can't insult me by turning it down."

I opened my mouth again, but nothing came out. I didn't want to insult him, after all.

"Anyway," Jeff said. "You're gonna need it. For a job. Soon."

I felt my mouth go dry. I felt my throat get tight. I licked my lips, trying to think of something to say. But I couldn't think of anything.

Slowly—almost as if my hand were working on its own—I slipped the Buster into my pocket.

That night, after dinner, I went upstairs to my room. I was feeling bad—really bad. Scared about what was going to happen. I wanted to get out of this. It had gone too far. I wanted to tell Jeff that I wasn't going to come to the barn anymore. But I knew in my heart that I wasn't going to tell him. I was afraid to tell him. I was afraid he would beat me up. I was afraid he wouldn't like me anymore. I was afraid I wouldn't feel cool anymore when I went to school and would go back to just being a PK.

I sat at my computer and I noticed Joe Feller was online. Joe's a big, shambling, friendly guy, kind of like a Saint Bernard dog in human form. We've known each other since we were little. His parents used to go to our church, and Joe and I used to hang together after Sunday school. About a year ago, Joe's dad got a job in Albany and they moved away. But Joe and I still chat online all the time. We've sort of developed this code, which is partly the usual chat abbreviations like LOL and IMHO and so on, but is also partly stuff we made up ourselves over time and just got used to using. So if I wrote our chat down word for word, it would pretty much look like alphabet soup to anyone who didn't know us. So I'll save you the trouble of translating and translate it for you myself.

It went like this:

ME: Are you there?
JOE: Always at the keyboard.
ME: Got a problem.
JOE: You fascinate me strangely.
ME: Did something dumb.
JOE: Tell all.
ME: Been hanging out with Jeff Winger.
JOE: ?????
ME: I know. And Ed P. and Harry Mac.
JOE: That IS dumb.
ME: I know.
JOE: That is dragnet.
ME: I know, I know.

(*Dragnet* is an old, old police television show that Joe likes because he thinks it's so old-fashioned and funny. The theme song goes, "Dum-de-dum-dum." So "dragnet" is Joe's way of saying something is really, really, really dumb.)

JOE: What do you do? With Jeff?
ME: Nothing. They show me stuff.
JOE: ?
ME: How to break into cars. Pick locks.
JOE: Cool!
ME: !!!
JOE: But dragnet.
ME: Right.
JOE: You should stop.
ME: Thank you, Yoda. Your wisdom astounds me.
JOE: But if you stop, they will kill you.
ME: Bingo.
JOE: Also, you will no longer be cool.

I knew Joe would understand. Like I said, we've known each other a long time.

ME: What do you think?
JOE: It's bad.
ME: I know.
JOE: Really bad.
ME: I know.

JOE: Dragnet.

ME: I KNOW!

JOE: You don't have to shout.

There was a long pause here. I stared at the monitor. As I've said, there was nothing much there but a bunch of letters: YHAP Rly? SA WDID . . . and so on. But I saw the whole conversation in my mind just as if it were all spelled out. It was not a pleasant sight.

The pause went on a long while—and then I saw something that made my heart grow heavy in my chest. In fact, it made my heart sink like a rock, *bang*, straight down to the bottom of my feet.

Three numbers appeared on the screen: 911.

I groaned out loud.

Nine-one-one was part of our personal code: it meant that a situation was so bad—that things had gotten so far out of hand—that there was no possible way out except to come clean and tell your parents about it.

And my heart sank when I saw that because I knew Joe was right. And telling my parents about hanging out with Jeff Winger was not going to be a good time.

ME: It'd have to be my dad.

JOE: Right.

ME: It will be bad.

JOE: Major bad.

ME: He will really give it to me. He will give me The Look.

Once again, there was a pause before Joe answered. Then . . .

JOE: Eat The Look. 911.

I stared at the screen for a long time, but finally I nodded. I signed off. I got up, carrying my heavy heart with me. My heavy heart and I shuffled to the door.

I stepped out into the hall—and was startled to see my dad standing right there in front of me.

My dad is tall, thin, long-faced, and bald. I remember when I was a little kid, it was always easy to draw him. I just made a very, very long stick figure with a long bald head. Oh, and round glasses. He wears round glasses too.

I stepped out into the hall and there he was towering above me—his back, anyway, because he was just passing by my room on his way to the stairs.

"Hey, Dad," I said.

He turned around as if he was as surprised to see me as I was to see him. He blinked behind his round glasses as if I had woken him from a dream.

"Hey, Sam," he said.

I knew right away that something was wrong. Usually my dad has a sort of serious-but-happy expression on his face. I know that sounds like it doesn't make much sense, but it does when you see it. I mean, my dad's not the kind of guy who always walks around with a great big grin or who's always making loud jokes and guffawing (like Joe Feller's dad, who's a salesman). He's more the type who's always thinking about something, so he looks serious, but he seems to like thinking about it, so he looks happy too.

But right now, he did not look happy. Not at all. In fact, even through the light glinting on his round glasses, I could see there was an expression of pain in his eyes.

"You got a minute?" I asked him.

He blinked again. He looked like he had to think very hard to come up with the answer. Then he said, "I was just heading out. There's an emergency over at the Bolings' house. Is it something urgent or can it wait?"

I hesitated. I knew what "an emergency at the Bolings'" meant. Mr. Boling was a close friend of my dad's—maybe his best friend. They had known each other since college, when Dad was a student and Mr. Boling was one of his professors. Mr. Boling had taught my dad a lot and even helped him decide that he wanted to become a preacher. Later, when Mr. Boling retired from the college, he had helped Dad get the job at East Valley Church here in Sawnee. I guess you might say Mr. Boling was Dad's mentor. He was a lot older than my dad, obviously. And now he had gotten sick. Really sick. As in: things did not look good. I knew my dad wanted to be with his friend in case this was the last time he'd get to see him.

So I sort of put on a relaxed voice and said, "Oh no, it's not urgent. Go on over to the Bolings'. We can talk later. I hope things turn out all right."

My dad smiled sort of sadly. "I'll see you later, Sam," he said.

He turned and went down the stairs.

I stood alone in the hallway and sighed. I guess I was a little relieved I didn't have to tell my dad about Jeff Winger, but mostly I was disappointed because I'd already worked up the courage to tell him and I knew I really needed his advice. I didn't think my mom would be as helpful. It's not that my mom isn't smart or anything, it's just that she tends to give advice that would be good if you were going to take it, but you're just not going to. I mean, she'll say stuff like, "Report him to your teacher," or "Just explain to him that it's not right for him to take your lunch money." That sort of thing. My dad's advice is more practical is what I'm saying.

So I stood there and I heard the front door close downstairs as my dad went out to see his friend. And then I sort of put my hands in my pockets, wondering what I should do. Then, without really deciding, I kind of wandered down the hall to my dad's study.

I'm not sure why I did that exactly. I just felt like it. It made me feel better to be in his study somehow.

The lights were off in there except for the small

reading light on his desk. He was always forgetting to turn that off when he went out. The light shone down brightly on the Kindle he'd been reading from and then sent a sort of faint glow out over the rest of the room. The rest of the room was mostly books, shelves of books on every wall except one wall that had windows overlooking the backyard. There were also a couple of chairs for people to sit in when they came to visit and talk.

The desk was big—a big old wooden thing that nearly stretched from one wall to another. I walked around it and plunked down in my dad's chair. The chair was big too—a big leather swivel chair with a high back. My mom had gotten it for Dad for Christmas a few years back. It was soft and comfortable.

I sat in the chair and swiveled back and forth. I had my right hand in my pocket. It was wrapped around the Buster. I rubbed its cool metal in my fingers. I was thinking: *What do I do, what do I do, what do I do?* Over and over again like that. Not a prayer exactly—I was too ashamed to pray. It was more like a chant in my mind. But I guess it was kind of a prayer too, since I was secretly hoping God would take pity on me and send an answer—fast.

As I swiveled and thought, my eyes went over the desk, the computer, the letter opener, the penholder, the Kindle under the reading lamp. Then I sort of swiveled around and looked over the books on the shelves, which were sort of sunk back in the shadows.

There was other stuff on the shelves too. Photographs of Mom and my brother and me. There was a drawing I'd done when I was, like, I don't know, five or something: a crayon drawing of a rocket ship. I don't know why Dad framed that and kept it, but he did. There was a drawing by my brother, John, too. And there was other stuff: tokens and souvenirs that people had given Dad or that he'd brought back from some trip or something. An old coin mounted on a block of wood. A carved cross from a church in Africa. Some of this stuff was hard to make out in the shadows, but I'd seen it so many times, I already knew what it was.

But then I saw something I didn't recognize, something I hadn't seen before. Maybe it was new, or maybe I just hadn't noticed it. It was a small statue of an angel. Even in the shadows I could tell what it was because its wings were spread. It was lifting a sword too, so I guessed it was the archangel Michael. He's the head of God's armies and does battle with Satan in the Bible, so they pretty much always show him with a sword.

Like I said, I'd never noticed the statue before, so I got up out of the chair and walked over for a better look. It was just a small statue, not much bigger than my hand. I picked it up and took a closer look at it. It was Michael, all right, with his angel sword raised up. And at the base of it, there were some words engraved:

RECTE AGE NIL TIME

The words gave me a strange feeling. I thought they were probably Latin, but I didn't know how to read Latin and had no idea what they meant. All the same, I got this weird notion in my head that the words were directed especially at me. Maybe I just needed advice so badly I was ready to find it anywhere, but still, I had this powerful feeling that the angel statue was answering that chant of mine: *What do I do, what do I do?* It came to me that if I could find out the meaning of those words, I would know.

I set the statuette down on the shelf and left the room. Headed back down the hall to my room.

My room is not at all like my dad's. It's a lot messier, for one thing. And there aren't as many books. Mostly the walls are decorated with posters, which are mostly from my favorite video games. Like one has "The Evolution of Mario," showing how Mario went from being all pixilated in the old days to being three-dimensional now. Then there's Batman from the *Arkham Asylum* game and the Prince of Persia and so on. Then there's my bed and stuff. And then there's my computer, which is a MacBook, on a big table that is cluttered with all my books and papers from school.

So I sat down at the computer. I called up Google and typed in the words I'd seen on the angel statue: *Recte Age Nil Time*.

The translation appeared on the monitor at once. I leaned back in my chair and took a deep breath.

Because now I didn't *think* those words were the answer to my prayer. I *knew* they were. I knew they were the advice I'd been looking for.

I guess in a funny way it was those words that started all the trouble. It was those words that changed everything.

The translation on the screen was:

DO RIGHT. FEAR NOTHING.

Someone in the Woods

Do right. Fear nothing.

Good advice. And I won't pretend I didn't know what the right thing to do was. Sure I did. It was the "fear nothing" part I was having a hard time with. How are you supposed to fear nothing? I mean, if you're afraid, how are you supposed to turn it off?

After school that day, I rode my bike up the long road toward the barn. My stomach felt hollow and cold like an empty canyon with a wind blowing through it. That was the fear, I guess. I was afraid of what would happen if I told Jeff I wasn't coming anymore—and I was afraid of what would happen if I didn't.

It was still afternoon. There was plenty of light, but the light was starting to get that kind of rich color it gets as the day shades toward evening. The road was rugged and broken. My tires bumped over the ruts and pebbles, and I had to work hard to keep the handlebars steady. I wove between deep holes in the macadam to keep the wheels on the smoother surfaces. It took a lot of concentration. I couldn't really pay much attention to the scenery around me.

The scenery was just trees mostly anyway, a sparse forest on either side of the pavement. When I did get the chance to glance up, I saw the light from the sinking sun pouring through the winter branches in beams. The woods were still and silent. The only sound anywhere was the rattle and bump of my bike going up the hill.

Then suddenly, there was a *snap*—a loud, startling crack.

Without thinking, I looked up toward the sound. The second I did, my front tire hit a rut. The handlebars twisted in my hands. I had to brake hard to keep from losing control. The bike stopped, my feet going down to the pavement to hold it steady.

I sat there, staring into the woods, staring at the place where the sound—that loud crack—had come from.

I had seen something—something moving there. Just before I stopped the bike, I'd seen a figure—a person—darting behind a tree. That sound I'd heard—it was the sound a branch makes when it's lying on the ground and someone—or something—steps on it.

My heart started beating hard. My eyes moved slowly over the trees.

Someone was out there. Someone was in the woods.

It was an eerie feeling, sitting there on my bike, alone on the road in the afternoon with nothing but trees on either side of me, knowing someone was there, hiding, watching me. I didn't like it.

My first thought was to start pedaling again and get out of there, get up to the barn. But I hesitated. I didn't like the idea of running away either—especially when something I couldn't see might be chasing after me. No, I thought it would be better to find out what was there.

So I shouted, "Hello?"

There was no answer. Silence from the woods. A big silence that seemed to fill up everything.

I was about to call out again when a movement caught my eye. A head peeked out from behind a tree.

I let out a sigh of relief. It was a girl. I recognized her right away. Her name was Jennifer Sales.

You remember Mark Sales, the track star, right? The handsome one Zoe Miller was always talking to. Well, Jennifer Sales was Mark's younger sister. His *weird* younger sister, to be more precise. *Weird* was definitely the best word to describe her.

She was a hunched, shy, quiet girl, a small girl, small and thin. My age, sixteen. She had long, straight brown hair that framed a pale, serious face. She was actually kind of pretty in a shy, bookish way. But she always seemed to be off in her own world, living inside her own head. She kept to herself at school and moved along the hallway close to the walls as if she were someone's shadow. When you did try to talk to her, a lot of times she'd say stuff that was . . . well, *weird*, like I say. Like she would rhyme words or string words together that didn't make much sense. She did it as if it were a joke—she'd say it was a joke if anyone noticed it—and she'd laugh as if she thought it was really funny. But sometimes I got the feeling she couldn't help doing it, that the words just came out of her before she could stop them.

A few kids had made fun of her once or twice, calling her names or laughing at her. But Mark set them straight and it didn't happen again. Mark was a good guy, but he was a big guy too, and you didn't want to get on the wrong side of him. He loved his sister. He said she was just different, that's all, like maybe she was a poet or something. Anyway, most of the kids in school were decent types and tried to be nice to her when they could. In the end, though, she just seemed to want to be left alone, and a lot of times she was.

Jennifer stared out at me from around the tree with big eyes—as if she were afraid of me, as if I might be a monster or something. Now that I knew who it was, I didn't want to annoy her or anything, but I was a little worried about her. I mean, what was she doing out in the middle of nowhere like this, out in the middle of the woods with no one else around? If it had been anyone else, it probably wouldn't have bothered me, but this being Jennifer—I don't know, I thought she might be lost or something.

So I called out to her. “Hey, Jennifer. How’s it going?”

The minute I said her name, she seemed to relax a little. She kind of edged out from behind the tree—although she still stood close to it as if she might need to duck back behind it at any second.

She lifted her hand in a shy greeting. “Hey,” she said.

“You all right?” I asked her.

She nodded. “Sure.”

I looked around me. There was no one else in sight. “Are you all alone up here?”

She nodded. “I’m just walking. And talking,” she added—mostly, I think, because it rhymed.

I didn’t have much else to say to her, and I thought of just saying good-bye and taking off again. But still, something about this just didn’t seem right somehow. It was a long way back to town on foot. I’d hate it if I left her alone up here and something bad happened to her.

“Are you all right?” I asked again. “Are you lost or something? Do you need me to walk you back to town?”

“No.” She pointed behind her into the woods. “I have my bike. My bicycle. My-cycle. So I can go around and around. And down. Down the hill. Home.”

You see what I mean about the way she talked. It was really strange. “Okay,” I said. But I still felt bad just leaving her here. “You’re sure you’ll be all right?”

Up till this point, Jennifer had remained standing next to the tree, one hand resting on it as if she wanted to make sure it wouldn't run away from her. She was wearing jeans and a pullover shirt with big horizontal green stripes on it. It was still pretty chilly, especially around this time of day, so she also had on a blue woolen jacket, although she kept it unbuttoned. The sun was behind her, the beams falling all around her. She stood in a little pool of shadow, a dark figure. It was hard to make out the expression on her face.

But now she stepped away from the tree. I heard the leaves crunch under her shoes as she walked slowly toward me. She stepped out into the road and kept coming, slowly, step-by-step as I sat on my bike watching her. She walked right up to me. She stood close. Really close. So close I could actually feel her breath on my face.

She leaned toward me, staring at me, studying me. I just sat there on the bike. I didn't know what to do or say. I let her look as much as she wanted.

"Sam," she said finally. It was as if she'd just figured out who I was. "You're Sam Hopkins."

"Sure, Jennifer," I said. "You know me. You're in my English class."

"I know you," she echoed. "I put you in my cell phone." She took her phone out of her pocket and held it up—still staring at me. "I put everyone in school in my cell phone."

"Well . . . great," I said. I didn't know what else to say.

She put the phone away again. "Your father's a priest," she said then.

"Well, we don't call them priests, we . . ."

"A priest is a father," she said. "Your father's a Father. Father Father. Farther and farther. My father's farther and farther away."

She murmured all this in a low, quick voice, and all the while she went on staring at me. It was really spooky. Then she smiled. And you know what? That was even spookier. It was a sort of small, secret smile. Her eyes glittered, as if she was about to share something with me, something very special that she'd never told anyone else.

"You know what I'm doing here?" she said.

I sat there on my bike, staring back at her. I was kind of hypnotized by her, by the way she was staring at me like that, and by her secret smile and glittering eyes. I slowly shook my head. "No," I said. "What are you doing here?"

She leaned even closer, edged even a little closer to me. And she whispered, "I'm looking for the devil."

I felt a chill go through me and I shivered. It was a strange thing to say, and the way she said it made it sound even stranger. Up there alone in the middle of nowhere surrounded by woods, just me and her, it was actually kind of frightening.

My lips parted as I tried to think of an answer.

But before I could, something even more frightening happened.

I heard an engine roar and turned to see Jeff Winger's red Camaro racing toward us.

8

A Revelation

I knew right away this was a bad situation. Jeff and his friends were bullies, and Jennifer was a natural victim if ever there was one. She was small, weak, odd, confused, and all alone out here in the middle of nowhere. The minute Jeff set eyes on her there was going to be trouble. I was sure of it.

I watched the chrome of the Camaro's fender plowing up the hill toward us. Then I looked back at Jennifer. She hadn't even turned at the sound of the car. She was still staring at me, still studying me, as if she expected to find something surprising hidden in my face.

I had this instinct to tell her to run away while there was still time—before the car reached us. But I didn't. I should have.

The Camaro roared right toward us—so fast that I edged my bike out of the way to make sure I wouldn't get flattened. But just before the car reached me, it stopped. The doors came open immediately. Jeff and Ed P. and Harry Mac got out and walked over to us.

Only then did Jennifer turn to look at them. It was as if she had just noticed they'd arrived. I heard her take a little frightened breath. I saw her eyes go wide. She was afraid. I didn't blame her. So was I.

I tried to talk in a normal, relaxed tone of voice. "Hey, guys," I said. "You heading up to the barn?" I guess I was hoping that if I pretended everything was all right, then somehow everything would be all right.

But Jeff didn't even answer me. He didn't even look at me. He walked up and stood in front of us with his friends flanking him, Ed P. behind his left shoulder, Harry Mac behind his right. He looked at Jennifer. He grinned his weaselly grin.

Jennifer quailed, afraid. She sort of pulled her arms close to herself as if she wanted to shrink away to nothing.

Jeff kept looking down at her, but he spoke to me. He said, "Hey, punk, who's your friend?"

I had to lick my lips before I could answer. They were very dry. "You know Jennifer," I said. "She's Mark Sales's sister."

Jeff gave a harsh bark of a laugh, right into Jennifer's frightened face. "Yeah, I know Mark Sales's sister, all right," he said in a sneering tone. Then he said to her, "You're the bug-head, aren't you? Huh? Your brother's smart. He's a little too smart, in fact. But you—there's something wrong with you, isn't there? You're a little bit . . ." He turned his finger in a circular motion around his temple to indicate "crazy." "You got bugs in the brain, haven't you?"

I saw Jennifer's eyes change. She might be weird, but she wasn't stupid. She knew when she was being insulted. Her pale face went even paler, her expression blank with hurt and fear.

"Bugs can be in a computer. A brain's like a computer," Jennifer said.

Jeff laughed at that as if she had told a joke. And of course Ed P. and Harry Mac laughed along.

"Bugs in a computer . . . ," Jeff said.

"Hey, look . . . ," I started to say, hoping to distract him.

But Jeff just ignored me. He went on talking to Jennifer. "The stuff you say, bug-girl," he said. "Where do you come up with that crazy stuff?"

"I buy it at the crazy store," she answered him. Her tone was defiant, but her eyes were flicking around this way and that as if she was looking for a way to escape. Her lips were trembling in fear.

For a second I saw a flash of anger in Jeff's eyes. He didn't like her smart-aleck answer. But a second later he laughed again and his pals laughed. "The crazy store," Jeff said. "I'll bet. I'll bet that's exactly right."

"Hey, Jennifer," I said. Quickly I climbed off my bike

and laid it down on the road. I stepped toward Jennifer, trying to maneuver myself between her and Jeff. "Maybe you ought to go home now," I told her. "You know what I'm . . ."

Jeff put his hand on my shoulder and moved me aside—not hard or anything—just sort of gently pushing me out of his way. He stepped even closer to Jennifer. There was no way for me to get between them now.

"Oh, she doesn't want to leave," he said, not looking at me, only looking down at her. "The fun's just getting started. Isn't it, buggy?"

"Listen, Jeff," I said desperately. "You know Mark doesn't like it when anyone . . ."

He turned swiftly, like a snake turning. The words died in my throat. "You think I care what Mark doesn't like?" he said.

"No, I . . ."

"You think I'm scared of Mark? I'm sick of Mark. Mark's pushed me just as far as I'm gonna go."

"I'm just saying . . . Look," I pleaded. "You know, she's . . . It's not right."

Jeff looked at me a long moment. It wasn't a nice look. I thought he might be about to knock me around again. But instead he smiled that smile. "It's not right? It's not *right*? What's that supposed to mean?"

"Well, you know . . ."

"No, I don't. Why don't you explain it to me, punk?"

"I mean, well, Jennifer, she's . . . You know. You shouldn't . . . She's . . ."

"O-o-oh," said Jeff, turning his smile back to Jennifer again. "I see what you mean. You mean *she's* not right. She's crazy, isn't she? She's got bugs in her brain. Don't you, bug-girl?"

And now Jeff made this crazy noise, this sort of high-pitched warbling sound—you know, to indicate that Jennifer was nuts: a way of making fun of her. Ed P. and Harry Mac laughed loudly. And Jeff kind of illustrated the crazy noise with his hands—waggling his fingers in Jennifer's face. Jennifer just sort of stared at the fingers as if she was mesmerized by them.

"Crazy, crazy, crazy," Jeff said.

And I said, "Hey, Jeff, listen . . ."

Then—very suddenly, very fast—Jeff slapped her.

It happened before I could do anything, before I could even think. Jeff was doing that thing with his hands, waggling his fingers in Jennifer's face, and she was staring at his fingers, and then the next second he kind of rolled his hands over and over, the way a boxer does when he's punching a bag. He rolled his hands over and hit Jennifer in the face with them four times really quickly, *whack-whack-whack-whack*, too fast for her to block them or get away.

Jennifer stumbled back from the blows and covered herself, cowering in pain, trembling in terror.

Ed P. and Harry Mac laughed and laughed, and Jeff

laughed and called at her, "How was that, bug-head? That was pretty funny, huh? Was that crazy enough for you? Why don't you take *that* to the crazy store?"

Have you ever had a revelation? You know, like, one minute you don't understand something and the next minute you do. Like maybe you're playing a video game and you can't figure out how you're supposed to climb up on this ledge that's out of reach and then all of a sudden the answer's obvious; it just comes to you as if from out of nowhere.

Well, that's what happened to me then. When Jeff slapped Jennifer, I had a revelation.

My revelation went like this: *Do right. Fear nothing.*

Before, when I was riding my bike up the hill, worrying about what I was going to tell Jeff, that idea had seemed complicated. Difficult. Even impossible. How could you just stop being afraid? How could you just do what was right when the consequences might be really painful?

Now, all of a sudden, in a bright brain flash, it came to me.

I thought: *Oh wait, I get it! Do right. Fear nothing. It's as simple as that!*

Jeff and Harry Mac and Ed P. were still laughing, and Jeff was making noises again as Jennifer cringed in front of him, her face red from his slaps and stained with tears. I could see that Jeff was getting all excited by his own cruelty, that he was planning to hurt her again, to hurt her more.

"Hey, Jeff!" I said.

He turned to me, grinning. "What do you want, punk?" he said.

I thought: *Do right. Fear nothing.*

And I slugged him.

Hey, under the circumstances it was the only thing I could think of. And sure, I knew what was going to happen to me next. But I wasn't afraid because . . . Well, because I understood the words on the angel statue. Do right. Fear nothing. It was just that easy.

Anyway, I slugged Jeff in the face, and it was a good one too—a good, solid punch, not like before when we were up on the ridge. This one came up from my knee with my whole body turning into it. My knuckles smacked hard into Jeff's cheek and sent him stumbling backward, his arms pin-wheeling, until he tripped and sat down hard on the ground.

"Run, Jennifer!" I shouted. "Run now!"

But she didn't—not at first. At first she just backed slowly away, gaping at me in wild-eyed terror.

"Run!" I shouted again.

"I don't want to leave-you-believe-you!" she cried out wildly.

"Believe me, leave me!" I shouted back. If I was going to get beaten up, I didn't want it to be for nothing.

Before I could say anything else, Harry Mac grabbed hold of me from behind, wrapping his powerful arms around me in a bear hug. Without thinking, I forced my elbow back into his belly. His belly felt like it was made of steel, but I guess I hit him in a good spot because the blow made him grunt and his grip on me loosened. With the strength of crazy panic, I yanked myself free of him.

"Run, Jennifer!" I shouted one more time.

Finally—finally!—Jennifer ran; at least she tried to. But just as she started to turn away, Ed P. went after her. You wouldn't have thought the lumbering thug could move so fast, but his arm snapped out like a whip and his big hand wrapped around her elbow.

I leapt onto his back. I put a stranglehold on him with one arm while I pummeled him with my free fist.

He lost his grip on Jennifer and she tore off into the woods. I caught a final glimpse of her, dodging through the trees at full speed, her coat spreading out around her like wings, her brown hair flying out behind her.

I was still clinging to Ed P. and he was reeling around, trying to throw me off. And now Jeff was on his feet and he and Harry Mac came at me at once. Jeff grabbed me from one side and Harry Mac grabbed me from the other. They pulled me off Ed P.'s back, and as I fell away, Ed P. took a blind, furious swing with his fist that caught me like a hammer blow on the side of the head.

I saw lights flash in front of my eyes. My knees went weak. Jeff and Harry Mac hurled me down hard onto the broken road.

The impact of the fall knocked the wind out of me. For a moment all I could do was lie there on my back, dazed. I saw the three thugs standing over me, looking down at me. Blood was pouring out of Jeff's nose from where I'd decked him. He wiped the thick stream away with his sweatshirt sleeve.

Then he grinned down at me, his teeth bloodstained. "Oh," he said. "Oh, punk. You are really going to get it now."

So that's how I ended up just about dead, lying in a pool of blood by the side of the road.

But that's only the beginning of the story.

PART TWO

THE THING IN THE COFFIN

JENNIFER HID IN HER ROOM, BUT SHE KNEW THEY WERE out there. The demon things, the shadow things. She could sense them, feel them, gathering on the other side of her closed door. She could hear them whispering, plotting together. She could feel them secretly changing the house so that no one could see the change but her.

She lay on her bed, on her side, clutching her pillow over her head so she wouldn't hear them. But she heard them anyway. Their whispers reached for her under the pillow like a skeleton's fingers . . .

Come out, Jennifer.

Come out, come out.

Come out and see.

The whispers crept over her, crawled over her like bugs, skittering into her ears like bugs, into her brain like bugs.

Come and see.

That's what the Winger creature had said. There were bugs in her brain, like bugs in a computer, whisper bugs sent by the devil because the devil wasn't on the level.

Come and see, Jennifer.

Don't try to hide.

You can't hide from us.

The bug-whispers crawled into her brain and took hold of her like skeleton fingers and the finger-whispers pulled at her—they pulled and pulled at her mind.

Come out, Jennifer.

Come out, come out, wherever you are.

Come and see how we changed everything.

You're the only one who can see it, Jennifer.

Come and see.

Under the pillow, Jennifer shook her head no no no. But she knew she couldn't resist for long. She had to get up. She had to go. She had to see.

Don't try to hide, Jennifer.

You can't hide.

We see you.

We know where you are.

She cried out and threw the pillow aside harshly, thinking, *All right already! All right!* She sat up angrily on the edge of the bed. *All right!*

She heard the whispers of the shadow-things grow gleeful and excited. There were more of them now and they were more powerful. She didn't want to start moving across the room but she couldn't help it, and as she moved, the shadows whispered gleefully:

Here she comes.

She's coming.

The bug-head.

She has bugs in her brain like bugs in a computer.

Even as she shook her head no no no, she did what they told her to do, what they made her do. She moved to the bedroom door, her eyes darting here and there as she did. She saw the Disney princesses staring at her from the calendar and the singers staring at her from their posters and her stuffed crocodile and her baby giraffe and her teddy bear—all of them staring and staring at her with their black, black eyes. They were supposed to be her friends. They had always been her friends. But they had all changed now and become stary-scary like the stary-scary-stereo. She was all alone with the shadow things. She had no friends now.

Yes, I do, she thought defiantly. *Sam.*

Yes. The name soothed her, like a magical charm.

Sam Hopkins.

Sam was her friend. Sam didn't stare. He wasn't a bear. He didn't care when her mind made her say the strange rhymey things. Magic Sam Hopkins. He hoppity-hopkined to help her like a magic Sam-kangaroo when Jeff Winger winged down on her like a Jeff-hawk and slapped her face mean mean mean.

She was at the door now. The whispers grew stronger, louder, more insistent. Jennifer put her hands over her ears to block them out, but the whispers battered at her, threatening to break through, to crowd into her brain . . .

Trying to fight them, she thought: *Sam Hopkins. Sam Hopkins. Sam Hopkins.* Thinking the friend-name three times to ignite its magic power. It worked—a little. When she slowly drew her hands from her ears, the whispers had faded.

Friend, friend, friend, she thought.

But even Sam's magic name was not strong enough to keep the whispers at bay for long. They had pulled back only to gather strength. Then they swarmed at her again, overwhelming her.

Come and see.

Come and see how we changed everything.

Now she knew there was no fighting the compulsion. The propulsion of the compulsion. She had to go. She had to see. She had to see what they had done to the house.

"Oh, Sam," she whimpered.

Why didn't he punch them like he punched the mean Winger boy?

But there were too many. They were too strong. Even magic Sam couldn't help her here.

Jennifer knew what she had to do. She drew a deep breath for strength. She reached out with a trembling hand and pulled the bedroom door open wide.

At once, the whispers stopped altogether. There was silence.

And Jennifer stopped. And she stared.

"Oh!" The sound came out of her on a long breath.

It was true. They *had* changed everything. With their skeleton fingers. They had stripped away the yellow paisley of the hallway wallpaper, leaving only the rough, splintery, unpainted wood beneath. They had scrawled their obscene whispers on the splintery wintery walls in blood-red paint, and they had slashed and splashed and dashed their weird symbols and their hateful, violent scenes everywhere around her.

"Sam-Hopkins-Sam-Hopkins-Sam-Hopkins," Jennifer whispered frantically very fast because she was so-scared-so-scared-so-scared.

She thought of running for Mark. Her brother. Her hero. Oh hear-oh Mark!

But no. She couldn't get to the end of the hall where Mark was. A tree blocked the way, a tree spreading its broad branches from the hallway wall to the landing banister and beyond, spreading its branches over a flat dark lake. The flat dark lake was wide and black and deep and threatening. That blocked her way as well.

And then there was the coffin.

The coffin sat right in the middle of the hall. Right there in front of her. There was no lid on it. It was open.

Jennifer didn't like the coffin. It scared her more than anything. She didn't want to go near it. She didn't want to look down into it and see what was inside.

But she had to. The whispers wouldn't let her alone. The whispers crawled into her brain like bugs and took hold of her with their skeleton fingers, drawing her on against her own will.

"Sam Hopkins . . ."

Even the magic friend-name couldn't make it stop. She had to go. She had to see. Step-by-step-by-step. Down the hall to where the coffin stood. Until she was standing over it, looking down. Down and down into the dark of the coffin, the dark that went down and down.

And then she saw. She didn't want to, but she did.

The thing inside the box had once been human, but it wasn't human now. It was dead and rotten now, a skeleton crawling with whisper bugs.

We are death, the bugs whispered out of the skeleton's mouth.

We are angels of death.

We will destroy them.

Destroy them all.

Jennifer stared down at it, whispering back, "Sam Hopkins," over and over as fast as she could.

But the magic friend-name wasn't powerful enough. The demon things kept whispering out of the dead creature in the coffin:

They will see our power.

They will be afraid.

Afraid of us.

Because we are evil.

Because we are death.

Jennifer stared down at the horrible thing while the whispers rose up to her. She wanted to run away, run away, run back to her room, but she couldn't. She couldn't move from the spot. And then . . .

Oh, then . . . then the thing in the coffin came to life!

It sat up suddenly and reached for her.

Jennifer started screaming—screaming and screaming. She couldn't stop. Even when the bedroom doors burst open, when her mother and brother came rushing out of their rooms . . . even as they put their arms around her, calling out to her, calling her name over and over, she couldn't stop. She went on and on.

The whisper-things were gone. The wallpaper was back on the walls. The coffin was gone and so was the thing in the coffin.

The house was back to normal.

But Jennifer could not stop screaming.

Going Home

I won't give you a blow-by-blow description of how Jeff and Ed P. and Harry Mac beat me up. Anyway, to be honest, it would be more like a blow-*after*-blow description because the three thugs pretty much just punched and kicked me, blow after blow, for what felt like forever. If I got an answering punch in there anywhere, I don't remember it. Mostly, I just tried to cover myself, rolling up in a ball, throwing my arms over my head, shielding what I could as best I could.

It was bad. It was really bad. But it could've been a lot worse. No, really, it could've been. For one thing, the thugs didn't play nice with one another. They didn't take turns. I know that sounds like a joke, but it actually helped me. If they'd taken turns beating on me, they would have each gotten in some solid blows. But acting together the way they did, they kept getting in one another's way. They bumped into one another and tripped over one another and sort of blocked one another without meaning to. It saved me from some of the real damage they could have inflicted if they'd come at me one at a time. Basically, if they'd been more polite, they would've been better thugs . . . But then, if they'd been more polite, they wouldn't have been thugs at all, would they?

So that was one thing that helped me. And another thing was the pickup truck. That road we were on—there was nothing up that way but some old farms, and most of those were abandoned—there was almost never any traffic passing by, especially during the week. Most days, Jeff and his pals would have been free to knock me around for as long as they wanted.

But today—what do you know?—a truck came. A battered old green Ford pickup. Looked like it was about a hundred years old. Came slowly, slowly, slowly up the hill from town, heading home to some farm or other, I guess.

I don't know how long the thugs had been working me over by then. I could hear their labored breaths above me, so I could tell they'd been at it for some time and were getting tired.

After a while the blows stopped altogether. I peeked up through my arms to see what had happened. I saw Jeff and Ed P. and Harry Mac puffing away, gazing off down the road. They looked concerned. I peeked down the road myself. That's when I saw the old green pickup trundling toward us from a distance.

There was a long pause. Then:

"What do you think?" said Harry Mac, breathing hard. I could hear by the tone of his voice that he was worried. Obviously, if you're going to beat a guy up, you don't want any witnesses.

Jeff took a moment before he answered. "Aw . . . ," he said reluctantly. "I guess that's enough. We don't need any trouble."

I saw him look down at me. He was already getting a black eye from where I'd punched him, and there were still bloodstains on his chin and his teeth. I could see the anger flashing in his eyes. He would have liked to go on punching me awhile longer.

"You ever tell anyone what you saw with us, this is gonna be like nothing," he said. He spat. "I thought you were gonna be one of us, punk, but I guess you don't have what it takes."

He was right about that, I have to admit. I knew that now. I didn't have what it took to be like him. And I was right in the middle of thinking, *Thank you, God*, for that, when Jeff gave me one last kick in the stomach. Then he and the others swaggered off to the waiting Camaro.

I lay there at the edge of the road, curled up on my side, clutching my stomach. Blood dripped out of my nose and down from a cut in my head. I saw the red drops falling onto the gray pavement and gathering there in a little pool.

I heard the Camaro's engine roar to life. For a second or two I was afraid that Jeff was going to drive the car right over me—just his little way of saying, "So long, and thanks for the memories." But no, I heard the tires screech, and when I dared to look, I saw the Camaro tearing away down the road, sending up a cloud of dust behind it.

I groaned. Then I groaned some more. I uncurled my body and lay flat on my back, trying to breathe. I stared up at the blue sky. I thought about my parents. I thought about how I was going to explain what had happened. I almost wished Jeff had finished the job. Almost.

My plan just then was to go on lying there for—I don't know—maybe a week or two—at least until the pain stopped, if it ever did. But I knew that the green pickup was still crawling up the road toward me. I thought if the driver saw me lying there, he might call an ambulance or something. I didn't want an ambulance. I didn't want to go to the hospital. I just wanted to go home. I just wanted to climb into bed and ache and bleed.

So—after throwing in a few more groans for good measure—I started moving again, rolling over, pushing up off the ground, trying to get to my feet.

I had just made it when the pickup finally pulled alongside me and stopped. The farmer behind the wheel looked to be as old as the truck, which, like I said, looked to be about a hundred. Peering out of his round, wrinkled face, his dark, sparkling eyes went up and down me. He had his tongue in his grizzled cheek as if he thought I was playing some kind of joke, standing there bleeding like that.

"Well," he said, "I'd hate to see what the other guy looks like."

I would've laughed, but it hurt too much. "The other three guys," I told him. "And don't worry: they look just fine."

The old man gave a hoarse chuckle. "I bet they do. What about you? Need a lift to the hospital?"

"No, thanks. I got my bike. I just wanna go home."

Looking out the truck's window, the old man chewed on his lip thoughtfully for a moment. "You're sure, now?" he said. "You're sure this isn't a police matter?"

Rubbing a point on my side where Harry Mac had gotten in one of his better kicks, I shook my head. "No. No police. I threw the first punch."

This time the old farmer didn't just chuckle, he laughed out loud. "Did you, now? Against three fellas? Well, you're a scrappy little guy, aren't you?"

"Oh yeah," I said with a painful sigh. "I'm definitely scrappy. I'm just not very smart, that's all."

He laughed again. "Well . . . I'm guessing you're a bit smarter now than you were half an hour ago."

I smiled as much as I could. "That's for sure."

"You take care of yourself, son. And while you're resting up, you might want to think about choosing your friends more carefully."

"Yes, sir."

He waved. Then, when he put the green pickup into gear, it gave a loud grinding sound that nearly drowned out his voice.

"Do right. Fear nothing," I thought I heard him say.

"What?"

But by then he was already driving away as slowly as he'd come.

I shook my head. I probably just imagined he said that. I hobbled over to my bike, picked it up off the road, and began the long trek home.

No way I could ride at first. My body was just too stiff and sore. I walked the bike down the hill. The sun sank lower and lower behind the trees. The daylight turned golden, then gray. After a while I'd stretched my muscles out enough. With a mighty effort I managed to get my leg over the bicycle seat. Then, gritting my teeth against the pain, I started to pedal.

The evening came on. I switched on my bike lights and coasted through the gathering darkness. I was glad no one passing by could see me now, could see the blood and bruises and dirt all over me.

And yet, you know, aside from that, and aside from the pain and all, it was a funny thing . . . I didn't really feel too bad. I felt . . . well . . . kind of good, in fact. Not good as in, "Man oh man, nothing makes for a happy day like having three thugs kick the living daylights out of you." But good in a different way. Good because . . . well, because Jennifer got away without being hurt. There was no question in my mind that Jeff was planning to hurt her—really hurt her. But she'd gotten away because of me. And now, too, I didn't have to go to the barn anymore. I could just go back to being my normal self, a preacher's kid like I was before. Only before, it had seemed like a problem. Now it sounded like the best life a dude could ever have.

So I was feeling pretty decent as I pedaled home through the cool evening—until, that is, I got near home and started to think about my parents again.

There wasn't any chance of hiding this from them. I might sneak inside and make it up to my room before anyone saw me. I might take a shower, change my clothes, clean up a little before coming down to dinner. But I was going to be wearing these cuts and bruises for a long time, and Mom and Dad were going to see them eventually. I hated to think what their reaction would be when they did.

Let me make a long story short. Their reaction wasn't good. It wasn't good at all. I don't like to describe my mom as being "hysterical," but hey, when you hit on the right word, you might as well use it. I didn't try to hide myself. I walked right into the kitchen where she was making dinner, and . . . Well, I don't remember everything she said, but I think it involved my being grounded for the rest of my life while the United States military was called in to unleash a massive air strike against Jeff Winger's house. Okay, maybe

I'm exaggerating, but that's what it sounded like at the time. Fortunately for me—and for Jeff and maybe for the United States military—my dad heard the commotion, came down from his study, and quickly took control of the situation.

Sitting in front of my dad's desk and telling him the truth about what I'd been doing for the last couple of weeks will probably win the award for "Worst Half Hour of My Life." Really, it made me wish I was back out on the road with Jeff and his crew using me for a punching bag. It wasn't that he yelled and screamed or anything like that. In fact, he didn't say a word. He sat quietly and let me tell the whole story without a single interruption. He didn't even *look* angry. He just sort of nodded every now and then as if he understood exactly what I was talking about. Which somehow made the whole experience even worse.

Finally, I got through it. It was a relief to stop talking. I sat there in the visitor's chair while my dad sat in the high-backed leather swivel chair. I looked at my dad and my dad looked at me and I wished God would just hit me with a lightning bolt and get the whole ordeal over with.

After a while my dad took off his glasses and massaged his eyes with his fingers. For the first time I noticed that he wasn't really looking too good. I knew he was worrying about his sick friend, Mr. Boling, and I guess he wasn't sleeping very well. His face looked kind of gray and old with dark rings under the eyes. Adding to his troubles made me feel about as small as it's possible to be without disappearing.

"I don't suppose . . . ," he said slowly. "I don't suppose you could have found some other way of dealing with Jeff— some other way besides punching him in the face, I mean."

I shook my head. This was the one thing I was sure of. After all, I knew when I swung on Jeff that I was going to be the one who got beaten up in the end. I wouldn't have done it if there had been any choice at all. "He was gonna hurt her, Dad," I said. "I could see it. He'd already slapped her for no reason, and he was gonna keep hurting her until he *really* hurt her. I could see it in his eyes."

Dad nodded. "Okay. I figured that. I figured by the time you got to that point you had no choice. But of course, *before* that happened, you had a lot of choices, didn't you?"

I sighed. "I know." I had to pause there for a minute. I'm sixteen. Too old to cry. But I sure felt like it. "I have no excuse. I pulled a dragnet."

"A dragnet?"

"Dumb de dumb dumb."

He gave a pale smile. "Ah."

"I was gonna talk to you about it," I said. "Remember? When I bumped into you out in the hall that time? But you've been so worried about Mr. Boling, I just didn't want to give you any more trouble than you already had."

"Oh, well, thanks a lot," he said drily. "That worked out well."

"Right. Sorry." I was about to tell him the whole story about how I'd come into his study, how I'd seen the statue of the archangel Michael on his shelf and read the Latin inscription and so on. But somehow it didn't seem important just then. It seemed beside the point.

"All right." My dad put his glasses back on. He leaned toward me, his elbows on the desk. "You did the wrong thing hanging around with Jeff and his crew. They have nothing to offer you. You know that now, right?"

"Oh yeah, definitely. I know it."

"So you ended up in a bad situation—which could've been a lot worse."

"Yeah."

"So"—he gestured at me, grimy and bloody as I was—"it looks like you got your punishment already. And it sounds like you learned what you needed to learn."

"Yes, sir."

"So all in all, I'm inclined to go easy on you. But you better hear me, son. If anything else comes of this, like Jeff comes looking for revenge or something or even threatens you—or anything at all—and you don't tell me about it right away, that's it, I'm going Old Testament on you, you hear what I'm saying?"

I swallowed. "Yes, sir." Dad had gone Old Testament only a couple of times I could remember, but it was not pretty business.

"But for now . . . ," he said.

Dad couldn't let me off scot-free because it would've driven my mom up the wall, but he did go pretty easy, all things considered. Grounded a couple of weekend evenings. Some heavy lifting, cleaning up the garage. Like the beating itself, it could've been a lot worse.

When Dad was done with me, I took a shower. Then I went to my room. I chatted with Joe online and told him what happened.

ME: I got beat up.

JOE: Yeah, I know. I saw the video.

ME: The video???

JOE: From Ed P's phone. He posted it on Facebook with the whole story.

ME: O no. The whole school will know about it by tomorrow.

JOE: By tonight. Now.

ME: Great.

JOE: Well, look at it this way: you may have been beaten up but at least you know it was your own stupid fault.

ME: Yeah. That makes me feel a lot better.

After a while I couldn't type anymore. I updated my Facebook status to "beaten up." Then, groaning, I lay down on the bed.

My mind was racing. I kept thinking over all the things

that had happened over the last couple of weeks. How Harry Mac had tripped me during my run, how I'd played chicken with the freight train, how I'd joined Jeff and his little crew in the barn. As I was thinking about it, I looked over and saw the Buster that Jeff had given me lying on my bedside table. I'd left it there when I'd emptied my pockets before taking a shower. I picked it up. Held it in front of me. My mind kept racing over the things that had happened.

I remembered Jennifer telling me, *"I'm looking for the devil."*

What did she mean by that—or was it just one of those crazy things she was always saying?

I remembered Jeff telling me, *"Mark's pushed me just as far as I'm gonna go."*

What was that about? What could a guy like Mark have to do with a guy like Jeff?

But before I could give it any real thought, there was a knock on my door.

Uh-oh, I thought. I was afraid it might be my mom, coming to blow up at me some more.

I set the Buster down on the table again. Then the door opened. It wasn't my mom. It was my brother, John.

John is the brains of the family. He's tall and thin like my dad. He kind of looks like my dad too. Same long face, same serious expression—only he still has his hair. He's one of those big brothers you have, you know, where when you go through school, all the teachers say, "Oh, you're

John Hopkins's brother. We expect great things from you." Not a pleasant experience, especially if you're not as smart as he is, which I'm not, or as good an athlete, which I'm also not.

John leaned in the doorway. "How you feeling?" he said.

"Like three guys beat me up. How are you?"

"Oh, you know. Working out which college I'm going to. Did Dad come down pretty hard on you?"

"Not too bad. He figured I'd already got what was coming to me."

"Yeah. Well, you did. That's for sure."

"I know it. You don't have to tell me."

"Well, listen, watch your back from now on, okay?"

"What do you mean?"

John straightened off the doorway. He was so tall, the top of his head nearly grazed the top of the frame. "Well, think about it, you know. Winger will never let this rest. You're a marked man now."

I didn't answer. I just looked at him. I hadn't thought about that.

"You mean, you think this isn't over?" I asked softly.

"No chance," my brother said. "Believe me. This is just the beginning."

Then he moved away, closing the door behind him.

Just the beginning, I thought.

I didn't know how right he was.

A Marked Man

If you thought I looked bad lying almost dead by the side of the road, well, you should've seen me the morning after. You ever see a piece of fruit—an orange, say, or a peach—that's gone rotten? You know, maybe it fell behind the sofa and nobody noticed it, and now you move the sofa and there it is and it's been lying there for weeks and it's all purple and yellow and discolored and saggy and swollen in some places and dented in others? Well, that's what my face looked like—and the rest of me didn't look much better.

The pain was worse than before too. Whatever had ached and stung when I went to sleep was now a throbbing torture. Plus I practically creaked like an old door when I tried to move. I would've liked to stay home for the day and recuperate, but there was no chance of that. If I even suggested to my mom I might need a day off, the whole hysteria of the night before would have started over again. Easier just to gut it out.

Riding my bike to school was no picnic. Every time the pedals went around, the pain shot up through my legs. Every breath I took hurt my chest. My backpack hurt my back and shoulders. Basically, everything I did hurt something somewhere.

I traveled mostly on the backroads, down quiet lanes with small houses on small squares of lawn. No one was around except a few delivery guys. That's the way I wanted it. I didn't want to have to answer any questions—not if I could avoid it.

But worse than the pain and embarrassment was the thought of what was going to happen next.

"You're a marked man now. This is just the beginning."

My brother's words repeated themselves over and over in my mind. I knew he was right. Jeff Winger was my enemy forever now, and he was not a good enemy to have. He was tough and mean and relentless, and he'd never forget. I could just imagine what it was going to be like at school. Always on the lookout for him. Always waiting for what was going to happen next. And then when something *did* happen, it wouldn't just be between me and Jeff anymore. Because I remembered what my dad had said too.

"If anything else comes of this, like Jeff comes looking for revenge or something or even threatens you—or anything at all—and you don't tell me about it right away . . ."

In other words, if Jeff started to terrorize me and I kept it to myself and tried to handle it without bringing in Dad, I'd have Dad after me too, which was worse. I think this is what they mean by being "caught between a rock and a hard place."

The entrance to the high school came into sight down the road. There's just a fence with a gate leading into a big parking lot. Then on the far side of the lot, there's your usual two-story, brick-and-glass high school building.

Painful as it was, I took a deep breath.

Do right. Fear nothing, I told myself.

I watched the school get closer and closer. I felt my stomach twisting with fear and suspense. I was pretty sure this was going to be a majorly bad day.

I put my bike in one of the bike racks on one side of the parking lot. I flinched as I straightened my backpack on my bruised shoulders. I took another deep and painful breath, ready to approach the school.

Here we go, I thought.

I walked through the parking lot toward the front of the school. There's a walkway there. The walkway leads from the parking lot over the front lawn, then divides in two and circles around a tall flagpole. The school bus stops at the curb at the head of the path and kids get out and start walking up. Some kids are dropped off there by their parents. The seniors park in the lot and come up the walk as well. And other kids walk straight in from the road or bike in and lock up their bikes in the racks and come to the walkway from the side like I did. In the end, though, everyone ends up on that front walk, the whole school crowd. It becomes like a big river of kids flowing toward the school—dividing in two to flow around the flagpole—then coming together again for the final stretch to the front door.

So I reached the end of the lot and started heading to the walkway to join the big river of kids. As I stepped over the curb, someone—I never saw who was first—started clapping. I didn't really notice it right away. You know, everyone was talking and laughing and there was all this general noise around and the clapping sort of blended in with that. But then another kid started clapping too. Then another. Then more. And after a while, I did hear it. You couldn't help but hear it. I looked toward the sound.

A group of seniors was standing at the head of the path, right next to me. There were about six or seven of them. They had stopped walking into school and were just standing there, clapping, as if they were standing on the sidelines of a football game or something, cheering on the team. But they weren't looking at a football game. They were looking at me. I checked. I glanced over my shoulder because I thought there might be someone behind me. But no, it was me, all right. They were clapping for me.

And now other kids turned to see what was happening. They followed the seniors' gazes to see what they were clapping for. And what did they see? They saw me! Beat-up-bruised-purple-and-yellow-rotten-piece-of-fruit me.

And those kids stopped where they were—and they started clapping too.

The applause spread from the parking lot all the way to the front door of the school. Everyone stopped where he was. The entire river of kids came to a standstill. Every kid there—there must've been hundreds of them—turned to look at me. They were all smiling. They were all nodding. They were all clapping. Hundreds of students from Sawnee High School giving me a welcoming ovation.

And okay, some of the applause was kind of ironic. Like, you know: *clap*, *clap*, *clap*. I mean, they'd all seen the video of me getting pounded into the earth on Facebook. They all knew I probably wasn't going to be starring in the next superhero movie. Unless it was called *Beatdown Man* or something. But at the same time the applause was ironic, it was somehow—well, not ironic too. Because I *had* stood up to Jeff and his thugs, after all. And while maybe Jennifer Sales didn't have all that many friends—or any friends—Mark Sales did. All the kids liked Mark. All the kids wanted Mark to like them. Mark was a track star, a High School Hero. So standing up for his sister made me kind of a hero as well.

The kids called to me as I passed by:

"Way to go, Sam!"

"Way to get kicked around the block, tough guy!"

"You're an all-American hero, my son."

"You're a great man—and you look like the back end of a baboon!"

"High five."

And all the while, the clapping continued.

I wasn't exactly sure how to react to it all. After a while I waved. Which was pretty idiotic, I guess. I mean, what was I? The president passing in his motorcade or something? But it was all I could think of. So I waved and bowed as ironically as I knew how and just kept walking past the applauding crowd.

"Nice going, Spider-Man."

"Gimme it low, buddy."

"Very cool bruises, dude."

Kids patted my back and shook my hand and grabbed my shoulder—which, let me tell you, was more painful than I can possibly describe. Still, even with the irony, it was pretty cool. The whole school clapping like that? Clapping for me? It was *very* cool.

I was practically grinning as I stepped to the front door with all the kids congratulating me on every side. Then I walked through the doors into the school.

And there was more. There were more kids, more applause. And also, Mark Sales himself was standing there. He was standing in front of everybody as if he had been waiting for me to arrive. Not just Mark but Nathan and Justin too—the other cool guys from the track team.

Mark stepped up to me with Nathan and Justin on either side of him as the other kids applauded. Mark did not look ironic at all. He lifted his fist and held it out to me. I bumped my fist against his. Mark smiled with his sparkling teeth.

"You're the man," he said. And remember, this is Mark Sales talking, so when he says you're the man, it means something because, well, he's the man. "Thanks," he added. "Thanks for taking care of my sister."

"No, no," I said, "forget it. What else was I gonna do?"

"I *won't* forget it, buddy," he said. "I won't ever forget it. Understand?"

Nathan and Justin bumped fists with me too. This was no small thing. Mark and Nathan and Justin were good friends to have. They were right up there with the most popular kids in the school, for one thing. And for another, they were big, tough athletes. Nobody dared to mess with them.

"Listen," said Mark. He leaned toward me. He dropped his voice. "If you're worried about Jeff—about what he might do—don't be. Understand?"

"Okay," I said doubtfully.

"I mean it," said Mark. "I had a conversation with him this morning. Jeff will not come near you ever again. Not ever."

"Really?"

"Really," said Mark. He said it like he meant it too.

I felt a strong wave of relief wash over me. It was one thing to know that Mark would stand with me if there was any trouble. That was very good news in itself. But to think there might not be any trouble at all—nothing to have to tell my dad about—that was even better. Much better.

"That's great," I said to Mark. "That's really great."

"All right," said Mark. We bumped fists again. "Gotta get to class. See you at lunchtime, all right?"

"Sure," I said. Was that an invitation to eat lunch at Mark's table? Also very cool.

As Mark and Nathan and Justin swaggered away, I just stood there for a moment, looking after them, amazed. Other kids went by, patting me on the back. Girls smiled at me and waved. I thought, *Hey, instead of being a marked man, it turns out I'm Mark's man. Cool.*

Smiling to myself, I headed to homeroom.

The whole day went like that. People smiling at me, congratulating me, kidding me. Even the teachers. I mean, the teachers couldn't actually say anything out loud—that might make it sound like they approved of fighting and, of course, no one approves of fighting. But they kind of gave me these smiles as I passed them in the halls. And Coach Jackson even gave me a thumbs-up, though he hid it close to his chest as he walked by so no one else would see.

So here was this day I thought was going to turn out to be some kind of nightmare, and instead it was one of the best days I ever had. The highlight? That's easy. Right after second period I made a pit stop at my locker to empty one group of incredibly heavy books out of my backpack and replace them with another group of even heavier books. And as I was in the process of doing that, I glanced up and saw Zoe Miller coming down the hall toward me.

I was too shy to actually say hello to her, so I sort of averted my eyes, pretending I hadn't seen her. But she came right up to me. Just sort of stood there next to me, holding her books.

"Hi, Sam," she said.

I believe I've already mentioned Zoe's high cuteness factor. The black hair, the green eyes, the smile that looks like she invented smiling. Close up like that—and directed at me—it all had a very powerful effect. The powerful effect was that I forgot how to speak English. Or anything else for that matter. I had to think about it for a very long ten seconds before I finally managed to come up with the stunningly clever reply: "Hi." Then, in a flash of inspiration, I added, "Zoe."

"We both have history next," she said. "I thought we might as well walk over there together."

If I could've remembered any words, I might have said something like, "Sure, that'd be great, Zoe." But I couldn't, so I didn't. Instead, I just sort of nodded at her like a bobblehead Sam Hopkins doll.

Then we started walking together down the hall side by side.

"So you're, like, the star of the whole school today," Zoe said as we went. "Everybody's talking about you."

I shrugged. Fortunately, my language skills were slowly beginning to return to me. "It's kind of dumb, I guess," I said. "I mean, everybody's congratulating me for getting beaten up!"

"I don't think that's dumb," said Zoe.

"You don't?"

"No. Under the circumstances, I don't think it's dumb at all."

Well then, I guess I didn't think it was dumb either.

"I bet your parents were really angry about it, though," Zoe went on. "Especially your dad."

"Actually, no, my dad was pretty cool about it. My mom burst into flames a little, but my dad sort of understood."

"Wow, really? I would have thought—you know, him being a preacher and all, he'd be all, like, turn the other cheek and everything."

"Well, he is, sure. But he says that's supposed to stop you from fighting out of pride or anger, you know. It's not supposed to stop you from standing up for what's right when you have to."

"Huh," she said. "That is cool."

We turned a corner and started down the hall toward our classroom.

"You know what's kind of funny?" Zoe went on. "I always felt a little nervous about talking to you because of your dad."

"Really? I always kind of wondered about that . . ."

"Yeah, I don't know why. I guess . . . I guess I sort of felt like because you were all, like, religious and everything, maybe you'd expect people to be perfect . . ."

She turned that smile of hers on me, not to mention those green eyes, and I wanted to tell her she actually *was* perfect. But instead I said, "Look, could you do me a favor?"

"Sure. I guess. Like what?"

"Just . . . don't be nervous around me anymore. Okay? Because if you're nervous, then I get nervous, and when I get nervous I act all stupid and then you'll think I'm stupid when I'm really just nervous because you're nervous."

Zoe nodded thoughtfully. "I have no idea what you just said."

"No, me either. But that sort of proves my point."

She laughed. "Okay. I guess I won't be nervous then. And you won't expect me to be perfect."

"Right," I said. *Although you are*, I thought. Only I didn't say that, because I was too nervous.

Zoe and I were both smiling as we walked into the classroom. In fact, to be honest, I went on smiling a long time after that. In fact, I had to force the smile off my face eventually so I wouldn't look like a clown with rigor mortis.

But the smile kept coming back. Especially after school was over and I was biking home by myself. I kept thinking about the day—thinking about it so much I almost forgot how sore I was, almost forgot how much every part of my body was throbbing and hurting. Almost. I kept seeing images of the kids applauding outside the school . . . Mark Sales bumping fists with me and telling me Jeff wouldn't bother me anymore . . . And Zoe and me walking to class together . . . And Mark and Justin and me having lunch . . . And Zoe and me walking to class together . . . although maybe I already mentioned that.

Anyway, I was smiling and remembering as I was biking home thinking about it all.

And then a strange thing happened.

I had just come onto Maple Street, my street, only a couple of blocks from where I live. The afternoon was cloudy, gray, getting dark kind of early. There was a wind rising and it looked like it was going to rain. This one stretch of Maple I was on was thick with trees, but there weren't that many houses. With the sky getting dark and the dead winter branches swaying and whispering in the wind, it was a little bit spooky-looking.

Maybe it was just because of that, but I began to feel that somebody was watching me. I had that feeling you get, you know, on the back of your neck, when somebody stares at you from behind. I glanced over my shoulder, but there was nobody there.

I didn't stop. I figured I was just letting myself get spooked. In spite of what Mark said, I guess I was still a little worried about Jeff, worried he might wait for me in some secluded spot—like this one—in order to take his revenge.

I rode a little faster the rest of the way home, even though my body was still aching like crazy from the beating.

When I got there, I walked around to the side of the house. There's a broad alley of grass there and just at the end of it, at the corner of the house, there's a little covered bike port next to an old willow tree. It's a deserted little corner. Getting dark now as the rain clouds moved in above. The willow tree waving and whispering in the wind. I still had that strange feeling that someone was watching me. I kept looking around me, but there was no one in sight.

I wheeled the bike into the port and locked it up. Then I turned to go into the house.

And there was Jennifer Sales, standing right next to me, staring.

What Jennifer Saw

I nearly jumped out of my own skin—that's how startled I was to see her. It was as if she'd appeared out of nowhere, and the way she was staring at me with that pale, serious face of hers—just standing and staring without saying anything—well, it was eerie. Very. It was like having a ghost stare at you.

"Oh!" I said, nearly choking on the sound. "Uh . . . hi, Jennifer."

She went on staring another long moment. Then her lips turned up in a shy little smile. She lifted her hand in a shy little wave. "Sam Hopkins," she said. And then she repeated my name: "Sam Hopkins."

"That's me, all right."

She smiled and nodded for a long time. Then she said, "Thank you for stopping Jeff. The Winger. From hurting me. He was mean."

"Yeah, he was," I said. "I'm sorry he did that. I'm really glad you got out of there all right."

"Because you helped me."

"Well . . ."

She lifted her hand and reached for my face as if to touch the bruises there. I guess I kind of flinched a little. The bruises were still really tender.

But in any case, Jennifer didn't touch me. Her finger just sort of lingered close to my cheek, then dropped back to her side.

"They hurt you," she said sadly. "They hurt you because of me."

"They hurt me because I busted Jeff in the grille. It wasn't your fault."

Jennifer smiled. "You were my Sam Hopkins friend," she said.

It sounded so funny I laughed. "Well, good. I'm glad to be your Sam Hopkins friend."

Jennifer looked this way and that, as if she wanted to make sure there was no one around to hear her. There wasn't. We were alone in that little grass alley at the edge of the house next to the bike port and the willow tree.

Jennifer dropped her voice and leaned toward me. "I said your name last night," she confided to me as if it were her great secret.

"You . . . what? What do you mean?"

"I said your name," she repeated, even softer than before. "When the demons came to my house."

I don't know if you've ever seen a weeping willow tree in winter. It's kind of a spooky tree to begin with. In summer it has those branches that hang down mournfully to the ground. But in winter, when the branches are bare, they sort of stick out every which way, all unruly like a witch's hair. Then when the wind comes through them, they shudder and snicker and whisper almost as if the witch were coming to life.

The wind came through the willow now and the weeping willow shook and whispered. With that and with what Jennifer said about the demons and with her staring at me after she said it, I felt as if something cold and yucky had run up my back, like an insect with icy feet. I shivered like the tree.

"Demons, huh?" I said. I hoped maybe Jennifer was making some kind of joke, but I didn't really think she was. "You get those a lot around your place?"

She nodded. "They come in at night. When no one else can see them. They change everything."

"Yeah, I guess they would."

"They put a coffin under the tree."

"Sorry?" The bowing branches of the winter willow swayed and whispered and I glanced at it—just to make sure there were no demons there right now. "What tree are we talking about exactly?"

Her eyes got wide. She leaned in even closer, her voice even more soft and secret and serious. "The one in the hall outside my bedroom. It's a demon tree. A low-spreading oak over the tarn."

I licked my dry lips. I found my own voice getting softer too, like Jennifer's. "What's a tarn?"

"It's like a lake. A flat, black, round lake under the spreading branches of the tree. The demons come out of it and they gather there. They write evil symbols on the walls. And they put a coffin under the tree."

"Wait," I said. "This is in your hallway? In your house?"

Eyes big and round, she nodded.

"And you saw this?" I asked her. "You saw this coffin there?"

"I saw the thing that was in it too," she said.

"In . . . ?"

"The coffin."

Okay, well, that didn't sound good. In fact, this was really starting to creep me out in a major way at this point. I mean, I didn't mind Jennifer saying silly-sounding stuff that rhymed or whatever. But this sounded downright crazy. Or something. A tree in her hall? With a coffin under it? With a thing in the coffin . . . ?

And just then the clouds seemed to grow even darker in the sky, and the air around us seemed to get darker too. The wind blew down the alley of grass, and the willow shifted and rattled as if something were hiding under its branches. I thought I felt the first drops of rain touch my bruised face.

"Sam Hopkins," Jennifer whispered.

"What?" I said.

But she didn't answer. It was as if she just wanted to say my name out loud.

"What was in the coffin, Jennifer?" I asked her.

"It was dead," she answered.

"Yeah, I was sort of afraid you were going to say that."

"And then it sat up."

"What?"

"It reached for me. It had skeleton fingers."

For a second I just stood there, just gaped at her. I mean, I'd heard stories like this before, of course. My brother used to tell them sometimes when we were camping out in the backyard—ghost stories, you know, to scare me before I went to sleep. And I've read comics and seen TV shows where scary stuff like this happens, skeletons getting out of their coffins or whatever. And sure, it creeps me out. But I always know somewhere inside me that it's just a story, right? Just a comic or movie, not something that could ever happen in real life.

But this was different.

I'm not saying I *believed* what Jennifer was saying. But I did believe that *she* believed it. I could tell just by looking at her that she wasn't lying or making it up. Somehow she had actually *seen* this stuff. Or dreamed it. Or something.

And somehow that made it scarier than a movie, scarier than a comic book or a story. Because Jennifer was real. She was standing right there in front of me, staring at me with her spooky eyes.

"Sam Hopkins," she whispered. Which made the whole thing even scarier.

I shook my head. "Why do you keep saying my name like that?"

"It's magical."

"It is?"

"Yes. There's magic in a friend's name."

"Oh." I guess I could understand that. Sort of.

The wind blew up again. This time as it came down the grass alley, it carried a full rainfall with it. I felt the damp spray against my face, stinging on the sore places. I heard the rain begin to patter in the branches of the trees all around me. And the willow branches rattled and whispered.

Jennifer felt it too—the wind, the rain. She looked up at the sky for a long moment. "Something terrible is coming," she said.

"Just rain," I told her.

But she shook her head, still studying the darkening clouds above. "No. Something else. Something bad. Soon. Very soon."

I looked up too, trying to see what she saw.

When I looked down, Jennifer was gone. No, wait—there she was—down the alley, backing away from me, backing over the grass along the house, shaking her head.

"Something terrible is coming," she repeated.

"What?" I asked her. "What is it? Coming when?"

Jennifer glanced up at the sky one more time, then back at me. She shook her head, a desperate look in her eyes. "Sam Hopkins," she whispered.

Thunder struck and the rain poured down.

Jennifer turned and ran away.

PART THREE

THE CASTLE OF THE DEMON KING

THIS MUST BE THE CASTLE OF THE DEMON KING, JENNIFER thought.

Her mother said no. Her mother said it was only a hospital—St. Agnes Hospital—for sick people. But Jennifer had her suspicions.

The building loomed darkly against the dark gray sky like a castle in a movie. And who would live in such a dark, dark castle but a dark, dark demon king?

That's what Jennifer was thinking—but she didn't say it to her mother, of course. Her mother would just tell her these thoughts were crazy. Her mother would say she had to ignore them or make them stop. And Jennifer did try to make them stop. She tried to force them out of her mind the way you would force intruders out of your house. But they wouldn't go. Even when she managed to silence them, she felt the bad thoughts standing like black shadows on the moonscape of her mind, staring at her, waiting for their chance to speak again.

"I had a long chat with the doctor on the phone and she sounded very nice," Jennifer's mother said.

They were walking up the front path now. Every time Jennifer looked up, the castle—the hospital—got larger and larger, spreading over her the way a monster would spread over you just before it snapped down on top of you and devoured you whole.

But it was not a monster, not a castle, Jennifer told herself. Just a great brick building of a St. Agnes Hospital where the doctor sounded nice on the phone.

"She told me she just wants to ask you a few questions," Jennifer's mother said. "Nothing scary is going to happen."

Jennifer glanced at her mother, trying to gauge whether or not she was telling the truth. Jennifer wanted to believe her, to trust her, but maybe she was in league with the demons. Maybe that's why she kept telling Jennifer there *were* no demons. A trick. To throw her off track. A trick-track.

But no, her mother just looked saggy and old, like a paper bag Jennifer had seen once blowing across the Shop N Save parking lot.

Shop N Save. Hopkins Save. Sam Hopkins Saved Me. Saggy and baggy at the Hopkins Save, Jennifer thought.

That seemed very clever to her, very insightful. She wanted to tell the joke to her mother. But she knew it would only make her mother look confused and worried, so she kept silent.

They pushed through the castle's—the hospital's—big glass doors.

Run away, Jennifer!

The voice spoke very suddenly, very clearly in her mind. It wasn't a whisper at all. It was a voice so clear that at first she almost thought it was her mother speaking again beside her.

Something terrible is going to happen . . .

Jennifer shook herself, like a dog throwing off water. She threw off the voice, tossed it right out of her mind.

"Sam Hopkins," she whispered aloud.

"What, sweetheart?" said her mother. "Oh yes, the Hopkins boy. He was very brave, wasn't he?"

"He's my friend," said Jennifer, shivering.

"That's nice," said her mother, weary and baggy like the bag blowing at the Shop N Save.

Inside the castle they waited in plastic chairs in a big room. There were lots of other people waiting too.

Jennifer looked at a magazine. She looked at it very hard because she was afraid if she looked up she would see the demons watching her. In the magazine, there were pretty girls with bright smiles. Jennifer stared at them and the girls sent thoughts telepathically into her mind.

Don't look up, Jennifer.

If you don't see them, they can't hurt you.

Jennifer stared at the pretty smiling girls and didn't look up and didn't see anyone she shouldn't.

Only at the end of their wait, only after the nurse came and said Jennifer could go in and see the doctor now, only when she had left her mother behind in the chair, her mother smiling saggy-baggy in her chair, only as Jennifer followed the nurse to the door did she glance back over her shoulder and catch one glimpse of one terrible creature standing darkly among the other people who were waiting and reading their magazines. The terrible creature seized on the moment of Jennifer's glance and whispered across the big room to her—whispered silently with its eyes:

Run away, Jennifer. Something terrible is going to happen soon. You have to tell Sam. You have to warn Sam Hopkins, your friend.

Jennifer gasped, then forced herself to look away and followed the nurse through the door.

Now she was in the doctor's office.

The doctor—if she really *was* a doctor—and of course she was;

her mother had told her she was and she had sounded nice on the phone. Why would her mother lie to her? Unless she was one of *them* . . .

The doctor was a small woman with a nice face.

Nice face, rice cakes, ice skates, Jennifer thought.

She was wearing a black sweater and a gray skirt. She came around her desk and held out her hand to Jennifer. It was a very small hand, like a child's. Jennifer shook it.

"I'm Dr. Fletcher," the doctor said. "You must be Jennifer."

Yes, Jennifer thought, *I must be. Because if I could be anyone else, I would!*

Dr. Fletcher and her rice-cakes-nice-face sat in the swivel chair to one side of the desk. Jennifer sat in the armchair across from her. Dr. Fletcher held a yellow pad on her skirt. She held a pen in her hand. This worried Jennifer. Was Dr. Fletcher going to write down what she said? Was she going to report her to the demon king of St. Agnes . . . or someone?

"Your mother says you've been having some frightening experiences lately," Dr. Fletcher said.

Jennifer hesitated. She was afraid. She was afraid if she told the truth, the doctor would think she was crazy and lock her in a padded room wearing a straitjacket. But on the other hand, she was afraid of the whispers in the night and the coffin under the tree and the creature who had stared at her across the room outside.

"Something terrible is coming. Soon."

Maybe the doctor could help make these things go away.

"Sometimes I get afraid," Jennifer said.

"What makes you afraid, Jennifer?"

Jennifer wasn't sure what to say. She shook her head.

"Are there unusual things happening in your life?" Dr. Fletcher asked her. She swiveled in the chair. She held the notepad on her skirt. She held the pen in her tiny, childlike hand, waiting to write down Jennifer's answers. "Are there things happening that haven't happened before?"

Jennifer nodded cautiously.

"Do you see things that worry you?" the doctor asked. "Do you see things that other people can't see?"

"Sometimes, yes," Jennifer managed to say. *Rice cakes, ice skates, mice on skates.* Mice on skates—that was a funny idea—but she knew she couldn't say it out loud or the doctor really would think she was crazy.

"Do you hear voices other people can't hear?"

Jennifer bit her lip and nodded. How did the doctor know? Who was she? Who was she really?

Dr. Fletcher reached out with one of her small hands and touched the knee of Jennifer's jeans. "It's all right," she said, with her nice-rice face. "I know you're scared. What's happening to you feels very frightening."

"What's happening to me?" Jennifer blurted out, her voice cracking. She had worried about this so much, so long, she could hardly bear to ask the question out loud. She clamped her lips shut to keep from saying anything else.

Dr. Fletcher had brown hair, but she was too old to have brown hair so it must've been dyed. Was it a disguise? Dyes disguise from eyes that spy. Was the so-called doctor hiding from someone?

"I'm not sure yet what's happening to you, Jennifer," Dr. Fletcher said, taking her small hand back from Jennifer's knee. "We're going to try to find out. Then I hope we'll be able to help you feel better."

In spite of her suspicions, Jennifer liked the doctor. In spite of her fear, she wanted to trust her. She confided in her: "I'm afraid something terrible is about to happen."

"Something terrible like what?"

Jennifer shook her head. She wasn't sure. "Soon," she said.

"You feel you can predict the future? That you know what's going to happen before it happens?"

Jennifer's eyes roamed over the walls, looking for any signs that the demons had been here. Had they put the wallpaper up just for her, just before she came in? It was flower wallpaper. And there were flowers on the doctor's desk. And there was a calendar next to the flowers.

"Sunday," Jennifer said. When she looked at the calendar, the word came into her head like a sound.

"Sunday?" the doctor asked.

"Something terrible is going to happen Sunday." Suddenly she knew this. She did not know how she knew it, but she did.

"Did the voices tell you this?"

Jennifer nodded.

"And did you see who was speaking?"

"I saw the thing in the coffin. It reached up to grab me." Jennifer saw no point in hiding the truth anymore. "In the hallway under the tree. I have to warn Sam. It's Sunday. Sunday. I remember now."

Dr. Fletcher took the notepad off her skirt. She laid it down on a lampstand next to her. "All right," she said. "We're going to have to do some tests."

"Tests?" Jennifer said. Her heart beat hard. She was afraid. What kind of tests would they do? Would they have to take pieces out from inside her to study them?

"It's all right," the doctor said. "It won't be painful. We're just going to take some pictures of your brain to make sure there's nothing wrong in there."

"You won't have to take it out, though?" Jennifer asked. "My brain, I mean. You won't have to remove it to take the pictures?"

Dr. Fletcher gave her a kind rice-cake smile. "No. We'll just take pictures of it. We won't take out your brain."

Jennifer pretended to laugh. "I knew that. I was only joking."

Dr. Fletcher stood up. "All right," she said. "You wait right here and I'm going to arrange to have the pictures taken. Don't be afraid, Jennifer. We're going to take good care of you, all right?"

Dr. Fletcher went out of the room, closing the door behind her. So now Jennifer was alone in the office. Swallowing hard, she looked around.

The office was a big room. There were bookshelves on the opposite wall. There was the desk with a great big window behind it. There were also the two chairs: the swivel chair and the one Jennifer was sitting in.

The lights were on in the office, but the office was shadowy—maybe because the venetian blinds on the big window behind the desk were closed. Jennifer wondered why the blinds were closed when it was only afternoon. Was there something out there she wasn't supposed to see?

She turned back to the door. Still shut. Where had Dr. Fletcher gone? What were these tests she was going to take? She said they weren't going to take Jennifer's brain out, but that didn't make sense. How could they take pictures of her brain without taking it out?

Jennifer bit her lip and her eyes filled with tears. Any minute, the doctor would come back and then the tests would begin.

She glanced at the window again. Maybe the demons were just outside the window, getting the testing machines ready. And the knives . . .

She couldn't stand the suspense. She got up from her chair. Quickly she went around the desk to the big window. She opened the slats on the venetian blinds and peeked out through the glass.

There were no machines out there that she could see. There was just the parking lot. Right there, right outside. She could see the road beyond. The gray sky through a line of trees.

But the machines were waiting. The knives were waiting. Somewhere. Any moment, the doctor would come back and take her away for her tests.

Brain. Pain. Windowpane.

Something terrible is going to happen. Soon. Sunday.

Run, Jennifer!

The voice spoke again, loudly, right beside her, and almost before Jennifer knew what she was doing, she had seized the rope that worked the venetian blinds and yanked it down, drawing the blinds up to expose the window. The window lock was easy to work, even with her fingers trembling. Then the window was open wide.

Jennifer started climbing out. Her heart pounded in her chest so hard she thought it would explode. Any moment, she thought, the doctor would come back in and catch her and call the demons to put her in a straitjacket and take her away so they could cut her brain out. She knew her mother would tell her that was a crazy thought, that she shouldn't have thoughts like that . . .

But maybe that was because her mother was one of them.

All this flashed through her mind so fast she hardly knew what was a fantasy and what was real. She just knew that something terrible was going to happen and she had to get out, she had to escape, she had to run, run, run away.

And so that's exactly what she did.

Track Day

That Saturday we had the first track meet of the year. Sawnee High running against Ondaga and Hamilton.

Meet days were always big days in our town. Other sports like football and soccer were popular enough, but track meets were something special. For some reason, our little section of the state held three state-champion schools: Sawnee, Empire, and Cole. The rivalry between them was intense and everyone paid attention. And because everyone followed the team, the town had built this really cool track-slash-soccer stadium—Sawnee Stadium—out by the river. Every Saturday of the season, before the meet started, the road—Stadium Road—would be packed with traffic, a long line of cars waiting to get through the gates. Next to the road there were woods, and on the other side of the woods there was a big parking lot. And on the other side of the parking lot, there was the river sparkling in the sun and a grassy slope by the banks where people could spread blankets and have picnics before the meet.

Beside the slope was the stadium itself. It looked like an ancient temple or something, only made of red brick instead of white marble: brick pillars between tall, arched entranceways and a brick tower flanking the pillars on either side.

By 10:00 a.m., big crowds of people were filing in between the pillars. The flags of the school were flying on top of the walls and fluttering in the high spring wind. It was a real scene, very awesome.

Even more awesome: This Saturday I wasn't just one of the crowd. Mark had invited me to hang out with the team and watch the meet from field level. I was down there with him and Justin and Nathan and the other guys as they stretched out, getting ready for the first event. It was exceptionally cool being down on the field, watching the people file into the gleaming silver bleachers above me. The red clay of the track seemed incredibly red down there, and the green of the soccer field in the middle of the circular track seemed greener than anything.

I stood and watched the seats get full. After a few seconds I realized Mark was standing next to me in his warm-up suit. I looked up at him. He was watching the crowd too.

"Next year, they'll be coming to see you," he said.

I felt kind of embarrassed when he said that—because it's exactly what I had been daydreaming about just then: maybe next year all those people would be coming to see me.

Now Nathan and Justin came over and stood with us. They were breathing hard from their stretches and bouncing on their toes to keep loose.

Nathan was a tall, narrow blond-haired guy with a round face. "There sure are a lot of them," he said.

Justin was smaller, compact and muscular. He had very pale skin, very red hair, and a lot of freckles. "They look small, don't they?" he said with a laugh.

I laughed back. "I guess we look small to them too," I said.

Nathan kind of snorted and slapped me on the shoulder—which reverberated painfully through my still-aching frame. "No, dude, we're the big guys."

The three of them laughed. Mark poked a finger into my chest—which also hurt. "Next year—right? You'll be a big guy too."

I tried to look like I believed it, but with my whole body still sore from the beating Jeff and his thugs had given me, it was hard to think that I would ever be as fast or athletic as Mark and the others. It was hard to believe that everyone might one day line up and file into the stadium to watch me. I was happy just to be hanging out with them.

It was a good day, a good meet. Watching Mark run from field level like that made me doubt even more that

I could ever run the way he did. The starting gun would fire—*bang!*—and it was like he was the bullet being shot out of it. Down the track he went like some amazing machine, his arms and legs like pistons, his speed almost unbelievable and unbelievably steady. The other runners fell behind him within a few steps and never caught up. He won both the 100 and the 400, and he and Nathan and Justin and one other guy—Tom—teamed up to win the relay too.

Afterward, the team went out to Burger Joint for a celebration. The whole team, some of their girlfriends—and me. Everyone laughing and shouting and kidding one another and remembering the best moments of the meet. I sat at the head of the big table, next to Mark and Justin and Nathan. I was so swept away by the fun I was having, I forgot my aches and pains and even the bruises that still marked up my face.

The talking and shouting got louder and louder, the guys congratulating themselves on their brilliant victories.

Finally, Mark said, "You guys, you guys." And immediately everyone got quieter. Everyone listened when Mark spoke. "You guys," he said, "enjoy the day, but don't get ahead of yourselves. This was just a warm-up for next week, remember."

Everyone around the table nodded. "That's right, that's right."

"Hamilton and Ondaga are nothing," said Justin.

“They’re not nothing,” said Mark. “But they’re not Empire, and they’re definitely not Cole.”

Those were the big meets every year. Sawnee against Empire and Cole. The first was scheduled for next Saturday. Only a week away.

“Empire and Cole,” said Justin. “They need to learn a lesson, no question.”

“Cole is nothing,” said Nathan.

“Cole has the Hammer,” Mark said. The Hammer was the trophy for the county championship. “They went to state.”

“Yeah, ’cause they cheated,” said Nathan with a sneer. “You know they did, Mark. If we’d had the guts to put up a challenge . . .”

“If the principal and the school board had backed us,” said Justin.

“If the *town* had backed us!” said Nathan.

This conversation had been going on for a year now. There were rumors that some of the Cole guys had used performance-enhancing drugs. Mark had led a delegation to ask our principal to challenge their victory, but the principal had declined, saying he would assume Cole won fair and square unless there was solid evidence they hadn’t. He didn’t want there to be bad blood between the schools.

“Whatever,” said Mark. “Come the big meet, we have to show them all what we are. Don’t forget that.”

I looked around the table. Everyone was quiet, nodding. See, Mark was not just the hero of the day. He was the hero of the team, the team leader. You could tell it just by looking at him. He had this—I don't know what the word is—this *presence* about him. Like a movie star or something. It was partly that he ran so fast and won so much. But partly it was just the way he sat and looked so sure of himself. Whatever it was, it was like there was an aura around him that made him stand out from the rest of us, that made everyone stop talking and listen whenever he had something to say. Even when other people talked, the other guys sort of glanced over at Mark to see what he thought, to see if he approved of what was being said, if he agreed or disagreed. As I watched him, I couldn't help but wonder to myself: *What would it be like? To be* that *guy, you know? To be the guy everyone looked up to. To have everyone want to know what* you *thought, what* you *wanted . . .*

As I biked home that afternoon, I sort of fell to daydreaming about it. I daydreamed that people looked at me that way, that everyone in school asked themselves and one another: "What does Sam think about it? Where does Sam stand on that issue?" I thought, *Maybe if I got on the track team, I would eventually become the center of everything like that . . .*

But I doubted it. It was just a stupid daydream. No matter how much of a celebrity I was at the moment, I knew it was temporary. I didn't have Mark's aura and I never would. I wasn't tall or handsome or sure of myself like he was. I couldn't imagine anyone ever caring one way or the other what I thought about anything.

Technically, of course, I was still grounded, so when I got home I had to go back to cleaning out the garage. If you've ever read the story of Hercules and the Augean stables, that's what it was like—although I don't remember Hercules being all sore from getting beaten up when he did that, so maybe it was easier for him. Anyway, I shoved the last box into the attic just before dinnertime. After dinner, because of the whole being-grounded thing, I stayed home with nothing much to do. I watched some TV, then hauled my battered flesh upstairs and fooled around on my computer. I tried to find Joe for a chat, but he was out. I tried to reach Cal, another friend of mine, but he was out too. It made me feel pretty alone, but then, that's what being grounded is like, as you may know.

But then something cool happened. I was still sort of hanging at the computer, cleaning up my tunes, leaving a couple of messages on other people's walls, whatever, when a chat message came up.

Z-GIRL: Wuzzup, Sam?

I sort of caught my breath. Z-girl. Her picture came along with the message. I could hardly believe it. I typed back:

ME: Zoe?

ZOE: Hey.

ME: (trying to sound cool and collected) Hey. Zup?

ZOE: Hanging. Babysitting my brother. You?

ME: Same. Well, no brother. But just hanging. Still grounded cuz of the fight.

ZOE: Stinx 2 b U.

ME: No doubt. Cud be worse tho. Didn't c u at the meet.

ZOE: Didn't go.

ME: Mark ruled. Won two events and the relay. 50 in the 400.

ZOE: Cool.

I narrowed my eyes. Seemed like sort of a bland response, you know? When you're chatting online, of course, you can't hear a person's tone of voice, so sometimes it's hard to know what they're feeling exactly. But I would've thought the news of Mark's track heroics would've gotten something out of Zoe more like "Cool!" or maybe even "Cool!!!!"

ME: You don't sound too impressed.

There was a pause. I have to admit I sort of watched the screen in suspense. Whenever I saw Zoe with Mark and the other track guys, she always seemed really at ease, really friendly with them. I guess I always figured if Zoe wasn't already Mark's girlfriend, she would be eventually. Was I wrong?

Now the answer came back.

ZOE: I'm kind of off Mark.

My reaction to this was, let's say, complicated. I mean, I won't lie: It made me kind of glad to think that Zoe wasn't going out with Mark. That she was free to go out with . . . someone else, say, if the situation should arise. On the other hand, I didn't know how anyone as smart and nice as Zoe could be off anyone as cool and great as Mark. I mean, Mark was my friend now too, and I didn't want to think that Zoe had done something wrong to him. Like I said: complicated. I started typing again.

ME: What, did you guys have a fite or something?
ZOE: No, no. Nothing like that.
ME: Mark's a good guy, no?

This was me being loyal to Mark—but also trying to find out more about what was going on.

ZOE: I guess. He can be kind of arrogant sometimes.

I sat back from the computer, surprised. Really surprised. Nathan and Justin—they always struck me as a little arrogant, I have to admit. A little snide, you know. Sneering at other people, other teams. But Mark? I didn't think of him as arrogant at all. I mean, yeah, he was sure of himself. Why wouldn't he be? Dude wins three events, runs a fifty in the 400? I mean, come on. It gives him the right to swagger a little bit, doesn't it? I thought Zoe was being unfair and I felt like I ought to defend Mark.

ME: He's the man, thazzall. Everyone looks up to him. Wants to know what he thinks. Wants him to like them. Maybe that makes him sure of himself, but not arrogant.

There was hardly a pause at all, then Zoe wrote back:

ZOE: Jeff Winger's the same way.

My mouth actually dropped open as I read that.

ME: ???????

ZOE: It's true. Think about it.

ME: *Jeff Winger's the same way as Mark???*

That's what I was about to type. But I hesitated with my fingers hovering above the keyboard.

Because I did think about it. And after a second or two, I could sort of understand what Zoe was saying. I mean, if you thought about it a certain way, all the things I said about Mark Sales were true of Jeff Winger too. Ed P. and Harry Mac looked up to Jeff the way the track guys looked up to Mark. They listened when Jeff talked—and when they talked, they glanced over at him to see what he thought about it. Same kind of thing.

But that didn't make Jeff Winger and Mark the same kind of people. It just meant they were both leaders, in their own way. But consider who they led and what they led them to do. Jeff was a thug leader who led thugs. Hanging out in some abandoned barn, teaching one another how to break into places and steal things. Mark was a good guy who led other good people. Training and working out and winning meets.

So why was Zoe saying all this mean stuff about Mark? As I thought about it, I glanced over at the window. I saw my reflection on the dark pane: me and my still-banged-up face, sitting at the computer, chatting with Zoe. Which suddenly struck me as pretty amazing. Not that long ago, I could hardly work up the courage to talk to her, and now here I was chatting back and forth like we were old friends.

I put my hands on the keyboard, about to type a response.

But before I could, my cell phone rang. A number appeared on the readout, but I didn't recognize it.

I typed SB for stand by. Picked up the phone.

"Yo," I said.

A voice came over in a whisper: "Sam Hopkins."

I was so surprised my mouth opened for a long time before I could get a word out. Then I said, "Jennifer?"

"I'm here."

"What? Where?"

"Here," she whispered. "Outside."

I shook my head, confused. "Outside what?"

"Outside your window."

"What?"

"You have to come down. Right now."

I turned in my chair to the window. I saw my own reflection again, holding the phone, staring, stunned.

I heard Jennifer's weird whisper come over the line to me like the voice of a ghost:

"Help me, Sam Hopkins. Help me."

Help Me!

As I sat there stunned into silence, holding the cell phone to my ear, words appeared on the chat screen.

ZOE: Sam?

I glanced back to the monitor. Zoe. I typed SB again.

Still holding the phone, I got up and went to the window. I pressed my face close to the glass, but I couldn't really see much below. So I opened the window and stuck my head out. I felt the night air wash over my face, cold and damp.

My window looks out on the little grass alley that runs along the side of my house, the place with the bike port and the willow tree where I'd had my conversation with Jennifer a little over a week ago. The sky was cloudy and there was no moonshine, but the light from downstairs spilled out of the house windows. By that glow I could make out the shape of the bike port just below me and even the witch-hair shape of the willow branches off to the side.

I didn't see anyone down there.

I was about to pull my head back in and shut the window.

"Sam Hopkins?"

I started at the sound and banged my head against the windowsill.

"Ow!" I clutched the back of my head, rubbing at the pain.

And again, from outside: "Sam Hopkins."

"Jennifer?" I called back softly.

I caught a motion out of the corner of my eye. Then I saw her. She was standing near the willow tree. Her silhouetted figure was hidden in the lacework shadows of the tree's branches so she was almost invisible.

I stared harder. "Jennifer?" I said again.

She answered with a gesture: she held her finger to her lips. "Shh." Her voice reached me through the chill of the night. "Shh."

"What are you doing down there?" I asked.

"I need to talk to you," she said. "I need you to come down."

"I can't. I'm grounded. You have to come in here."

"I can't. They're after me. They'll catch me."

"What? Who?"

"Come down. I need you, Sam!"

I thought about it for a minute. Then I pulled my head inside and shut the window. My heart was beating fast. I sensed that something was terribly wrong.

I moved back to the computer. There was Zoe's latest chat message:

ZOE: Sam? Are you there? Is everything all right?

I hated to break off with her. I hoped she wouldn't be angry at me. But I didn't know what else to do. I typed back:

ME: G2G.

Then I put my phone in my pocket. I went to my door and peeked my head out. I could hear the TV on downstairs and figured my mom and dad were watching something before going to bed. I shut the door. I went back to the window. I took a breath. Then I opened the window again and climbed out.

Okay, it wasn't as dramatic as that. The fact was, there was a rainspout that ran right next to my window. You could grab hold of it and slide down to the ground pretty easily. I figured if I hurried, I could get down and back before my parents even knew I was gone.

Flinching against the stiffness and pain in my thug-hammered body, I slithered out over the frame, grabbed the spout, wrapped myself around it, and was down on the ground—in that alley of lawn beside my house—in a second.

I shivered as my sneakers touched the soft earth. I hadn't put a coat on or anything and it was cold out there. It had been clear and spring-like all day, but now there was a heaviness in the air as if more rain was coming. I felt the chill tighten the skin around my bruises.

I moved to the willow tree. It was a spooky tangle of shadows in the dark. Jennifer stepped out of those shadows as I approached. Her eyes were big and bright. They caught the light from the living room and glowed.

"What are you doing here?" I said.

"I escaped from the castle," she whispered, looking all around her as if someone might hear.

"What? The castle?"

"St. Agnes. They told me it was a hospital. But I know."

"You ran away from a hospital?"

"I had to. I had to tell you."

"Tell me what?"

"It's tomorrow, Sam," she said. "It's Sunday. I know now."

"What do you mean? What's tomorrow?"

She reached out to me but didn't touch me. Her hands just hovered there in the air between us. "Don't you remember? I told you that something terrible is going to happen. Something terrible under the tree by the tarn."

I did remember. I remembered a lot of crazy talk about demons and coffins in the hallway outside her bedroom.

"Yeah," I said. "I remember. So?"

"Well, it's going to happen tomorrow. I know that now. I can hear the demons planning. No one else can hear them, but I can."

I didn't know what to say. I didn't know what to think. It sounded so crazy, but she seemed so convinced it was all true.

"Jennifer, look, I don't really understand what you're talking about."

"We have to hurry. We have to stop them."

"Stop what? What are we supposed . . . ?"

But before I could finish the sentence, the darkness was pierced by a bright beam of light. It came from behind me, shot past my shoulder, and caught Jennifer's face, making her terrified expression suddenly shine chalk-white in the darkness.

"Jennifer!" A deep voice boomed her name.

I turned and saw a figure standing at the head of the grass alley. A big man, holding a huge flashlight, shining it directly at Jennifer. As the man came forward a step or two, I saw he was a police officer. I could make out the shape of his hat and his utility belt with the gun hanging from it. I also noticed a red glow from the flasher of the patrol car that was parked in front of my house.

"It's the police, Jennifer," said the officer as he came forward. "We've been looking for you."

Jennifer stared into the flashlight beam, her mouth

open, her eyes wide. She was shaking her head back and forth, *No, no, no.*

Then she looked directly at me. "Help me, Sam!" she barely managed to whisper.

For a moment I froze, not sure what to do. She looked so frightened. But I knew the officer must be there to help her.

"Don't be afraid," I told her. "It's just a policeman. He's not gonna hurt you."

"Your mother's worried about you, Jennifer," the policeman said. "She wants you to come home."

"Sam!" Jennifer cried out, her voice cracking. "Please! Please! Don't let them take me!"

She reached out to me again. This time I caught her hand in mine.

"Listen to me, Jennifer," I said. "It's all right. It's going to be all right. It's a policeman. He just wants to take you to your mom."

"No! You don't understand. My mother's in on it."

"What?"

"She took me to a doctor! They're going to take my brain out!"

It would've been funny except she was so scared, so convinced it was true, that I felt sorry for her.

"You're my friend, Sam!" she said. Then she babbled: "My friend to the end hopping Sam Hopkins magic. You can't let them take out my brain!"

"Jennifer, shh." I held her hand, trying to calm her. "No one's going to take out your brain. They just want to help you, that's all."

"They don't understand. About the demons. About the plan. They don't understand about the terrible thing. It's going to happen tomorrow, Sam. You understand. But they just think I'm crazy."

I had a pretty good idea what had happened now. All of Jennifer's weird talk, her rhyming words and crazy sentences—it all must've gotten so strange that her mom had decided to take her to a hospital. Somehow, Jennifer had got this ridiculous idea in her head that the doctor there was going to take out her brain—and so she had run away. She had come to me because she thought I was her magic friend. And the policeman was just here to take her back to her mom so they could get her help.

"Listen to me, Jennifer," I told her. Holding her hand, I moved closer to her. The policeman came closer, shining his light on her. With her face glowing white, Jennifer stared into my eyes, her own eyes so wide and frightened that it really was pitiful to see. "I'm your friend, right?" I said. "I'm on your side, you know that."

"Friend Sam. Magic friend hopping to help me helpkins," she babbled.

"I'm telling you as your friend: you have to go with the policeman," I told her.

"No! Don't let them take me," she pleaded.

"You have to go. They want to help you, that's all," I insisted. "There's something wrong with you, Jennifer. You know that. There's something wrong in your head."

"They'll take my brain!"

"They're not going to take your brain! They're just going to—I don't know—give you some medicine or something to make you feel better."

"No, no, no!"

And all the while, the policeman cautiously came forward down the alley, closer and closer, step-by-step.

Jennifer tried to pull away from me. "I have to go," she said.

"Don't," I said. "You're not safe like this. Don't go."

"Something terrible is going to happen tomorrow."

"It'll be all right," I told her.

"It won't! It won't! Don't let them take me, Sam; you're my friend."

"Jennifer, I am your friend, but you don't understand . . ."

Just then, the policeman reached us. He stretched out a hand and put it gently on Jennifer's arm.

"Jennifer, you have to come with me," he said in a kindly tone.

Jennifer flipped out. She just went totally nuts. She started fighting and screaming and trying to pull away, and nothing I or the policeman said would calm her or convince her that the policeman just wanted to help. She attacked the cop. Struck at him with her fists, scratched at him with her fingers curled like claws. He had to dodge her and wrestle with her, pulling her arms behind her back so she couldn't hurt him.

"No! No! No!" she screamed.

"Jennifer, stop fighting!" I shouted. "They just want to help!"

But she wouldn't listen. I don't even know if she could hear me over her own panicked screaming.

"No! No! Sam Hopkins! Sam Hopkins! Help me, help me!"

It was awful to hear. Really awful. The way she was crying out for me to help her. The way the policeman had to fight her to keep her from hurting him or herself. I felt so bad for her. I wanted to do something for her. But what could I do? I knew the policeman was doing the right thing. I knew he would take her back to her mom and her doctor where she could get help. But it didn't matter what I knew. I still felt bad just standing there, helplessly, while she cried out to me in terror.

"Sam, don't let them take me! Sam, please!"

Now another policeman was running down the alley to us. And a moment later, my dad, hearing the screams, burst out of the house and now he was running toward us too.

The first policeman held Jennifer's arms behind her back while the second put handcuffs on her wrists. I knew they were doing it to keep her from hurting herself, but it looked terrible, as if they were arresting her to take her to prison or something.

I reached out my hand instinctively to protect her. But now my dad was there and he put his hand on my shoulder, drawing me back.

"Help me, Sam!" Jennifer screamed, tears streaming down her terrified face.

"Jennifer, listen . . . !" I tried to tell her.

"Sam, help me!"

"Dad, what's wrong with her?" I shouted out. I thought I was going to start crying too. "What's wrong with her?"

"She's sick, Sam," my father said. The quiet sound of his voice helped to calm me down. "She's sick. There's nothing you can do for her."

Jennifer was in handcuffs now, but she was still struggling like mad. One policeman was holding one of her arms and another officer held the other. There was no way she could get away, but she kept fighting all the same. She twisted in the officers' grasp and tried to pull free, shaking back and forth, her hair flying wildly all around.

"Sam, don't let them! Don't let them, Sam!"

My father squeezed my shoulder. "It's all right, Sam. This is the right thing. There's nothing you can do."

I knew he was right. But it sure felt terrible. I stood there watching helplessly as the two policemen carried Jennifer away. She twisted and kicked in their grasp, still screaming my name, still crying as they brought her down the alley to the front of the house. There was a second police car there now, drawn up to the curb where I could see it.

My father put his arm around my shoulder. We stood together watching as the policemen carried Jennifer to the end of the alley and brought her to the car. One cop went on holding her while the other opened the car's rear door.

They worked to lower Jennifer into the backseat, and just as they did, just as they were about to shut the door, she screamed out in a ragged, tearful voice:

"Sam Hopkins. Sam Hopkins. Sam Hopkins. It's the magic word!"

It just about broke my heart.

A Demon of My Own

"What's wrong with her, Dad?" I asked again.

We were inside now. We were sitting in the living room. My dad was in one of the armchairs; my mom was in the other. I was on the sofa, massaging my side. All the excitement had set my bruised ribs to aching again. The patrolmen had driven Jennifer away.

"Well." Dad took off his round glasses and pinched the bridge of his nose. He looked really tired. He had been up late the night before, sitting with his sick friend, Mr. Boling. He hadn't even bothered to come down on me for sneaking out of the house. "She obviously has some kind of mental illness," he said. "Some variation of schizophrenia, I guess. I've seen it before."

I had heard of schizophrenia, but when I thought

about it, I realized I didn't really know exactly what it was. "What's that, like, split personality or something?"

"No." My dad sighed and put the glasses back on. "It's this really tragic disease. Genetic partly—it tends to run in families. It's not very common, but when it does show up, it frequently shows up in young adults. They hear voices, get strange ideas. Sometimes they even see things. They get confused about what's real and what isn't."

"Jennifer saw demons in her hallway," I told him. "And a coffin with something inside that came to life and reached for her."

"Poor girl," he said.

"Her poor mother," said my mom. "Raising those two children all by herself—and now this. God help her."

I sat staring down at the rug. I still felt pretty miserable. I kept hearing Jennifer's voice in my head. I kept hearing her scream.

"Help me, Sam! Don't let them take me! Help me!"

"I couldn't make her understand that the police were trying to help," I said out loud.

"Yeah," said my dad. "I know it feels bad, like you let her down. But you didn't. You did the only thing you could to help her. Doing the right thing—you know, it isn't about *feeling* like a good person. It's about doing what's best for someone else—which sometimes doesn't feel very good at all. That's a hard thing to learn, Sam. A lot of people never learn it."

To be honest, I wasn't sure I understood it myself.

"Will the doctors be able to cure her?" I asked.

Dad shook his head wearily. "There's no cure for schizophrenia yet. But they have some medicines that can help. Sometimes they help a lot. If she's lucky, she'll be one of those cases."

I nodded. That made me feel a little better, though not much. There was still the memory of Jennifer's voice:

"Something terrible is going to happen, Sam. Tomorrow. I know that now. It's going to happen tomorrow."

"Jennifer came here to tell me that something terrible was going to happen," I said. "She said it was going to happen tomorrow."

"What do you mean?" my father said. "Something terrible like what?"

"I don't know. She said she heard . . . demons planning it." It sounded pretty crazy when I said it out loud. I added lamely: "She was pretty sure of it."

"Well . . ." My dad stood up. He stretched his back, his hands on his hips. "I wouldn't worry about that. Schizophrenics often think they have secret information about conspiracies and so on. It's part of the disease. The important thing is that she goes to a doctor before she really hurts herself or someone else."

I nodded. "I guess," I said.

But I still felt pretty bad.

I went to bed early that night. It had been a long day. The track meet, Burger Joint, Zoe, and Jennifer. My body hurt, I was exhausted, and I was down in the dumps.

But tired as I was, I couldn't sleep. I lay in the dark a long time with my eyes open because every time I closed my eyes, I saw Jennifer again. I saw her face, terrified, chalk-white in the darkness. I saw her struggling with the policemen as they carried her away. Even with my eyes open, I could hear her screaming.

"Help me, Sam! Don't let them take me!"

"Sam Hopkins! It's the magic word!"

I thought about what my dad said, about how sometimes doing the right thing feels bad. I thought about how bad I had felt when I was hanging around with Jeff Winger up at the barn. Then I felt bad because I was doing something wrong. Now I felt bad because I'd done something right. What kind of a rotten deal was that?

Finally, my eyes started to get really heavy. They drifted shut and I finally managed to fall asleep . . .

But when I did, I had a horrible dream. Here's how it went:

I was riding in the backseat of a car. I knew I wasn't supposed to be there, but I couldn't escape. A guy was sitting up in front driving. I thought it must be Jeff Winger, but I was afraid to see his face. I looked out the window, hoping to find some way out. All I saw outside was scenery passing: rolling hills, trees, a lake.

"Where are we?" I said.

The driver looked up at me in the rearview mirror. I saw there was something wrong with his eyes. My heart began to beat faster. I knew something really, really scary was about to happen.

Then it did. The driver spun around quickly to look at me. And I saw it wasn't Jeff Winger at all. It was a demon. His face was gray with a long snout like a rat's. He had dripping fangs and laughing, fire-red eyes. He was about to speak.

"See . . . ?"

But before he could finish, I came awake with a start. I was breathing hard, as if I'd been running. My heart was thundering.

I looked around my bedroom. It was morning. The sun was pouring in through the window, glinting on the shiny surface of the Super Mario poster on my wall. What a relief to see daylight! What a relief to see Mario!

Then my relief vanished. I sat up, putting my feet over the side of the bed onto the floor. I remembered my dream. The demon. Its terrifying face. It had been about to speak to me, about to tell me something. I had this awful feeling in the pit of my stomach that I knew what that something was.

Something terrible is going to happen. Today. Today. Today.

I made a noise and shivered. *It was just a dream*, I told myself. *It wasn't real. It didn't mean anything. I was just upset about what had happened the night before and so my mind turned it into a bad dream, that's all.*

That's what I told myself.

I washed up and got dressed and headed downstairs. As I did, I noticed something strange. It was quiet in the house. Nobody was moving around. There were no voices anywhere. There was no noise at all. That just doesn't happen in my house early on a Sunday morning. My dad has to get up super early to get ready for the eight o'clock service. And even though there's no choir until the ten o'clock, my mom usually wakes up with him to make breakfast and get ready to sing in her service and host the women's discussion group later and so on. Most Sundays, when I wake up I can hear my parents talking and the breakfast pots and dishes clattering. Or if I wake up a little later, I hear my brother taking a shower and my mom singing to get her voice ready.

But this morning: nothing. No voices at all. Silence through the whole house.

I went on downstairs. Into the kitchen. There was my brother, John. He was sitting by himself at the kitchen table, eating a piece of toast with one hand and holding his iPhone in the other so he could read the latest news on his sports app.

He glanced up at me, chewing his toast. "Hey. How you doing? How's the bod?"

"A little better, actually. Not as sore."

"You still look like garbage."

"Thanks."

"You recover from last night?" he asked.

"Yeah."

"That was pretty gnarly stuff, that girl screaming like that."

"Yeah, it was. Where is everyone?"

"Mom and Dad had to go out. Their friend Mr. Boling died last night."

"Oh man, that's too bad. He was, like, Dad's best friend."

"Yeah, I know. It's sad. But the guy was really old and really sick. Dad said he was totally peaceful about it at the end. Just said he was ready to go home—and went. It's the way it is, bro."

"Sure. I know that."

And I did know. People die. And it's not like I was grief-stricken about it or anything. I mean, I didn't know Mr. Boling all that well and, like John said, he was a really old guy and it was his time to go. Still, I remembered the weary look on my dad's face last night, and I felt bad he had to lose his old friend. I knew he'd be sad about it.

For a while the news about Mr. Boling pushed Jennifer out of my mind. I forgot about my dream completely—like I said, it was just a dream after all. I made myself some toast and then got over to church for the ten o'clock service.

Mary—Dad's assistant minister—had taken over the

service for him so he could go be with the Boling family. Mary was a small, squat woman with short salt-and-pepper hair. She had a loud, high, happy-sounding voice. She was kind and cheerful and everyone liked her. I found her sort of comical sometimes—everything she said sounded like she was singing opera—but I liked her too.

The church was crowded this morning. My brother and I squeezed into a pew near the front. I was a lector and had to get up and read one of the Scripture passages for the day.

The service went on and I waited for my turn to read. As I did, I sort of got lost in my own thoughts—about Jennifer and Mr. Boling and Jeff Winger and all the stuff that had been happening this last couple of weeks. Then John stuck his elbow in my side and I realized it was my time. I jumped out of my pew and hurried up the aisle to the podium.

I used to get nervous reading in front of everyone, but I didn't much anymore. Most of the people in the church had known me my whole life, and it wasn't like they were going to laugh at me if I made a mistake or anything. I was a little embarrassed about my bruised face, but I figured the whole town must have heard about what had happened by then. I had the Old Testament portion today and I started reading, "When the Lord restored the fortunes of Zion, we were like those who dream . . . ," and so on.

When I was done, I got down and went back to my pew and sat next to John and the service continued.

And as it did, my mind started to drift again.

"We were like those who dream . . ."

I started thinking about that. I started thinking about dreams in the Bible. The dream that told Abram about God's plan for Israel. The dream that told Joseph there was going to be a famine in Egypt. The dream that told the wise men to go home by another way . . .

My dreams were never like that. They never predicted the future or anything. Most of the time they didn't even make any sense. All the same, I began thinking about the Bible dreams, and then I began thinking about the dream I had last night. How I was driving in the car where I wasn't supposed to be. Looking for an escape route but seeing nothing outside except the scenery. Then that driver suddenly turning to look at me with his rat-demon face . . . about to say something . . .

The congregation around me started to stand up to sing the next hymn. I stood up too—and as I did, something occurred to me. I stood there holding the hymnbook but staring into space. My lips parted, but I didn't sing.

I remembered the demon driver in the dream. He hadn't been *about* to say something. He *had* said something.

He had said: "See . . . ?"

See what? I thought. What was there to see?

I had been looking through the window for a way to escape—just as I had done when Jeff Winger and his thugs threw me into their Camaro and drove me up to the barn in real life. I had been looking out the window and there was nothing to see outside but scenery. Hills. Trees. A lake.

"It's a demon tree. A low-spreading oak over the tarn."

As Jennifer's words sounded in my brain, I felt as if the church—the old stone church with its high gray walls, the colored banners between the tall windows, the choir singing and the people all around me singing along with them—all of it seemed to disappear, to fade away from my consciousness into a kind of surrounding darkness.

In that darkness I stood alone in a single beam of light falling through the windows. And I heard—not the hymn people were singing—but Jennifer's voice:

"A tarn is like a lake. A flat, black, round lake under the spreading branches of the tree. The demons come out of it and they gather there. They write evil symbols on the walls. And they put a coffin under the tree."

A low spreading oak over a flat, black, round lake.

I had seen that. Not just in my dream. In real life. I remembered now.

It happened when Jeff and his thug pals had driven me up the hill to the barn that first time. I had been looking out the window of the red Camaro, trying to figure out where we were going, hoping for a way to escape. But there was nothing out there. Nothing but a hillside of grass and an oak tree spreading its branches over a flat, black, round lake.

"The demons come out of it and they gather there. They write evil symbols on the walls. And they put a coffin under the tree."

It was real! The place Jennifer was talking about—it wasn't just some kind of fantasy she was having because of her schizophrenia. It was a real place. I had seen it with my own eyes. Which meant maybe . . .

"Something terrible is going to happen. Sunday."

Today.

Maybe . . ., I thought, *maybe that's real too.*

Something Terrible

I blinked—and suddenly my surroundings came back to me. I was in church. In the pew, standing next to my brother with the hymnal in my hands. The high gray walls whooshed back into my consciousness. So did the colored banners and the tall windows with the sun pouring through. The people stood on every side of me, their voices rising as they sang the hymn:

O young and fearless Prophet of ancient Galilee,
Thy life is still a summons to serve humanity . . .

But all I could think was: *I gotta get out of here!*

I had to get back to that road, back to the place where I'd seen the tree and the lake—the tarn—that Jennifer had told me about. It wasn't in her hallway. It wasn't in her mind. It was just outside of town. And it was real.

"Something terrible is going to happen. Sunday."

Today. Now.

I tried to think. *What should I do?* Was there someone I could tell? My brother? The police? Was there someone to whom I could give a warning?

But what warning? What would I tell them? That a crazy girl had seen demons in her hallway? That she was running around town afraid her doctors would take her brain out? Oh yeah, and by the way, she made a prophecy that might come true . . .

"Something terrible . . ."

I knew no one would believe me if I told them any of that. No one would believe that Jennifer had seen anything but a schizophrenic hallucination. Even I didn't believe it. Not really. I just felt a need—an urgent need—to get out of there, to get to the road where I'd seen the tree and the tarn and find out . . . what was going to happen next.

It would be nothing, I told myself. Of course. It was all just some silly coincidence. Jennifer had seen the oak and the lake and they had gotten tangled up in her hallucinations, that's all—the way my thoughts and worries had gotten tangled up in my dreams.

But now another memory came back to me. I

remembered when I saw Jennifer in the woods—that day I was biking home from the barn, that day I got into the fight with Jeff. I remember I asked her what she was doing there.

"I'm looking for the devil," she said to me.

I didn't know what it meant then. Really, I didn't know what it meant now. I just knew that when I remembered it, my throat went dry. My feeling of urgency increased. I had to get out of there. I had to go to the lake . . .

Now the hymn was ending. Now Mary was carrying the Bible down the aisle in order to read from one of the four Gospels. She came to a stop right next to me. She opened the book and started reading.

"Six days before the Passover Jesus came to Bethany . . ."

She always read the Gospel passage in an especially loud, trumpeting sort of voice. It practically rang in my ears.

"There they gave a dinner for him . . ."

I couldn't leave the church now. I couldn't just push past Mary in the middle of the Gospel reading and take off up the aisle. I swallowed hard—or tried to. Now the reading was over. Mary was marching back up the aisle toward the altar. Taking her place behind the high pulpit to deliver her sermon. What could I do? I couldn't walk out on her sermon either. Not for this. Not because I happened to remember a tree that looked like the tree in Jennifer's visions . . .

"Something terrible is going to happen."

"Something terrible is going to happen," said Mary from the pulpit.

"What?" I said, astounded that Mary's ringing voice had echoed Jennifer, had echoed my thoughts.

People in the pews looked back to see who had spoken. My brother whispered, "Keep it down, dumbo."

I stared up at him in stupid silence. I turned back to Mary and stared up at her.

"Jesus knows this," Mary went on, "and that's why he speaks as he does in the Gospel today . . ."

I felt like I was in a dream. Mary's words were just part of her sermon. But still, they echoed my thoughts, they echoed Jennifer's prediction, and they struck me as a message, a sign of some sort.

Was *I* crazy too? Or was someone trying to tell me something?

I really had to get out of here. I had to get to the tree, to the tarn.

The sermon seemed to go on forever. I couldn't listen to it. I couldn't think of anything except Jennifer's desperate voice:

"Something terrible . . ."

Finally, Mary was finished. She leaned into the pulpit microphone. She said a heartfelt "Amen."

"I gotta go," I said to John.

I guess John must've thought I was slipping out to use the bathroom. He didn't say anything as I ducked into the aisle and hurried to the back door—and out.

It was a cold day. A strong wind was blowing. Gray clouds moved quickly over a bright blue sky, dragging their shadows across the ground. I felt the force of the wind in my hair and against my cheek as I pushed my aching legs and ran top-speed over the green church lawn to my house—then around the side of the house to the port where I kept my bike.

Moments later I was pedaling as hard as I could through a powerful headwind. Glad to feel my body finally working better, healing. Making my way to the edge of town, down the country lane, to the base of the hill where the broken road led up into the countryside.

I felt strange and guilty being out on the road at a time when I was usually in church. As I traveled I started to think that maybe I was being ridiculous. Maybe I was acting as crazy as Jennifer. Or maybe—maybe I felt so bad about standing around helplessly while the police carried Jennifer away last night that I'd invented this whole situation—this dream, this sense of urgency—to make myself feel better, to make myself feel like at least I was doing *something* to help her.

But it didn't matter now. No matter what, I had to get to that tree. I had to get to the tarn. I had to see whether there was really a coffin there, whether there was really something terrible about to happen—and if so, whether or not I could stop it.

I reached the hill and started up the road. I hadn't been there since Jeff Winger and his boys beat me up. And you know what? I wasn't happy to be there now. I was afraid I might run into Jeff—or Harry Mac or Ed P. What would happen if they saw me in the middle of nowhere like this without Jennifer's brother, Mark, to protect me?

The wind pounded me as I pedaled hard up the long, winding incline, grunting with the effort. I scanned the scenery all around me. The rolling hills of grass. The stands of trees. Farmhouses and barns here and there—most of them standing empty and dark and abandoned.

I told myself I was going to feel awfully stupid once I saw that there was nothing to worry about. How was I going to explain to my brother why I had gone running out of church like that?

Then I saw it. Just as I remembered. A low oak stretching its branches out so far that it was wider than it was tall. And underneath it . . .

"A flat, black, round lake."

A tarn, just as Jennifer had said.

I laid my bike down by the side of the road and started up the grassy slope on foot. I couldn't run the whole way. I was too tired from pedaling. But I jogged as far as I could and then walked quickly, passing first through a thicket of trees and then into the open grasslands of the hill.

It was a weird scene out there. I was all alone. No one in sight anywhere as far as I could see. The sky looked huge and the clouds seemed to fly through it as if in a fast-motion film. The sun dimmed and grew bright again as the clouds passed. The grass bent in the wind, and the wind whispered through the trees behind me and rattled their bare branches. The whole place seemed somehow alive.

Up ahead, I could see the low oak bow and sway and rattle in the wind.

"*It's a demon tree.*"

That's what Jennifer had told me.

"*The demons come out of the tarn and they gather there. They write evil symbols on the walls. And they put a coffin under the tree.*"

I looked around over the empty hill. I didn't see any demons. I didn't see any coffin either. But I could see the lake now more clearly as I got closer. A small, round lake, as Jennifer had said—little more than a big puddle really. I could see its flat surface riffled by the wind, the little waves moving steadily across the surface, as if something were underneath the water, agitating the waves, rising, about to break through . . .

"*They put a coffin under the tree. The thing in the coffin was dead. And then it reached for me. It had skeleton fingers.*"

As I remembered Jennifer's words—as I moved up the hill toward the tree and the lake—I started to get really nervous. I had this sense that something was behind me, following me, reaching for me from behind with its skeleton fingers . . .

I whipped around to check, still moving backward up the hill.

Nothing was there, of course. Just the empty slope. The waving grass. The waving trees at the bottom. The shadows passing over as the clouds raced by above.

Do right. Fear nothing.

I turned and ran up the slope.

I reached the oak at the crest. The wind pushed through it from behind, making its wide branches sway forward almost as if they would surround and take hold of me. I bent forward, my hands on my knees, my head down, trying to catch my breath after the climb. I looked into the riffling lake where the water rose and fell.

No demons in sight, that was for sure. No coffin. Nothing "terrible" seemed to be about to happen. I was just being silly. Following the visions of a schizophrenic. Following my dreams as if they were real. I was just trying to make myself feel better about the fact that there was nothing I could do to help Jennifer.

I straightened. And then I saw the old barn.

It had been hidden behind the oak, down the far slope of the hill, out of sight from below. I saw it now through the moving branches.

I stepped around the tree and peered down the slope. I

felt something twist inside me as I got my first good look at the barn.

It was not a pleasant place to look at. It was old, empty, abandoned. The paint had long since worn away, and the boards were rotten and splintery. The barn's door was closed, a wooden bolt holding it in place. But the wind made the door buck and knock as if someone—or something—were pushing on it from behind.

I looked around me. The emptiness of the hill seemed chaotic with the racing shadows of the clouds. It was an eerie, lonely place to be and I wanted to get out of there fast—now. I told myself: *I've done my job. I've checked things out. Nothing terrible is happening.* After all, Jennifer hadn't mentioned the barn in her vision. Just the tree and the lake.

But even as I told myself to turn around and run back to my bike, I started moving down the far slope of the hill toward the barn.

Do right. Fear nothing.

The closer I got to the place, the spookier it looked. Big. Dark. Empty. And it seemed to expand and shudder with the wind. The door kept knocking against its bolt, straining against its hinges. The closer I got, the more I expected the door to burst open and something—Jennifer's demons, maybe—to come rushing out at me.

I reached the barn. Again, I had that feeling that someone—something—was creeping up behind me. Again, I looked around. Again, I saw nothing.

I turned back to the door and put my hands on the bolt. Felt the door moving and straining against my hand like a living thing.

I lifted the bolt. I pulled the big door open. The barn yawned wide and dark in front of me.

There was the coffin.

I wasn't nervous anymore. I was scared out of my wits. My stomach was in knots. I had to use all my willpower to keep from running away.

It's not really a coffin, I told myself. *It's just a crate. It's just an old crate in an empty barn.*

And that was true. It wasn't shaped like a coffin. It just looked like an old shipping crate or something.

But I couldn't help noticing that it was just the right size to hold a body.

"The thing in the coffin was dead. And then it reached for me. It had skeleton fingers."

I ought to go, I told myself. *I ought to get out of here, get some help. I ought to call the police.*

But what would I tell the police if I called them? There's an empty barn with a box in it? There's a schizophrenic girl who says something terrible is going to happen? And I had a dream? And there are dreams in the Bible?

No. It would sound ridiculous. In spite of all my fears—in spite of my horror-movie imagination—nothing had really happened. Nothing terrible. Nothing at all.

The problem was, I still felt I couldn't leave here before I was sure everything was all right.

So I stepped into the barn.

The daylight disappeared behind me. The barn's shadows closed over me. The place was big and empty and the shadows were dark. I could vaguely make out piles of garbage—farm tools, lumber, auto parts, crates—lying against the wall. I couldn't help feeling that there were things moving unseen amid those weirdly shaped piles—but I told myself it was just my imagination.

I stepped closer to the box in the center of the dirt floor.

"The thing in the coffin was dead. And then it reached for me."

I shook my head rapidly, hoping to get rid of Jennifer's words.

But now, as my eyes adjusted to the darkness, I saw something else. Something on the walls. Writing. Slashed symbols. I turned and saw a picture of a grinning skull. A picture of a grinning devil. The word *DEATH* splashed in huge letters.

"The demons come out of the lake and they gather there. They write evil symbols on the walls."

My breath caught and a sound came out of me—a sound I didn't like to hear—a frightened whine that made me sound like a little boy scared of the monster under my bed, trying not to call for my mommy.

What was this place? What was that box? What was happening?

I really wanted to run. I wanted to run so badly it was almost like my legs were going to start moving without me. But I kept thinking of what Jennifer had said—had repeated over and over:

"Something terrible is going to happen. Sunday."

Today. Now.

Do right! I screamed at myself in my mind. *Do right and fear nothing, Sam!*

If something terrible was going to happen—and if I was the only one who knew—and if I could do something to stop it—then I had to find out what was going on and do whatever I could.

I took another step toward the box.

And something inside it started to move.

I stopped dead-still. My mouth hung open. I thought I must be imagining things. But there was no way. No way I was imagining this. Clearly, from inside the box, came the sound of thumping. I even thought I saw the box tremble a little—as if something was twisting around in there.

And then . . . another noise . . . I wasn't sure what it was at first. Then I was. It was a voice. Muffled. Straining to speak. A human voice.

This was no demon. Someone was in there! Someone was trapped in that box. Struggling to get out. Calling for help.

Do right!

I had forgotten all about the bruises and sore spots on my body now. I rushed forward. The box had a lid on top of it. The lid was just boards hammered together. There were ropes running through the spaces between the boards and the spaces in the crate. The ropes were knotted to hold the lid in place.

I knelt in front of the box and began to try to untie the knots as fast as I could. It wasn't easy. My hands were shaking like crazy. I felt the shadows of the barn moving all around me. I felt the symbols on the wall watching me: the grinning death's head, the grinning devil, the strange symbols, the slashed words . . . *DEATH* . . . I felt sure something was hiding behind the piles of garbage on the walls, watching me . . .

And all the while, from inside the box, the thumping noise continued, growing more rapid—more desperate, I thought. The muffled voice tried to call out, cracking in its strain. It sounded panicky and fearful.

I pulled frantically at the rope—and finally, finally, the knot came loose. I grabbed hold of the lid and shoved it off the box.

My eyes had adjusted to the darkness now. I could see clearly what was inside—*who* was inside the box.

It was Harry Mac. Jeff Winger's muscleman crony. The guy who had chased me onto the railroad bridge. The guy who had helped Jeff beat me silly down by the road. He was tied up with ropes. He was gagged with an old bandanna. His eyes were white with terror. His face was streaked with blood.

Struggling against the ropes that tied him, he cried out to me frantically from behind the gag. I couldn't make out the words, but I knew he was trying to scream for help.

I reached forward to pull down the gag, but before I could, I heard a noise behind me.

I turned and saw a silhouetted figure charging at me out of the shadows.

And suddenly, the wind rose. The barn door blew shut. Darkness.

The next second, something struck me—hard—on the side of the head, and I toppled over into a deeper darkness still.

Something Even Worse

I don't know how long I was unconscious. It didn't feel like very long at all. At first, when I woke up, I couldn't remember anything. I couldn't remember where I was or what I had been doing. I could hardly think about anything except the pain throbbing in my forehead.

I was aware that it was dark. I was aware that I was uncomfortable, my face pressed into the cold, rough dirt. I was aware that, somewhere, the wind was blowing—roaring all around me. There was another sound too—a high-pitched wail far away—almost hidden inside the wind. What was it?

But before I could figure it out, I became aware of a louder noise: the door rattling, banging on its hinges . . .

Then it came back to me. Where I was. What had happened. The tree. The lake. The barn. The coffin. The figure charging through the shadows . . .

Harry Mac!

I started to sit up quickly—but the minute I did, the throbbing pain above my eyes became a lancing knife of agony. I cried out, clutching my head. Stars and purple blotches flashed in front of me. I sat there on the barn floor, half-upright, holding the bruised place, my body wavering back and forth as I fought down nausea.

The wind kept blowing. And that high-pitched keening sound hidden in the wind grew louder, steadier. What was it?

Harry Mac . . .

I fought down the pain. I had to help him. I turned to the box in the center of the room. I could just make it out in the shadows that grew lighter and darker as the door moved in the wind, as it let in sunlight from outside and then blocked it again.

But the box was still there, just as I'd left it. The lid was as I'd left it too, thrown off, leaning against the side.

Flinching at the pain, I moved to the box, took hold of the side, drew myself up over it. I looked down into it.

Harry Mac was still there, still bound, still gagged, still staring up at me with his white eyes. I reached in and grabbed his shoulder.

"Harry Mac, you all right?"

He didn't answer.

"Harry . . ."

I tried to lift him, but he was limp, too heavy. I leaned

forward into the box and tried to get a better grip. And as I did, I saw . . .

"Oh!" I said. The breath rushed out of me.

Harry Mac was still staring at me, but now I realized: His eyes were no longer filled with fear. His eyes were empty. Completely empty.

Harry Mac was dead. A round bullet hole showed darkly in the center of his chest.

I fell back from the box, scrambling away. The images and words on the wall seemed to swirl around me on every side. The grinning skull. The grinning devil. *Death.*

As I scrambled back, my hand touched cold metal. I saw something lying under my fingers. A pistol.

The door rattled. The wind blew. That high-pitched keening sound grew louder and louder, closer and closer.

I knew what it was now. It was a siren.

The police. They were almost here.

Prime Suspect Me

Detective Freddy Sims was fat and bald. With his round belly and round head, he looked kind of like a snowman, only with big, bushy gray eyebrows. Also, he had these big unsnowman-like saggy bags under his eyes and thin lips that curled at one corner into a sort of permanent smile, as if he found the whole world kind of stupid and annoying but kind of funny at the same time.

He came into the room where I was sitting. It was a small room in the police station. It was white with soundproofing tiles on the walls and ceiling. There was nothing in it but a long table and chairs and a video camera hanging up high in one corner. I had seen a lot of rooms like this on television police shows. In the shows, police detectives interrogated people in rooms like this until the people burst into tears and confessed to murder. As you might guess, I was not happy to be there.

At least I wasn't alone. After they arrested me at the barn, the police called my dad. He came straight from the Bolings' house, still wearing jeans and a checkered flannel shirt. His eyes looked damp and bright as if he were in pain. I guessed he was. First his best friend dies, then his son gets mixed up in a murder? Not a good day for my dad.

Dad and I sat next to each other at the table. I tried not to pick at the bandage that was taped to my head behind my right ear. It covered the place where I'd been slugged, which was still throbbing and aching despite a lot of extra-strength aspirin.

The snowman-shaped Detective Sims sat across from us. There was a black folder on the table in front of him. Along the side of the folder, there was a label that read "Macintyre, H." Macintyre was Harry Mac's full last name.

Sims pressed the tips of his pudgy fingers together and looked down at them with that permanent little smile of his—as if he found his hands kind of silly somehow. Then he looked up at me. He went on smiling.

"You're Sam Hopkins?" he asked—as if that was kind of amusing too.

"Yeah," I said. My voice shook a little. Even though I hadn't broken any laws, I was nervous to be talking to the police.

"As I understand it, our officers found you alone in an abandoned barn with the dead body of Harry Macintyre. Is that correct?"

"Yeah, but . . ."

Detective Sims held up a fat finger, telling me to be quiet. I was quiet. "They tell me Mr. Macintyre had been shot with a 9mm automatic pistol."

"I know, but . . ."

"The pistol in question was also in the barn."

"Yeah, but I never . . ."

"And it had your fingerprints on it."

"Yeah, but I don't know . . ."

"Now you and this Mr. Macintyre—they tell me the two of you are known to have had a fight recently, yes?"

"Yeah, but . . ."

Detective Sims held up the finger again. "And as I understand it, Mr. Macintyre and his friends beat you up pretty severely."

"Yeah, but that's the thing . . ."

"You know what the word *motive* means, don't you, Sam?"

"Yeah, but . . ."

"Let me use it in a sentence for you so I'm sure you understand," said the snowman detective, still smiling away. "Sam Hopkins got beaten up by Harry Macintyre, so Sam's motive for murdering Harry was revenge."

There was an explosion of horror inside me. "I didn't

murder Harry Mac!" I nearly shouted the words, the idea was so scary. "I wouldn't murder anybody."

"So what exactly were you doing at the barn with a dead body and a gun?" asked the detective.

"I already explained that to the officers who brought me here."

"Well—now explain it to me."

So I did. I told him how Jennifer had had a hallucination about demons and then I had had a dream and then the Bible had mentioned dreams and I'd remembered how I'd seen the tree and the lake and I went there because Jennifer said something terrible was going to happen and Harry Mac was in a box there and got killed.

When I finished talking, there was a long, long silence. Detective Sims tapped his fingertips together. He went on smiling. His bushy eyebrows bounced up and down on his round, bald snowman head.

"That's your story?" he asked me finally.

"That's what happened!" I insisted.

"A crazy girl had a hallucination about demons and whatnot. Then you had a dream. And it all came true."

"Well . . . Yeah! Basically. Yeah," I said. I was starting to feel sick to my stomach. Was it really possible the police could think I'd killed Harry Mac?

Detective Sims nodded. "Okay," he said. "Okay. That's your story then." He reached for the black folder and drew it closer to him. He opened it and scanned the top page inside.

"Now let me tell you another story," he went on. "We'll see which one sounds more plausible. In my story, Jeff Winger and Harry Macintyre and Ed Polanski are a gang of thieves. They steal cars and burgle houses, then deliver the swag to a crew in Albany, who sell it off and give them a piece of the profits. Jeff brings you in and starts giving you lessons on how to be a thief too. But somehow you and Harry Mac have a falling-out, and Harry convinces the others to cut you out of the action. They give you a beating and send you on your way. So you decide to get your revenge on Harry, hoping the others will let you come back into the crew. So this morning at approximately eleven o'clock, you abducted Harry Mac. You took him to the barn. And you shot him dead."

I opened my mouth to try to answer him, but I couldn't. It felt like there was something blocking my throat. All I could think about was getting taken off to jail. Charged with murder! Locked up for life! I just sat there with my mouth hanging open.

Finally, my dad spoke for me in his usual quiet, serious, and thoughtful way.

"Detective Sims," he said, "you can see my son was struck very hard on the back of his head, can't you?"

"Yes, of course I can, but . . ."

My father did to the detective what the detective had done to me: he held up a silencing finger. "You must know he couldn't possibly have done that to himself."

"Well, no, but . . ."

"So that means you know someone else was in the barn with him."

"Yeah, but . . ."

"Someone who must've abducted Harry Mac because at the time he was abducted, my son was in church, reading in front of the entire congregation."

Detective Sims shrugged. "Okay. So maybe he had an accomplice who did the actual kidnapping, but . . ."

My father's serious face creased with a small, quiet smile of his own. "Only you know that's not true, don't you, Detective?"

This time the detective didn't answer at all. He went on smiling as before, but I could tell that, behind his smile, he was annoyed.

I watched almost without breathing. What was Dad talking about? Why was he making the detective mad?

"You knew my son was hanging out with Jeff Winger," my father went on in the same quiet tone. "You knew Winger and his thugs beat my son up. That's the sort of thing you might have heard around town. But you also knew Winger gave my son lessons in breaking locks and stealing cars. That's inside information. I'm guessing you had an informant in Winger's gang, someone who was talking to you about the whole thieving operation."

"Reverend Hopkins . . . ," Detective Sims began.

"I'm guessing that informant was Harry Mac," my father said.

For the first time, Detective Sims stopped smiling. His cheeks turned red—just slightly, but I could see it. And his eyes got dark too. He still looked like a snowman, but now he looked like a really, really angry snowman.

And I was thinking: *What? Harry Mac? An informant? How did my dad figure that out?*

"You know what the word *motive* means, don't you, Detective?" my dad said then. "Let me use it in a sentence so I'm sure you understand: Harry Mac was informing on Jeff Winger and Ed Polanski, so Winger wanted to shut him up and that was his motive for killing him."

My dad and Detective Sims sat looking at each other through another long silence.

And now the horror inside me was almost instantly transformed into hope. I realized what had happened, what my dad had done. And I thought, *Whoa! Dad! Bring it on!* My dad was a better detective than the detective.

Finally, Detective Sims cleared his throat. "I'm not saying your son acted alone. But his fingerprints were on the gun and . . ."

"My son was knocked unconscious, Detective," my father said. "Anyone could have wrapped his hand around that pistol. In fact, why knock him out in the first place unless you wanted to do exactly that?"

"Wanted to do exactly what?" said Detective Sims.

"Frame my son for murder," said Dad. "I mean, if my son had fired that gun, wouldn't there be powder residue on his hands? Blood-spatter stains on his shirt? Did you find anything like that?"

Again, Detective Sims didn't answer. And again, I thought: *Whoa, Dad!* Powder residue? Blood-spatter stains? Where'd he learn about that stuff? My dad never even watched cop shows on TV.

And Dad said, "My son couldn't have been there to abduct Harry Mac—he was in church at the time. And he obviously didn't fire the gun that killed him. That pretty much leaves my son's version of events as the only plausible version there is."

Detective Sims looked at my father across the table and said nothing. There was nothing he could say.

Now my dad turned to me. "Sam, do you have anything else you want to tell the detective?"

I thought about it. "No," I said. "I told him everything I can think of."

My father's chair scraped against the floor as he pushed back from the table and stood up. He was so tall, he looked to me like his head was going to brush the ceiling. He looked down—way down—at Detective Sims. "Are you going to arrest my son?" he asked.

I held my breath as I waited for Detective Sims to answer. After what seemed to me the longest silence of all, the detective finally said, "No. No, not today. But if he gets in any more trouble—if he even gets in my way—we're going to take up this issue again. I may not have him on murder—not yet. But I've got enough to charge him with being part of Winger's gang."

"Except you know he wasn't," my father said. "Because Harry Mac was your informant, and he told you what happened."

Detective Sims didn't answer.

"Well, in that case, I'm taking him home," said my father. Then to me he said, "Let's go, Sam."

Believe me, he didn't have to tell me twice.

18

Prophets and Madmen

I followed my father out of the interrogation room into the detective room—and there was Jeff Winger.

The detective room was a windowless office with lots of flyers and papers pinned to bulletin boards along the wall. There were three gray desks crowding the floor. There was a detective sitting behind one of the desks, talking on the phone. At another desk, there was a detective tapping at a computer. Jeff was sitting next to him.

Jeff was in handcuffs. He looked totally miserable. His head was hanging down and his weaselly eyes weren't darting around every which way like they usually did. They were just staring at the floor.

Until I came in, that is. When Jeff heard the interrogation room door open, he looked up. He saw me at the same time I saw him. He stared at me—and his eyes looked so dark and so unhappy, I actually felt sorry for him even though he'd beaten me up. He didn't have a dad to get him out of trouble—and he was in a lot of it.

I paused for a minute and just stood there looking at Jeff as he looked at me. Then my father stopped walking. He turned back and took hold of my arm.

"Come on, son," he said.

And I left the detective room with my dad as Jeff Winger sat there in handcuffs, watching me go.

I kept my mouth shut until Dad and I were in the Passat, driving out of the police station parking lot.

"Dad!" I said then. "That was so awesome! That was so cool! You turned that detective guy inside out! He never knew what hit him!"

"Well," said my father quietly. "Then that makes two of us."

I was about to say something else, but my mouth fell shut with a snap. I hadn't really had time to think about how all this had seemed to my father. Me running off without telling anyone. Getting in more trouble over Jeff Winger without saying anything to him. And it was real trouble this time too. This wasn't just some fistfight out by the side of the road. Harry Mac was dead! Murdered. And for a minute there, before my dad unleashed his death-ray intellect on Sims, I was feeling like I was the prime suspect.

"Listen, Dad, I'm really sorry. I'm, like, the worst son ever. I didn't mean to—"

"No, no, no," said my father, holding up his hand as he drove. "I can see what happened. I'm not sure you did exactly the right thing, but I can see you didn't do anything actually wrong—not as far as I can tell anyway."

I was quiet then, thinking about everything that had gone on. The Passat cruised down a tree-shaded lane of houses. It was Sunday quiet out there, the lawns and sidewalks empty, no one in sight. The afternoon sun shone through the late-winter branches, sending patches of light and shadow over the windshield.

"How could it happen?" I said after a while. "How could Jennifer's hallucination come true?"

My father shook his head. "I don't know."

"Do you think . . . ?"

I couldn't find a way to put it into words, so after a minute my dad glanced at me. "Do I think what?"

"Well, do you think Jennifer might be some kind of, like, prophet or something?"

"A *prophet*?" He repeated the word as if he'd never heard it before. "What do you mean?"

"Well, there are prophets in the Bible, right? People who had visions about what was going to happen . . ."

My dad gave an unhappy sort of laugh. "Well . . . I think the prophets in the Bible were just very wise people who knew how to listen to God in their hearts and who understood that actions have consequences."

"But the prophets did have visions, didn't they?"

"Yes, some of them."

"So, I mean, isn't it possible that Jennifer could be somebody like that? I mean, maybe her mom is taking her to the doctor and giving her medicine and whatever, and really she's fine—she's just seeing visions of things that haven't happened yet."

I watched my father as he thought this over. The corner of his mouth turned up in a smile as he drove, but it was a very sad smile, I thought.

"Listen, Sam," he said finally. "Jennifer is a sick girl. She has a mental disorder and she's having hallucinations. How those hallucinations managed to get you to that barn just as Harry Mac was being murdered—well, that I don't know, but . . ."

He stopped. I thought there was something he wanted to say, but now he was the one who couldn't figure out what words to use.

"But what?" I said.

"Aw, Sam . . . ," my father said with a sigh. "I've devoted my life to my faith, so you know what I believe. I believe there are powers beyond the ones we see, but . . ."

"But what?"

"Well, the world is not a magical place, that's all. The things that happen are pretty predictable, and they can usually be explained in ordinary terms. People do bad things and bad things happen that we can't control. People hurt each other. They get sick. They grow old and . . ." He shrugged.

And die, I thought. *Like Mr. Boling.*

My dad glanced at me and I looked away—because he looked so sad. I guess he was. I guess that's why he sounded so sad.

"Well, then . . . how do *you* explain what happened?" I asked him now. "How do you explain that Jennifer had a hallucination about a coffin with someone alive inside it—and then I went off to that place and there was a box with Harry Mac alive inside it, just like she saw? And what about her telling me that something terrible was going to happen on Sunday—and then it did?"

"I don't know," Dad said. "I can't explain it. Maybe it was just some kind of coincidence or . . . something. I don't know." He brought the Passat to a stop at a stop sign. He stayed there a second in order to turn and face me. "What I do know is that Jennifer needs medical help. She's not a prophet, Sam. She has a disease, that's all. Those are hallucinations she's having. Not visions."

I wanted to argue with him, but I decided against it. He looked like he wanted to stop talking about it now.

I wished I could've stopped talking about it too. But there was no way. When we got home, I had to tell the whole story all over again to John, who was kind of annoyed about my running out of church like that without telling him. Then that night, when my mom got home from the Bolings' house, I had to tell it to her. She practically went through the ceiling like a bottle rocket.

Then the next day in school, Monday, everyone wanted to know about it. Zoe asked me about it on the way to history class. Mark and Nathan and Justin made a big deal about it in the cafeteria, pulling kids over to their table and getting me to tell them the story even if they already knew the details. At night, a radio station even called the house for an interview, but Dad wouldn't let them talk to me.

More news came out the next day. We heard how Jeff Winger and Ed P. had both been charged with killing Harry Mac and a whole lot of other stuff too, like stealing cars. I guess that meant my dad was right and Harry Mac had been killed because he was talking to the police about what Jeff was doing. A couple of days later we heard that both guys had gotten lawyers. They were going to be tried as adults and faced long sentences in prison, maybe even life.

I only got a little news about Jennifer. Mark didn't want to talk about it much. He told me his sister had been put in the secure ward at St. Agnes Hospital because she was so upset. He said they were waiting for the antischizophrenia medicine to kick in. Then they hoped she would calm down and they could put her with the rest of the patients.

It wasn't until the end of the week that things started to quiet down a little bit. And by Friday people were finally talking about something else—namely, the big track meet against Empire and Cole. In fact, people were so excited about it, I went the whole day without anyone asking me a single question about Jeff or Harry or Ed. I was glad about that. Really glad. I thought maybe the whole thing was over. In fact, that night after dinner, I went on my computer and sent a message to Joe:

ME: Well, I guess that's the end of it.
JOE: Guess so.
ME: I even got my bandage off. I almost look normal.
JOE: That'd be a first.
ME: I'm really glad it's over. It's been awful.
JOE: Well, like you said, it's over now.

Just then, my cell phone rang. I didn't recognize the number on the readout. I picked it up.

"Sam Hopkins, Sam Hopkins," a voice whispered to me breathlessly.

"Jennifer?" I said. My heart began speeding up. What now?

"I have to tell you what's going to happen next," Jennifer said.

"Next?" I said—or tried to say through my dry throat. "What do you mean? Jennifer, where are you? Did you run away again?"

"I can't run away. I can't, Sam Hopkins. They locked me up. They locked me up in the demon castle."

The demon castle? I thought. "The hospital?" I said. "St. Agnes?"

"They gave me medicine so I wouldn't hear, so I couldn't see. But I *can* hear, Sam. I *can* see. I see with my eyes. Through the lies. I see who dies."

"Jennifer," I said. "You're not making any sense."

"I see what's going to happen, Sam."

I licked my dry lips. I tried to remember what my dad said. She was just sick. She was just having hallucinations.

But I remembered Harry Mac in the box too, like a man in a coffin, just as Jennifer had said.

"What do you see, Jennifer?" I asked her. "What do you see is going to happen?"

There was a long pause. And then suddenly—and this was just really terrifying—suddenly Jennifer whispered very quietly:

"So many dead, Sam! So many dead!"

PART FOUR

BUSTER

JENNIFER SLEPT AND DREAMED AND WOKE AND SLEPT again. The demons had her locked away. Locked in their demon castle. She could hear them. Invisible. Gathering. Whispering. Planning . . .

Now we're free.

Now she can't stop us.

Now Sam Hopkins can't stop us.

We can do what we want.

We can kill.

We can kill them all.

She lay curled on the bed in her room. She tried to stay awake to listen. She tried to stand. She tried to go to the door, to catch them out, the way she sometimes did at home. But here in the castle, the wizards had given her a potion. It made her sleepy. The sleepiness made the whispering demons sound far away. She had to listen very hard to hear them. But she could still make out their words.

Tomorrow.

Tomorrow, we'll kill them all.

Tomorrow, they'll see our power.

Don't tell Sam.

"Have to tell Sam," Jennifer murmured into the mattress. But she couldn't move. She couldn't get off the bed. She couldn't even keep her eyes open . . .

Her eyes came open wide suddenly. She had been asleep again. Lost in a terrible dream. Blood-soaked death. Bodies everywhere.

She rolled over onto her back. She stared up at the ceiling. She listened.

Nothing.

The whispers had stopped.

Quickly, Jennifer sat up. She shifted her legs over the side of the bed, sat gripping the edge of the mattress with her fingers. The drowsiness still sat heavily on her. She stretched her eyes wide. She shook away the sleep. She looked around.

She was in a new room. Not the room they'd put her in at first, when the police had caught her, when they'd carried her away from her magical friend and brought her back to the demon hospital. They had locked her up then. And given her their potions that made her sleep so she couldn't stop sleeping.

"We're going to give you medicine to make you feel better," said Dr. Demon Fletcher with the nice-face rice cakes. "We're going to make the demon whisperers go away. Don't you want that?"

Jennifer did. She wanted it so much, more than anything.

All that was days ago now—she wasn't sure how many. She wasn't sure when they had taken her out of the locked room and brought her here. She sat on the edge of the bed and looked around. Her new room was small but pleasant. There was the bed and a desk and a chair. There was a notebook on the desk and a marker for her to write with. There was a small calendar. It was Friday.

Friday, Jennifer thought—and shivered. Now she knew.

This room was not as homey as her room at home, but it felt safer somehow. There weren't all the animals and posters and princesses staring with eyes to see who lies, to see who dies . . .

And Jennifer noticed something else too. It was quiet here. Very quiet. The whispering had stopped. *Maybe*, she thought—hardly daring to hope—*maybe the medicine had worked.*

Jennifer stood up in the weird silence. It was hard to stand because the drowsiness sat on her shoulders like a stone gargoyle. It made her feel like a gargirl, heavy as stone.

There was a small window on the wall behind her. She moved to it, unsteady on her heavy gargirl legs. She pressed her face close to the glass, staring out.

It was dark. It was night. But there was a spotlight on and she could make out some things in its glow. She could see the courtyard of the hospital, one story below her. Grass. Paths. Benches. A tall tree in the middle. The hospital walls rising on every side of it in shadow. Dark walls like the dark battlements of a demon castle.

Did they think they were fooling her when they called it a hospital?

Jennifer scanned the courtyard. No one there except . . .

Except every time she looked in one direction, she caught a motion out of the corner of her eye in the other direction. But when she turned to look in that direction . . . nothing. No one.

Because they were moving in secret. That's why. That's why there were no whispers. They were keeping quiet. So she wouldn't hear, wouldn't see.

Jennifer turned. She had to blink a few times because the gargoyle sleepiness was hanging on her eyelids, trying to force them closed, just as the gargoyle was sitting on her gargirl shoulders, trying to drive her back down onto the bed.

All the same, pushing her heavy stone legs forward, she went to the door. She tried the knob. Was she locked in here too?

No! The doorknob turned. The door opened.

Jennifer stepped out into a hallway. Almost at once, a lady was there, walking toward her. The sight of the lady startled Jennifer and suddenly she felt less sleepy, more awake.

The lady had a brown face. She wore white clothes. Was she an angel? No, just a lady. She smiled.

"Hi, Jennifer," she said. "How are you?"

Jennifer tried to smile, but her face felt stony too. Who was this white-brown angel lady? What did she want?

"Are you hungry?" the woman asked.

Jennifer realized that in fact she was hungry. She nodded.

The angel lady smiled. "It's past dinnertime now, but I figured you might want something to eat when you woke up so I saved you a little something. Go into the common room and I'll bring it to you there."

She pointed down the hall at a door. Jennifer tried to smile again, did better this time. She was feeling more awake. She moved in the direction the woman pointed.

She listened carefully as she walked down the now-empty hall. There were no whispers. No noises. Maybe the demons had gone away as Dr. Fletcher said they would. As she walked, she turned her head, turned it quickly, this way and that, trying to spot them, trying to see if they were hiding in the shadows, bad-ohs in the shadows, but no, there was no one. Maybe it was safe here. Maybe the medicine had made them go away. Maybe . . .

She reached the broad doorway into the common room. And stopped. And stood stock-still, gaping in horror.

Her dream had come true and death was everywhere. Bodies were everywhere, all over the common room. Murdered corpses, their flesh ripped by bullet wounds. They lay on the chairs, their blood staining the upholstery. They lay sprawled on the floor in red puddles of blood. Everywhere Jennifer looked . . . the dead, the dead!

She drew back, moving her hand to her mouth, about to scream, when all at once . . .

"Here we go!"

Startled, Jennifer let out a little cry and turned to see . . .

Just the angel lady, coming toward her with a tray. A sandwich. A glass of juice. A cookie. On a tray. Angel smiling.

"Go on in," she said, nodding toward the common room.

Jennifer looked again. She let out her breath in a long sigh.

Everything was fine now. The dead were gone. The blood was gone. The common room was empty. Big comfortable chairs. Two sofas. A television set on the wall. Everything was normal except . . .

Except the clock. The round clock high on the wall. The hands of the clock were spinning, spinning quickly. Hours going by. Days.

Tomorrow, Jennifer thought. *Tomorrow.*

"Go on in," said the lady again.

Jennifer stepped through the door into the common room. Everything was normal now, but she could smell gun smoke. She could smell blood. She could smell death.

"I'll just put this right over here," the woman said.

We're going to kill them all, whispered a demon suddenly in Jennifer's ear.

Jennifer put her hands on her ears to close out the whisper—but then quickly took them away again because she didn't want the angel lady to see.

Tomorrow. Tomorrow.

She had to call Sam. She had to warn Sam.

"Is there a phone somewhere?" she asked—she spoke the words before she even thought them.

The lady set the tray down on a small table by one of the armchairs. She straightened and looked at Jennifer. "Well, there is," she said, "but you're only supposed to use it at certain times . . ."

"I . . ." Jennifer tried to think of an answer—and the answer came into her head as if out of nowhere. "I want to call my friend. He hasn't heard from me in days. I want him to know I'm all right."

The lady hesitated but then smiled, a white angel smile in her brown face, and said, "Well, since you just got out of the secure ward, I guess it's only right to let you call a friend. You want to eat first or . . . ?"

"No," said Jennifer, the right words just coming to her. "I'm afraid it'll get to be too late and he'll be asleep."

"Okay. Well, let's see what we can do."

The lady led her out of the common room. Down the hall. As Jennifer walked behind her, she heard whispers, whispers, whispers but couldn't make out the words they said. She thought they were laughing.

"Here we are," said the lady. "Just go back to the common room when you're done and your sandwich will be waiting for you."

The lady unlocked the door of a small room. Inside there were several desks with dividers on them—walls that rose out of the desktops, protecting them from the other desks. On each desk there was a telephone. No one else was in the room.

"No more than five minutes, all right?" said the lady in white. "That's the rule."

"All right," said Jennifer.

The lady in white left her there alone. Jennifer sat down at one of the desks. She lowered her head low, low, low, almost pressing her cheek to the desktop so she was hidden away, so no one could see her over the dividers, and she couldn't see anyone, couldn't see the rest of the room.

She reached for the phone. Her hand was trembling. She was trying to stay calm. She dialed Sam Hopkins's number. She knew it by heart.

"Hello?" Sam said.

Jennifer was so happy to hear his voice. She said his magic name. Said it twice."Sam Hopkins. Sam Hopkins."

"Jennifer?" said Sam.

"I have to tell you what's going to happen next," she said quickly. She had to talk quickly before the demons found her. "I can see. I can see with my eyes. Through the lies. I see who dies. I see what's going to happen, Sam."

There was a pause. Then Sam asked, "What do you see, Jennifer?"

She tried to tell him. About the bodies in the common room. About the moving clock. Tomorrow. It was going to happen tomorrow. She began to grow excited as she tried to make him understand. She lifted her head. Holding on to the phone, clutching the phone in her shaking, quaking, sweating hands, she stood up.

Her breath caught in her throat.

There it was again. Death. Everywhere. The bodies. Everywhere. The blood in pools. Bodies splayed over the desks and sprawled on the floor. And the clock on the wall, spinning.

Tomorrow.

Jennifer tried to cry out, but her voice would not rise higher than a whisper.

"So many dead, Sam!" she whispered. "So many dead!"

"Jennifer." Sam's frightened voice came back to her. "Who's dead? What's happening? Tell me what you see."

"Tomorrow!" The words would barely come out of her. "Tomorrow! So many!"

"Jennifer, tell me what you see!"

She was about to try to explain it to him, but now the door to the telephone room opened. The lady in white, the angel lady, came in.

Jennifer looked at her and then looked around the room. All the dead were gone. Everything was back to normal. Jennifer could only stand, staring.

"Time to go," the angel lady told her.

And she walked over to Jennifer, took the phone from her slack hand, and gently hung it up in the cradle.

The Worst Night of My Life

Suddenly the phone went silent.

"Hello?" I shouted. "Hello?"

But there was no answer, nothing. Jennifer had hung up. She was gone.

I lowered my cell from my ear and stared into space. I thought: *So many dead. Tomorrow. So many dead.*

Something on my computer caught my eye.

JOE: Sam? U still there?

I hesitated for only a second, then I typed in quickly:

ME: G2G.

And I dashed out of the room.

"Dad! Dad!" I shouted.

I plunged down the stairs two at a time, so fast I nearly tripped and fell headlong to the bottom. My feet skittered over the floor as I came off the last step. I had to grab hold of the banister post to keep from falling.

"Dad! Da—"

"Whoa, Sam. What's happening? What's wrong?"

Dad was there, right in front of me. He took hold of my shoulders to keep me from going down.

"Jennifer called me," I said to him. I could barely get the words out, they were jumbling together in my mind and in my mouth. "Jennifer . . . she . . . on the phone . . ."

"All right, all right, slow down. Tell me what happened."

My father—so much taller than I was—blinked down at me through his glasses from high above. My mom had also come into the room at the sound of my shouts and she was standing behind him. John was at the top of the stairs now, looking down. They were all watching me, waiting to hear what I was about to say.

I took a breath, trying to slow down my racing brain so I could get the words right. "Jennifer called me on my cell."

"From the hospital?" said my father.

"I guess. Yes. I don't know. Yes, probably. She said she'd had another . . . another vision."

My father straightened a little in surprise. He was still holding on to my shoulders. "A vision. What do you mean?"

"She said, 'So many dead. So many dead.' She kept saying it. She said it was going to happen tomorrow."

I don't know what I expected to happen next. I guess I thought my dad would leap to the phone and call the police or something. But instead of getting more excited—as excited as I was—he seemed to sort of relax. He let go of me. He put his hands in his pockets. His mouth kind of bunched up all on one side.

"Look, Sam," he said, "we talked about this. Jennifer is a very sick girl. She has hallucinations . . ."

"I know, but . . ."

"She's not a prophet, Sam. She's not seeing into the future. That's not the way things work. It doesn't make sense."

"But last time her hallucinations came true."

"Her hallucinations didn't come true . . ."

"Harry Mac . . . ," I started to say.

"Harry Mac was killed by his fellow criminals after he informed on them to the police. That had nothing to do with demons or coffins or prophecies. It was just a crime."

"But Jennifer saw it! She saw it was going to happen!"

My father smiled kind of painfully. He glanced over his shoulder at my mother. She sort of shrugged.

"She didn't see Harry Mac get murdered, Sam," Dad explained patiently. "You know she didn't. What she saw was some demons and a coffin and all kinds of crazy stuff: a hallucination. I admit that somehow that made you think of the place where Harry was killed. But that doesn't mean . . ."

"But it couldn't have been a coincidence!"

"On the contrary," Dad said. "I think it was obviously some sort of coincidence. I don't think there can be any other explanation. And anyway, the people who are responsible are in jail. They're not going to hurt anyone else."

I couldn't believe I was hearing this. I couldn't believe my dad was saying it. I stared at him with my mouth open. Why couldn't he see what was happening? Jennifer had had a vision—a vision of death coming tomorrow—"*so many dead.*" It was going to come true just like the other one. I knew it. I was absolutely sure.

Someone had to find out what it meant. Someone had to stop it from happening.

"Dad . . . ," I started.

"Sam," he said, "what is it exactly you want me to do?"

"Well . . . shouldn't we maybe call Detective Sims at least? Shouldn't we tell him what Jennifer said?"

"I don't think we should bother the detective," my mother said quickly, a worried look on her face. "He almost charged you with murder, Sam. We should stay away from him as much as we can. We don't need any more trouble today."

But my dad, after a minute's thought, said, "No, I think that's fair. I think Detective Sims would want to know about this. I'll call him in the morning."

"In the morning?" I nearly shouted. "We only have till tomorrow!"

"Well, Detective Sims has probably gone home for the night . . ."

"Well, can't you call 911?"

"I'm not going to call 911 to report a hallucination," Dad said, starting to sound impatient. But then I could see him think the whole thing over some more. And he said, "But I'll call the department now and tell whoever's there."

My mom and I stood in the living room and listened while my dad called the police. We heard him ask for Sims. Then we heard him say, "Well, is there some other detective on duty?" After a wait, I guess someone came on, because my dad explained it to them: exactly what I'd told him about the phone call and what Jennifer said. He spoke in his usual quiet, reasonable voice. He didn't sound panicked or even concerned. He just sounded like he thought it was something they ought to know.

Finally, he hung up.

The minute he did, I asked him: "What did they say? What did they say?"

"It was another detective. Brody. He said he would tell Detective Sims about it in the morning."

"In the morning?"

"He didn't sound very concerned."

"But Jennifer said . . ."

"I know, I know what she said, Sam. But this Detective Brody was familiar with Jennifer's case. He says the doctors are now fairly certain she's suffering from schizophrenia. He says it's unlikely anything she says has any relation to reality. And frankly, Sam, I have to agree with him."

"But she knew about Harry Mac!" I insisted.

This time my father only looked at me without saying anything. He didn't have to say anything. I could read what he was thinking right there on his face. He didn't believe for a second that Jennifer was having visions of real things that would really happen. He thought it was just madness. Schizophrenia.

"Don't worry, all right?" he said. "The police are on it, and they'll take care of it in the morning."

But I did worry. I worried a lot. In fact, for the next couple of hours, that's pretty much all I did: worry. I went back up to my room. I paced around. I lay down on my bed. I stared up at the ceiling. I got up and paced around some more. The whole time, all I could think about was Jennifer—Jennifer whispering. I could hear her, almost as if she were standing right there next to me.

"So many dead. Tomorrow. So many dead."

My dad hadn't heard that. He hadn't heard the fear in her voice. I had. And I couldn't stop hearing it. Jennifer's words brought all these pictures into my head. Pictures of dead people lying all over the place. Bodies. Blood. And okay, some of these pictures, I guess, were from horror movies I'd seen on TV, but all the same, they were pretty realistic looking. And the more I thought about them—the more I paced back and forth—the more I remembered Jennifer whispering over the phone—well, the more realistic these pictures started to seem.

It was after ten o'clock now. I heard my parents come slowly upstairs. I head their voices on the landing.

"What a week," my father said heavily.

"Joy comes in the morning," said my mother, which was something she always said when someone was having a hard time.

"I sure hope so," said my father. "Because, really—what a terrible week."

Then I heard their bedroom door close and their voices became muffled and were finally silent. The house was quiet around me. I felt alone. Really alone. Like maybe I was the last person left in the world.

And I was scared too. More scared, I think, than I had ever been in my life. Because somehow I had managed to convince myself completely that Jennifer was telling the truth. I felt absolutely sure that the bodies and the death she had seen were real, real things that were really going to happen in the future. Tomorrow. I felt sure that Jennifer was having visions like the prophets in the Bible did.

The dead—so many dead—tomorrow.

Somehow this disaster already seemed real to me.

There was not a doubt in my mind that it was going to happen. You have to understand that. You have to—because that's the only way you'll be able to understand what I did next.

20

Thief in the Night

Do right. Fear nothing.

I waited till everyone else was asleep, then I crept out of the house. I took two things with me: a flashlight and the Buster—the lockpicking tool Jeff Winger had given me. I wore my autumn coat with the two big pockets. I put the flashlight in one pocket and the Buster in the other.

It was cold outside. Cold and dark. There was only a sliver of a moon, and mostly it was buried under a steadily moving blanket of clouds. My bike had a light on it, but I kept it off at first. There were streetlights to see by, and I thought if the police spotted me—a kid out on his own at that hour—they would stop me and ask me questions. That was one thing my mom was right about: I didn't want to deal with the police any more than I already had.

I pedaled fast, taking the back lanes. The town was

asleep. The lights in the houses were out. There were very few cars on the road. There were no pedestrians.

St. Agnes Hospital was a long way away. I had looked up the address online. It was a good hour's ride at least on Route 33. When I reached the two-lane, I switched my lights on and set myself to pedaling as fast as I could.

I tried not to think, but I did think—and everything I thought of made me more and more afraid. I thought of the dead people Jennifer had seen. I thought of what the police would say if they caught me on the highway. I thought of what my father would say if the police picked me up and brought me home. I thought of what my mother would say. Then I thought of the dead again and what would happen if I didn't get to Jennifer in time.

They weren't happy thoughts.

I rode on. The forest closed around me, edging up to the highway on both sides. I sensed the depths of its darkness and began to imagine lurking presences among the trees, watching me pass. At one point, out of the empty horizon, a pair of lights shone suddenly. A big truck passed me, heading back toward town. I saw the driver in the lighted cab. I saw him look at me as he went by, his eyes narrowing. I thought about him getting on his radio and calling the police: *There's a kid out here on the road . . .*

Then the truck passed, its backwash of wind making my bike waver back and forth unsteadily.

I kept pedaling. It was a good thing I'd been running

so much, practicing for track tryouts. My legs were strong, but even so, they ached like crazy. My wind was good, but even so, I was panting pretty hard. I needed to rest, but I kept thinking, *No, go a little farther, just a little farther . . .*

Then, all at once, there it was.

As I came around one bend in the highway, the trees parted on my left. There was an entranceway. Just a small space. A gate. No lights. The opening was nearly hidden by the forest shadows and I almost went right by it. Then I caught sight of the sign: St. Agnes Mental Health Facility. That was the place.

I stopped my bike, my feet on the ground. I looked through the gates. There was nothing visible but a long driveway leading over a hill and out of sight. In the darkness it didn't look like an inviting journey. Not at all.

I thought to myself: *There's still time to turn back. If you're quiet about it, no one will even know you left.*

Then I thought to myself: *Do right. Fear nothing.*

Man, right then I was sorry I'd ever seen that little statue of the archangel Michael on my father's shelf. I was sorry I'd ever seen those Latin words.

But it didn't matter whether I was sorry or not. I knew I couldn't turn back. I had to try to get to Jennifer. I had to try to stop whatever was coming.

I got off my bike and walked it into the trees. I laid it down in the woods, out of sight of any traffic that might pass. Then I kept walking, hoping to find a way around the gate.

I had imagined there would be all kinds of obstacles: high walls, electric fences, even guards and dogs patrolling the place to keep the mental patients from escaping. In fact, it was nothing like that. When I came out of the trees, I was on a little lawn. A driveway ran beside it. I stayed on the grass but followed the drive. When I came over a small hill, I saw the hospital. It was that easy.

As I approached the building, though, my stomach did that thing again, like I was going down in an elevator too fast. The hospital was a broad structure of brick. It was only two stories tall, but there was a castle-like roof on the front of it, giving it an extra two stories. Then the walls went out on either side a long way. There were lots of large windows in the walls and lights on in some of the windows, but a lot of them were dark. The building loomed black against the silver sky. The darkened windows stared down at me emptily like a skeleton's eyes. The big central door was closed tight and made the place look forbidding. Now and then, I saw a shadow passing through a lighted window upstairs, and I knew that there were people inside and that they were awake, moving—and would be watching for intruders.

I moved carefully through the night. I moved close to the building and then followed its wall around to the side. I was looking for a way in—some way aside from barging right through the front door.

I passed a series of big windows. I pressed my face to

them and peered inside. They were mostly offices, dark and empty. Then when I got to the rear corner of the wall, there was a row of smaller windows, closer to the ground. All of these windows were dark too. Looking to my right and left to make sure there was no one to see me, I drew close to the smaller windows. I knelt down and pressed my face against one of them. I couldn't see anything, so I took out my flashlight and shone it through the window glass. As I expected, I was looking into the hospital's cellar. I saw a kind of tiled room with a large bath in the center of it. I moved on to the next window. This time I saw a trash can with brooms sticking out of it. There was a tall shelf with towels and sheets on it. There was a pair of green overalls hanging on the wall.

That was the window I wanted.

I took the Buster out of my pocket. Jeff Winger had taught me his trade well. In under fifteen seconds I had the window lock picked and opened. I guess I would have been a good thief, if I'd stuck with it.

But just as I was pushing the window up, I thought: *What if there's an alarm?*

It was too late. The window rattled upward. I held my breath, waiting for the siren.

No siren. No alarm. Silence.

I grabbed hold of the sill and scrambled up and in through the window.

I dropped to the floor. My sneakers muffled the sound

of my landing. I crouched there, listening. For a long moment I couldn't hear anything except the beating of my own heart and my quick, nervous breathing. Then, as I calmed down a little, I started to hear the noises of the building: air moving through vents; footsteps in hallways above me; distant, muffled voices fading in and out.

I shone my flashlight around. As I expected, I was in a large supply closet: a small room with shelves of towels and linens, garbage cans on wheels, brooms, a couple of trolley-carts, and so on. There were also overalls—not just the ones hanging on the door, but a few others on hangers, dangling from a rod.

I moved quickly to the overalls and started looking through them for a pair in my size. The best ones I found looked big, but it was as close as I could get. I was just beginning to peel them off the hanger when I heard a noise. Someone was close and quickly getting closer.

I froze. It sounded like a trolley-cart on wheels. It was coming down the hall toward the supply room door.

Quickly I doused my flashlight and ducked behind the overalls. It was the only place to hide, and they didn't hide me much. I knew my sneakers were sticking out from underneath the overalls. Anyone who came in would probably see me.

The cart noise came closer and closer—and sure enough, it stopped outside the door. I held my breath. If I was caught now—here—they would take me back to the police, and I didn't think my father would be able to talk me out of jail this time. It finally—finally!—occurred to me just how stupid I had been to do this, to come here. I realized—finally!—just how big a risk I was taking. Suddenly, *Do right; fear nothing* didn't sound like such good advice after all.

I nearly groaned aloud in fear as the doorknob on the supply room door began to turn. The door began to open. Wider. Then a man's voice spoke—just outside.

"Dave?"

The door clicked shut again. The next time the voice spoke, it was muffled. Another man's voice answered, also muffled. Even though I strained to hear, I couldn't make out what they were saying.

I stayed where I was. I tried to swallow but couldn't. My throat was too dry. I waited for the door to open again—all the way this time.

But the next thing I knew, I heard the wheels of the cart start rolling once more over the hallway floor outside. This time, though, the noise got softer and softer. Yes! The man with the cart was going away! After a while the sound of it was gone altogether.

I breathed for what felt like the first time in minutes. Then I started to move again, quickly now.

I snaked out from behind the overalls. I was too afraid to turn the flashlight back on, so I just felt my way around. I found the overalls I'd had before. I started to pull them on over my clothes. They really were big, bigger than I'd thought. I had to roll the cuffs up over my sneaker heels so I'd be able to walk. Then I had to roll up the sleeves so my hands would be free. Even so, when I was finished, the overalls hung like a tent canvas around me.

I went to the cart—the one with the big trash can and brooms on it. I took hold of its handle and rolled it to the door.

With one hand on the cart handle, I used my free hand to draw the door open. I stuck my head out and peeked around. There was a hallway. Empty. I took a deep breath. *Here we go*, I thought.

Then I pushed the door open all the way and pulled my trolley-cart out into the hall.

I had gotten into the hospital at least. Now all I had to do was find Jennifer.

21

Sales, J.

I tucked my chin into my chest to hide my face. I pushed the cart along the hall, moving as quickly as I could. Sure, I was in disguise, but it wasn't much of a disguise, was it? I mean, if someone walked by me really fast without paying too much attention, they might not notice anything peculiar. But the second anyone took a closer look at me, I was pretty much toast. A smallish sixteen-year-old kid with his overalls rolled up at the cuffs and sliding down at the sleeves: I must've looked like a sixth grader dressed up for Halloween. If I was going to reach Jennifer—if I was going to find out what she'd seen and what she thought was going to happen—I was going to have to do it fast, before anyone spotted me.

Where did I begin to look? I didn't think there'd be any patients down here in the cellar. The halls were pretty empty. There were no nurses or aides or anything that I could see. Most of the doors were closed, and the few that were open revealed offices, baths, and a furnace room. I figured I had to get upstairs.

Luckily, there were arrows painted on the wall pointing to the elevators. Also luckily, I reached the elevator without bumping into anyone. Even more luckily, no one came by after I pushed the button and stood waiting for the elevator to arrive.

The door opened. The elevator was big, empty. My cart and I both got on. There were only two more floors in the building. I had seen the offices on the first floor, so I guessed that the patients' rooms would be on the second. I pushed the button for the second floor.

That's when my luck ran out.

The door had started to close when I heard a woman's voice: "Hold it! Could you hold the elevator, please?"

I froze. I prayed the elevator door would close before the woman reached it. But it just seemed to hang open forever. Then, slowly, slowly it started to slide shut.

And there was the woman now, coming into view, reaching for the door. *What should I do?* If I didn't hold it for her, it would look really suspicious. So quickly I reached out and grabbed the edge of the door. It slid back. The woman got on.

"Thanks so much," she said.

I nodded, trying to keep my head down so she wouldn't see how young I was. Also, the motion to hold the door had sent my sleeve rolling back down over my hand. It looked ridiculous.

But you know how people act in elevators: they don't look at each other much. The woman turned away from me at once and pushed the first-floor button. She faced the door as it shut. I quickly rolled my sleeve back up again.

The elevator ground upward, slow, slow, slow. The woman stood with her back to me. She was a tall, thin woman. I don't know how old—maybe thirty. She was wearing a suit, the skirt and jacket the same color. She had short brown hair. That was pretty much all I could see, standing behind her like that.

"Are these the slowest elevators in the world or what?" she said—but she still didn't look at me.

I was in a panic. I knew if I said too much, my kid's voice would give me away. If I didn't say anything, she'd turn and look at me.

So I made my voice as old-sounding as I could and grunted. "Yeah."

"They take forever," she muttered, but she was talking more to herself now.

Then the elevator reached the first floor. The door opened.

"Thanks again," the woman said. She turned her face my way, but she didn't really look at me. Then she was off the elevator, walking away.

I started to sigh with relief—but it caught in my throat

as two men stepped into the elevator to take the woman's place. They pressed the same button I had pressed—they were going to the second floor like me. They barely glanced my way. Like the woman—like most people in an elevator—they faced the door.

"I don't see how they can make any more cuts," one man said.

"I know. The staff is down to the minimum as it is," said the other.

"On the other hand, where's the money gonna come from?"

"Right—that's the big question."

The elevator stopped again. Second floor. The door opened. The two men got out and turned off to the left. I pushed my cart out after them. I couldn't take the chance of following them, so tucking in my chin, I started down the hall directly in front of me.

Turned out not to be such a great idea. When I looked up, I saw a hallway with doors on either side of it. But in the middle of the hall, there was an open space with a counter. Behind the counter I could see two people, one a guy and the other a woman. They were both large. They were both in white. Nurses or aides, I guessed. They glanced up at me as I came their way, so I figured it was too late to turn around without making them suspicious. I just kept pushing the cart toward them.

The corridor had a quiet, late-night atmosphere. As

I went along it, I stole glances at the doors to my left and right. The doors were wooden, heavy. Each one of them had a small metal label holder next to it. The labels had names on them: Sanders, T.; Monahan, G.; Callahan, B.; and so on. So there was my plan. All I had to do was keep walking down the halls and reading the names until I got to Jennifer's.

I pushed the cart down the hall, looking left and right as I went by the doors.

"How ya doin'?"

I nearly jumped at the sound of the voice, but it was just the male aide. I'd reached the counter where he was standing. He was a big guy like I said—very big and pale-faced with very broad, square shoulders that made him look like a tremendous block of cement. I didn't answer him. I just made a sort of greeting gesture at him with my head and kept pushing my cart along. When I was past him, I didn't dare look back to see whether he and the other aide were watching me or not. I half expected them to notice my baggy overalls, my young appearance—to call after me, "You there, stop!"

But they didn't. I just kept pushing the cart down the hall, kept reading the names on either side: Walters, C.; Christiansen, P.; . . .

I couldn't believe it. Somehow, I was actually getting away with this. If I could just find Jennifer before I was caught . . .

I reached the end of the hall and turned the corner. The next hall was empty except for a single nurse all the way down at the end. She was just coming out of one of the rooms. She crossed the hall and went into the room on the other side. Then everything was quiet. Not a voice, hardly a sound. Just the buzzing of machinery. The hum of fluorescent lights. And then the rattle of my wheels as I pushed the cart along more quickly, reading the names as fast as I could: O'Brien, T.; Porter, Q.; Sales, J.; Malloy, R. . . .

I stopped short, the wheels going silent.

Sales, J.

That was Jennifer!

I was so surprised to have actually found her, I almost didn't notice it. I looked around over my shoulder. Still no one else in the hall. I backed up to Jennifer's door.

My hand went into my overalls, into my coat pocket underneath. My fingers curled around the Buster. I figured they must lock the patients in at night and I'd have to break through. I reached for the doorknob with my other hand—and to my total surprise, the knob turned easily. It wasn't locked at all.

The door came open.

It was dark in the room, but the light from the hall fell in, a thin wedge of light. As I pushed the door open more, the wedge spread wider and wider.

I saw a desk. I saw a picture on the wall. I glanced down

the hall. No one there. I pushed the door wider. I saw the foot of a bed. More of the bed. Then . . .

"Sam Hopkins!"

My heart felt like it was going to explode. There she was—Jennifer!—sitting up at the head of the bed. She was clutching the blankets to her chin in fear. She was staring at me with eyes open wide. But in the next moment, the fear washed out of her expression as she fully recognized me.

"Sam Hopkins!" she said again.

You would not believe how loud her voice sounded in that quiet hospital.

"Jennifer, shh! Shh!" I whispered desperately.

She leapt off the bed and came rushing toward me. She was wearing a flannel nightgown, white with flowers on it. She had her arms spread as if she was about to wrap me in a tremendous hug.

"Sam Hopkins!" she said again—and though this time she whispered it, it still sounded awfully loud.

I held out my open hand at her like a traffic cop, trying to get her to stop, to stay where she was. I grabbed the trolley-cart out in the hall. Took one more quick look around out there to make sure no one was in sight.

But someone was.

The nurse. She had come out of the room she was in. She crossed the hall again and disappeared into the room on the opposite side.

Now I understood. She was checking on patients, one after another. Coming this way. At the rate she was moving, I figured I had about five to ten minutes before she reached Jennifer's room.

Quickly I pulled the cart into the room and shut the door, plunging the room into darkness.

I didn't see Jennifer reach me, but I knew she was beside me when she clutched my wrist in both her hands.

"You came for me!" she said.

"I never thought I'd find you," I told her.

"But you were magic."

"I'm not magic, trust me."

"You are."

"Whatever."

"When I was screaming, they put me in another place," she said. "They locked me in."

"Just keep your voice down, will you?!"

"The room was white. It was empty. I had to stay there until I was quiet."

"Shh!"

"They gave me medicine to make me sleep. But I didn't sleep. I just got quiet."

I wished she would be quiet now!

"Then they brought me to this room. It's better here."

"Okay, okay." I didn't have time to listen to her life story now. That nurse was doing her rounds, on her way. Who could tell how fast she'd get here? I needed to find out what was going to happen tomorrow—I needed to find out now.

Jennifer's two hands were still clutching my wrist. I clutched her two hands in my two. I shook her hands to get her attention. Even though it was dark in the room, there was some light seeping in around the edges of the window blind, and now that my eyes were adjusting, I could make out Jennifer's face. Her eyes were eager, focused on me. "Listen," I said. "Listen."

"I'm so happy," she said. "I'm so happy you're here, Sam Hopkins."

"Yeah, just try to be happy quietly, okay? We have to act fast. You have to tell me what you saw."

"Saw?"

"About the dead—remember? You said there were going to be so many dead. Tomorrow, you said."

"So many dead," she echoed in a low, awestruck voice.

"Where?"

"What?"

"Where, Jennifer? Where are the dead?"

She blinked, confused. She shook her head. "Everywhere."

"No, but where are they going to be?"

She shook her head again. She was still gazing at me with that eager look, but it was clear she didn't know what I was talking about.

I tried again. "Where did you see the dead, Jennifer?"

"In the common room."

"In the . . . ?"

"Then in the phone room later."

"Jennifer, that doesn't make sense."

"I know. It was awful. They were lying on the chairs and on the floor. There was so much blood."

I was so frustrated, I wanted to shake her. How long could I stand here talking to her before that nurse reached us, before she found me here and sounded the alarm?

I shook Jennifer's hands in mine again. I knew what was happening. She was telling me her hallucination, just like she did before out by the willow tree. It was up to me to figure out what it meant.

"Okay, okay," I said again. "So you saw the dead people lying around the common room."

"Yes."

"Did you see anything else?"

"Blood," she whispered.

"Yeah, yeah, besides the blood. I mean, did you see, like, a tree or one of those tarns or something, like you did before?"

She stared and stared at me with those wide eyes. Then she shook her head. "No. Just . . . bodies. Just blood."

This was no help, no help at all. "*Why* are there going to be bodies, Jennifer?" I tried asking then. "How are the people going to die?"

She looked at me now as if I was being silly, as if I didn't understand the simplest thing. "The demons! The demons are going to kill them."

Right, of course. The demons. Great.

I knew I was running out of time, fast. I had to get out of there before I was caught. But I'd come so far, I couldn't help but try to reach her one last time.

"Jennifer," I said, "is there anything—anything you could tell me—anything that would help me find the demons, that would help me find out who the demons are, or where they live or how to stop them?"

The question seemed to reach her. At last, she seemed to understand. There was a long moment of silence in the dark room. Jennifer's eyes drifted away from me, and I could tell she was thinking it over, trying to help me out, trying to think of some clue that would give me the direction I needed.

And then, in the shadows, I saw her face brighten. I saw the idea come to her. She turned back to me.

"Yes!" she said. "Yes, there is something . . ."

Wouldn't you know it—at that very moment, the door swung open. Light from the hallway flooded the room, catching us both.

I swung around and saw the nurse, standing in the doorway, staring at me.

All three of us—me, Jennifer, the nurse—stood frozen like that for one more second.

Then the nurse—without saying a single word—lifted a lanyard clipped to her uniform. There was a small black device at the end of the lanyard. It had a red button on it.

She pressed the button and an alarm went off.

22

Running for It

The alarm wasn't loud. In some ways that was the scariest thing about it—how soft it was. Instead of some high-pitched, shrieking siren that sounded like a woman trapped in a burning building, this was a mild, calm, repeated tone that sounded like it was all business. The second I heard it, I knew it was probably sounding on a device clipped to the pocket of every aide in the hospital. Probably on a direct line to the police station too. That meant the large block-of-cement guy around the corner was probably already on his way—not to mention several carloads of armed officers of the law. I figured I had less than thirty seconds before I was in custody.

That meant there was no time to think. There was no time for anything—unless I was ready to grow old in jail. I had to run for it. Now.

The nurse stood there, blocking the doorway. I grabbed hold of the cart handle.

"Get out of the way!" I shouted at her.

And at the same time, I started pushing the cart straight toward her.

I didn't push it too fast—I wanted to give her time to step aside so I didn't hurt her. But I didn't slow down either.

The nurse hesitated a moment as the cart barreled toward her. For another moment I thought, *Oh no, I'm going to knock her down!* But then, thank heavens, she moved—she didn't have much choice really. At the last second, just before the cart slammed into her, she dodged to the side and the cart went hurtling through the door right past her.

I ran out after it. Or, that is, I tried to run. But I couldn't—because Jennifer was still holding on to my arm with both hands. As I went forward, she stumbled after me so that I dragged her out into the hallway with me. I tried to shake free of her. But I couldn't.

"Jennifer, let go!" I shouted.

"No, no, no!" she cried, holding on.

"Let go of me!"

She wouldn't.

I looked up. Oh yeah, there he was, all right. Block-of-Cement Guy, larger than life. Charging around the corner full speed and racing down the corridor toward me.

The other aide who'd been at the counter with him—the one who looked like a female block of cement—was right behind him.

I had to make a choice: surrender and find myself back in the police station facing Detective Sims—or take Jennifer with me.

"Run, Jennifer!" I shouted.

Then I started running—and to my relief, so did she.

We raced down the hall together, side by side at first, Jennifer's straight brown hair flying back behind her. After a second, I took the lead, dragging Jennifer after me.

I might have outrun Block-of-Cement Guy by myself—I probably would have—but there was no chance of it as long as I was hauling Jennifer around behind me. At this rate, the aide was going to tackle me in about ten seconds. I had to think of something—some other plan—and fast.

But what? The elevator was no good—too slow. There had to be a stairway. That was it. I had to find the stairs.

We reached the end of the corridor. Block-of-Cement Guy was closing in behind us. I could hear his sneakered footsteps getting louder on the floor.

At the corner, I looked to my left: there was another corridor. To my right: Yes, there it was! The stairwell door.

Pulling Jennifer by the hand, I ran to it, yanked it open, dashed inside.

Now Jennifer and I were thundering down the steps. I clutched her hand in one of my hands. With my other hand I steadied myself on the banister as I flew downward two and three steps at a time.

I heard Block-of-Cement Guy bang through the door upstairs and come thundering after us.

The stairs switchbacked as we went down. We reached the first floor and went spinning around to get on the next flight. As we did, Jennifer tripped. She let out a scream. Her hand slipped out of mine. She went down two steps and was about to topple over. If she'd been wearing shoes, I think she would've kept going. But she was barefoot, I realized now, and that gave her some extra traction. Somehow she managed to spin around in front of me and grab the banister, holding herself up.

I just kept running past her. To be honest, I figured it didn't matter that much if she got caught. What would they do to her? They'd just put her back in the hospital, where she already was. I was the one in danger of going to prison if Detective Sims heard about this. I was the one who had to get away at all costs.

I kept running.

I reached the bottom floor, the basement. I could hear Block-of-Cement Guy's footsteps right above me—and more footsteps and more doors opening up there as more people came into the stairwell chasing after us.

I pulled open the door. Jennifer went flying past me, racing out of the stairwell. I charged after her, pushing the door shut behind me.

As I did, I noticed something. A keyhole on the outside of the stairwell door. Sure, they had to be able to lock the stairwell when they needed to. Maybe . . .

I yanked out the Buster.

I could hear the footsteps of my pursuers come down the last flight of stairs. I figured I only had seconds before they came plunging through the door. I figured—if I know how to open a lock, I must be able to close one too.

I pulled a lockpick out of Buster and went to work on the keyhole as fast as I could.

Inside the stairwell the charging footsteps reached the bottom of the final flight and raced at the door as I struggled to turn the latch with the Buster pick.

"Sam Hopkins!" Jennifer screamed behind me in a panic. "They're coming! They're coming!"

The pick clicked. The lock turned over. The stairwell door locked shut just as Block-of-Cement Guy ran into it with a thud—at least, I guessed it was him. The door rattled against my hand as the big aide tried to force the door open. He couldn't do it.

I heard him curse.

"He locked it somehow!" he shouted to the others behind him.

I didn't wait around to hear him curse again. After all, I'm a preacher's kid! I can't be listening to that sort of thing. So I took off.

By now, my overalls were starting to unroll. The

places where I'd rolled them up at the sleeves and cuffs had come most of the way down. My hands were swimming in the sleeves and I was tripping over the cuffs as I moved—like a little boy trying to walk around in his daddy's clothes.

But with the pursuing aides locked in the stairwell, I had a few seconds of freedom. I used those precious seconds to stumble down the hall, looking for somewhere—anywhere—to hide.

I found another supply closet. Good thing too, because just then I heard the bell of the elevator ring around the corner. I heard the door slide open and a big, angry voice say, "They must be down here somewhere."

I pushed into the supply closet—and Jennifer quickly crowded in behind me.

I shut the door.

"Sam Hopk . . ."

"Shh, shh, shh," I told her. I put my finger to my lips for emphasis, but it was too dark for her to see me, so I put the finger to her lips and she was silent.

I pulled out my flashlight and quickly passed the beam over the place. It was just like the room I was in before when I first came in: carts, garbage cans, brooms, supplies. As the flashlight beam went around, I saw Jennifer's face in the outglow. Her eyes were shining, her mouth was open. She looked . . . she looked *happy*, to tell you the truth. Excited. As if this were all some sort of big hilarious adventure. Well, like I said, she wasn't the one who would go to jail if she got caught.

There was no lock on this side of the door. But there was a big garbage can that seemed just the right size. I rolled it over and wedged the edge of it under the doorknob. That would hold people off for a couple of seconds anyway.

And they were out there looking, that's for sure. I heard the footsteps running down the hall. I heard the voices, loud enough so I could make out the words:

"I don't see them!"

"Start searching the rooms!"

"Someone unlock that stairwell door!"

I pulled down my overalls. Peeled them off my pant legs, threw them aside. I flicked the flashlight on, then off again—just long enough to find my way. Then I moved through the crowded supply room to the window.

The window was high on the wall, but the latch was on the bottom. I could reach up and get it, unlock it. Then I grabbed hold of the ledge and pulled myself up, using my head to push the window open as I went. I crawled out onto the ground and scrambled to my feet.

"Sam Hopkins!"

I heard Jennifer's desperate whisper below me. I looked back through the windows and saw her standing in the supply room, reaching her hands up toward me, the way a baby reaches when it wants to be picked up. It occurred to me that if I just left her here and ran for it, I might have a chance of getting away.

But then I remembered: Just before the nurse caught us in Jennifer's room, Jennifer had been about to tell me something. There was some clue, she said, that might help me find out about tomorrow, about the dead. If I left her behind now, I might never hear what she had to say. All this craziness and danger would've been for nothing.

I stuck my hand down through the window. Jennifer grabbed it. I pulled her up until she could take hold of the window ledge herself. Then I caught both her arms and dragged her up and through the window, out into the open air.

We both stood up—and immediately we heard the sirens. Police. They sounded close too. Very close. I figured they'd be coming up the hospital driveway in under a minute.

"Hurry," I said.

I ran to the edge of the building and peeked around until I could see the entrance and the long driveway.

We were already too late. A couple of aides had come out through the front door and were shining flashlights over the lawn, searching for us. I had to duck back quickly as one of the beams went sweeping past me.

Then there were the police. They were already in sight. When I looked down the driveway, I saw the red glow of their cruiser lights running up into the high branches of the winter trees down by the road. They were seconds away from the driveway. Soon they'd be coming into view over the hill.

"Sam Hopkins!"

Jennifer's voice had dropped to a low whisper, but even so, the sound of it made me jump, made me turn to her with my face scrunched up in a warning, too scared even to tell her to be quiet.

Jennifer didn't speak again. But she gestured frantically, pointing away from the front of the building.

I lifted my eyes, followed her gestures. I looked to the rear of the building. There were spotlights back there. They picked small swaths of lawn out of the surrounding darkness, bathing them in their soft glow. They also made it possible to see the brick wall that surrounded the grass. The wall wasn't high. I thought I could get over it.

Beyond the wall, as far as I could tell, there was nothing but forest.

I nodded once.

"Let's go," I said.

Jennifer and I ran off together.

23

What Happened in the Woods

A sprint across the grass. A running leap. I grabbed hold of the top of the wall and, grunting, pulled myself up. As the sirens sounded closer and closer, as the red glow of the police flashers lit up the surrounding forest, Jennifer, barefoot, raced to join me. I sat astride the wall and reached for her as she reached for me. Now her hand was in my hand. I pulled her up. I took one last glance across the lawn at the hospital. I saw aides pouring through the rear doors into the night, passing their flashlights over the back lawn, searching for us.

No time to wait around. I slid off the top of the wall and hung from it, as far down as I could—then dropped onto the forest floor on the other side. Jennifer did the same, but as she landed . . .

"Ouch. Ow!"

The sticks and rocks bit into her bare feet, and she flinched and stumbled, crying out in pain. I knew it was only going to get worse in the forest.

I glanced up at the wall. I could see the flashlight beams piercing the night above it as the aides crossed the lawn, searching. If we were going to escape, we had to go into the woods and we had to go now.

I lifted Jennifer into my arms. I was amazed how easy it was, how light she was. It was like picking up a doll. She put her arm around my neck and rested her head against my chest.

"Sam Hopkins," she said tenderly.

Oh brother!

I carried her into the forest.

There was no path, but the trees were spaced pretty far apart and the brush was fairly thin. We also got a lucky break from above: the clouds went sailing past and the moon came out. Its light shone down through the bare branches, making it easier to see. It wasn't hard to make my way through the darkness, even carrying Jennifer.

After a while the ground began to rise. I was gasping for breath by that time and my arms were starting to ache pretty badly. I knew I couldn't carry Jennifer much farther. I found a small space and set her down. I sat beside her. Looking back through the trees, I couldn't see anything but moonlit darkness. No one seemed to be coming after us. I figured we had some time.

I took off my sneakers. They were way too large for Jennifer, but I thought my socks might do her some good. I took those off too, and pulled them over her feet to give her a little more protection. As I did this, I felt her watching me with her big eyes. I glanced up and tried my best to smile at her.

"This oughta help your feet a little at least," I said.

"You're my only magic friend," she said.

I rolled my eyes. What are you supposed to answer when somebody says that? "Right," I said. "Sam, the magic friend, that's me."

I put my sneakers back on my bare feet, ready to go. But something else occurred to me now: it was cold out here. I hadn't noticed it before. When we were running, the motion had kept me warm. But I could feel it now—and I could see the gooseflesh coming up above Jennifer's wrists. She wasn't wearing anything but a flannel nightgown, remember.

"Stand up," I said.

She jumped to her feet as if this were the army and I was a general who had given her a command. I stripped my jacket off and put it around her.

"This'll keep you warm," I told her.

"But you'll be cold."

"I'll be fine. My fear will keep me warm."

She laughed. I think it was the first time I'd ever heard her laugh, and I looked at her in surprise.

"You're funny," she said.

"Oh yeah, I'm a laugh riot."

"You're good too," she said then, serious. "No one else helps me. When I'm with you, I feel better."

"Jennifer . . . a minute ago you were safe in the hospital; now you're on the run in the forest. I don't think I'm helping you at all."

"But you are," she said. "You are."

I rolled my eyes again. There was no talking to her. "Let's go."

We set off again, moving more slowly now. My guess was that the aides and the police would be in no hurry to go wandering through the forest in the middle of the night. They would do a thorough search of the hospital and its grounds before they came chasing after us. If we were lucky, they might even wait until morning before making a full search. But even if they didn't wait, I thought we might be able to evade them out here in the darkness of the woods, at least for a while.

So we went on at our own pace. We picked our way through the trees. It was an eerie scene, an eerie place to be. The naked branches stirred above us as the wind rose, their motions strangely rhythmic and alive. The moon dodged in and out of the clouds, sending weird, tangled shadows every which way. The crackle and squeak of the bending wood filled the forest, which was already loud with other noises: night peepers and crickets—and startling bursts of motion as animals and birds escaped from us through the brush. Now and then, there was a distant sound of traffic—a car or truck passing on the road. Once, a freight train let out a lonesome whistle, and my mind went back to how all this began: that desperate race over the rail bridge with Harry Mac after me. Poor Harry Mac.

When I thought it was safe, I paused a moment. I turned on my flashlight and passed it over the scene. The twisted branches and moving shadows went up the hill as far as I could see. I felt very alone, far away from my home, my ordinary life.

Finally, near the top of the rise, we came to a clearing. It was an open circle of ground surrounded by winter oaks. They were big trees with big branches that reached out to one another, creating a lacework canopy above our heads. There was a little brook gurgling along underneath them. As we entered the clearing, the moon came out. The branches of the trees cast dense shadows that moved back and forth hypnotically. The running water of the brook winked and sparkled with the silver light. Then the clouds raced over the moon again and there was only darkness and the whisper of the wind.

"Let's rest here," I said.

The moon appeared again as Jennifer sat down on a rock next to the brook. In the dim light I saw her reach her hand into the water and bring it up to drink out of her palm. I turned away, hugging myself and shivering. Now that we'd stopped moving—and now that Jennifer had my jacket—the cold was really beginning to get to me.

I tried to ignore it. I tried to think. All I could think was: *What am I doing here?* Was I as crazy as Jennifer? I had helped her escape from a mental hospital! Where the doctors were taking care of her! Why did I do that? I must've been out of my mind. I probably should've been in the hospital with her!

I turned and looked at her. She continued to sit on the rock and drink from the spring. She didn't seem worried or scared at all. Of course not. I was her magic friend. She trusted me. I made her feel better. Which only made *me* feel worse because . . . well, because look what I'd done to her! Was it all for some ridiculous idea I'd gotten stuck in my head? Some stupid notion that Jennifer was having "visions" instead of hallucinations? Was it all just nonsense I'd concocted for some reason?

Boy, if that's all it was, I was in real trouble now. With the police. With my father and mother. With everyone.

But then I thought: *Well, what if it's not nonsense? What if I'm right?* Then I had to find out what Jennifer knew, didn't I? I had to find out what she was about to tell me when the nurse burst in on us . . . That's why I'd taken her out of the hospital in the first place.

I took a deep breath. I had to try it, anyway.

"Jennifer," I said.

She looked up at me for a long time as if she were thinking deep thoughts. When she did speak, she spoke very gently. "Sam Hopkins," she said.

I came toward her. I rubbed my eyes, exhausted, trying to clear my mind. "Jennifer, do you remember what we were talking about in the hospital?"

She looked away again, down at the water. I saw her nod. "I remember."

"The demons, right?"

She nodded again. "They're not real, you know," she said.

I was startled. "They're not?"

"No. The doctor explained it to me. I have a sickness—in my brain. That's why I see them. The medicine is supposed to make me better, then they'll go away eventually." She raised her face to me, and at that very moment, a single broad beam of moonlight fell through the canopy of branches and touched her. It bathed her pretty, bookish features in silver-white and brought her mournful expression out of the darkness of the clearing. "I hate it, Sam. The sickness, I mean: I hate it so much. I can't . . . I can't break through it to be me again."

It made me hurt to hear her say that, as if someone had reached inside me and grabbed my heart. *What would it be like*, I wondered, *to be trapped inside your own sick mind?* "Maybe the doctors will be able to help," I said. It sounded pretty lame, even to me, but I had to say something.

"Maybe," she said sadly. Then her voice broke and she said, "Why did God let this happen to me, Sam?"

I lifted my hands and opened my mouth, but no words came. I didn't know how to answer her. I tried to think what my dad would say. I said, "I don't know, Jennifer. Bad things happen in the world, that's all. It's like—it's like the world is broken or something. I know it shouldn't be like this, but sometimes it is."

"Does God know I'm still in here? Does God know it's still me inside?"

"Sure he does! Of course he does! He's right with you. He's right there."

"Because I feel really alone sometimes."

"You're not alone." I moved to her, put my hand on her shoulder. "You're not, believe me."

She put her hand on my hand. "I know," she said. "I guess I know that, but . . . but I'm glad you're here too. I'm glad there's someone I can touch and see. You're my magic friend, Sam."

It was funny. A minute before, I'd been thinking about how crazy this was, how stupid I'd been to come here, to take her out of the hospital, into the woods like this. But suddenly just then, it didn't seem crazy or stupid at all. It made sense somehow, as if it was what I was supposed to do. Because I knew how Jennifer felt: even though you know God is with you, it's easier to feel him there when a friend shows up to be with you too.

So I said, "Yeah. Yeah. That's right, Jennifer. That's right. I'm your magic friend." Because I figured—well, I was.

Jennifer was quiet after that. We both were. I was thinking that maybe I'd gotten everything wrong. Maybe I hadn't taken Jennifer out of the hospital to talk to her about demons and hallucinations and whatever else. Maybe I'd taken her out just for this, just to tell her she wasn't alone. Maybe now I should take her back . . .

Then Jennifer whispered: "They have guns, you know."

I stared at her. I wasn't sure I'd heard her right. "They . . . ? What?"

Suddenly Jennifer jumped to her feet, surprising me so much I fell back a step. She stared at me. "I saw them. I remember now. I saw their guns."

Now she turned away, still staring, as if she saw something deep in the darkness of the clearing. She started moving. She moved past me into the farther shadows. Her hands were out in front of her, like a blind woman feeling her way in the dark. Her eyes were distant, empty. Her mouth was open, but no words—only a long, slow breath—came out of her. In a daze she walked away, as if I weren't even there.

"I heard their whispers. In the night. In the dark. In my room. I heard their footsteps. And I followed them."

I stood there, watching her. I had stopped shivering. If it was still cold, I didn't notice it anymore. The sight of her—a white shadow moving gracefully around the clearing, reaching for the invisible things she saw in the dark, mesmerized me—made me forget everything else.

"I followed them down the stairs and out the door," she said. "They went behind our house. They gathered there in the little shed. They whispered to each other. About death. They said, 'We're going to bring death on them, then they'll be afraid . . .'"

She moved around the edge of the clearing, circling me. I stood dumbstruck, turning to watch her go.

She reached a tree and took hold of it, leaned against it, peering past it as if she were hiding, peeking, seeing what she was describing to me.

"They had bags," she whispered. "They opened the bags. The guns were in them. I heard them whisper, 'We are the angels of death.'"

I didn't answer. I just listened. I couldn't tell: Was this real? Or just another hallucination?

"Who was this, Jennifer?" I finally asked her. "Who did you see?"

At the sound of my voice, she gasped and turned, startled, as if she'd forgotten I was there.

"Who did you see?" I asked again.

"Demons. They had to be. They had to be."

"Were they talking about Harry Mac? Was that the death they were talking about?"

She shook her head. "Harry Mac knew. He was going

to tell the police. They decided to put him in a coffin. Under the tree. By the tarn. Send a warning to the others. Then they would be afraid. They would never tell. Then nothing could stop them."

I shook my head. I didn't understand. "Was this Jeff Winger? Jeff and Ed P.? Are they the demons?"

"They would be afraid," she whispered. "Then no one could stop them. Because they would have the power."

"The power," I echoed her.

"The fire," she said. "The explosion. So many dead."

"What . . . ?"

I was about to ask more when there was a sound from the forest, a loud snap, a branch breaking. I looked toward the noise—Jennifer looked too—and I saw flashlight beams crisscrossing in the trees below us.

Our time was up. The police had come searching for us in the woods. Our tracks probably hadn't been all that hard to follow.

They were already pretty close. I could hear them calling to one another in the distance:

"This way."

"I've got the trail."

"Looks like they went up this hill."

Jennifer and I turned and looked at each other.

"They're coming," she said.

I nodded. "I know."

"They'll take me back to the castle, won't they?"

"It's not a castle, Jennifer. It's a hospital."

"A hospital, yes. Yes. I know that. I know that."

"The doctors there will help you. You have to go back."

"I know. I know."

"Then when the medicine works, you can go home again."

She nodded too, but she looked very sad, very forlorn. "Why did God let this happen to me, Sam?" she asked again.

And I told her again, "I don't know. But he knows you're in there, Jennifer. He's right there with you. You won't be alone."

She held tightly to the tree. Even in the darkness, I could tell she was crying. "Will you be there too? Will you come to see me too?"

I went to her. I stood beside her. The crisscrossing flashlight beams passed over the trees, illuminating the branches.

"Definitely," I said. "I'll definitely be there. I'll visit you. And when you come out of the hospital, you can visit me too."

"You're my magic friend, Sam."

"That's right," I told her. "I'm your magic friend."

Still holding on to the tree, she lifted her tearstained face to me. "You have to go now," she said softly.

"Yeah. But I'll come back."

"You can't let them catch you."

I nodded.

"I won't tell them it was you, Sam," said Jennifer.

"Okay."

Jennifer let go of the tree. I heard the voices calling to one another below us.

"There it is. Here. I've got the trail."

"Over here."

"I see it. Up the hill."

The flashlights swept the woods.

Jennifer slowly, reluctantly took off my jacket. She ran her hand down over it once, as if she were caressing it. She held it to her face and breathed in the scent of it. Then she handed it to me. I put it on. I was glad to—it really was cold out there. As I did, Jennifer reached down and tugged my socks off—first one foot, then the other. She handed the socks to me. I stuffed them in the jacket pockets.

"Thanks," I said.

Jennifer straightened. We looked at each other as the voices of the searchers got louder, closer.

"Don't be afraid," I whispered.

She gave me a little smile. "I can't help it sometimes," she whispered back.

I smiled too. "Me either."

Now I could hear the feet of the searchers crunching on the brush and leaves of the hill as they moved toward us.

Jennifer shivered. She hugged her shoulders.

"You better call to them," I said. "Let them know where you are before you freeze out here."

She nodded. Her voice shook with the cold. "Good-bye, Sam."

"I'll see you, Jennifer. I will."

She took a breath. Then she shouted, loud enough so that the searchers could hear her: "I'm here. I'm up here! I'm all right! I'm up here!"

That got their attention, all right. The sounds of motion quickened. Their voices became an excited babble, running together:

"You hear that?"

"There she is!"

"I heard her!"

"She's up the hill!"

"We're coming, Jennifer! We're coming!"

"Keep calling, Jennifer!"

I gave a short laugh. "Like I said: you're not alone."

I touched her hand. Then, quickly, I moved away from her. I reached the far edge of the clearing.

"Sam!"

I stopped at her whispered call. I turned around. Once again the moon picked her out of the darkness, her pale face glowing. The flashlight beams swung back and forth on the tangle of branches behind her.

"They're real, Sam," she said. "The demons. They're all real."

"Are they?" I still wasn't sure.

"You have to stop them."

I didn't know how to answer. "I'll try," I said.

The first searcher's flashlight came into view.

I ran off into the woods.

PART FIVE

MADNESS

24

What If . . .

First, the alarm woke me up. Then the police came. And I knew I was in more trouble than ever before.

I had not been home for very long. The journey back from the hospital had been slow and dangerous. Luckily, everyone had been so busy looking for me and Jennifer in the woods in back of the hospital, no one had found my bike in the woods out in front. I made my way to it quickly. With the glow of the police flashers visible from the nearby hospital driveway, I threw my leg over the saddle and started to pedal away down the two-lane.

It was slow going. The police were everywhere along the road. I had to listen for them—to listen for any traffic that might be them. Whenever I heard a motor approaching, I had to—quick—pull off into the woods, lay down my bike, and duck behind the trees until the gleaming white headlights went by and the red taillights faded into the darkness. Only when they were out of sight did I feel safe enough to take up my ride again.

It was nearly three in the morning by the time I got back to the rectory. As worked up as I was, I half expected to find the police waiting for me right there on the front lawn. Jennifer had promised not to tell them about me. But to be honest, I didn't think she'd be able to keep that promise. She was so sick, so confused, I figured once they started questioning her, she'd probably tell them the name of her "magic friend" without even meaning to.

But it seemed I was wrong. It seemed Jennifer had been as good as her word. At least, there weren't any cop cars waiting for me on the lawn when I got home. The lights were out in all the windows. Mom, Dad, my brother—no one even knew that I had gone.

I put my bike in the bike port and snuck inside as quietly as I could. Crept upstairs as quietly as I could. In my room I was dropping my clothes to the floor even as I staggered to the bed. I dropped onto the bed like a falling tree—*plonk*—face-first into the mattress. The last thought I had was:

"They're real. The demons. They're all real. You have to stop them."

A second later, I was asleep.

A second after that—or at least it seemed like it was only a second—the radio alarm went off and music was banging through the room, banging in my ears. I don't think I'd moved at all since losing consciousness. I barely moved now. My hand just reached out and hit the clock radio button to turn off the music. Then my hand fell and I just lay there, my face still plunked down into the mattress.

My thoughts picked up right where they'd left off the night before: "*They're real. The demons. They're all real. You have to stop them.*"

I didn't know what to think when she said that—and I still didn't know what to think. *Were* the demons real? Was that possible?

After all the trouble I'd gone through to get to Jennifer, I still didn't really know the answer to that question. I'd been too busy worrying about the police to think about it much on the way home. And when I got home, I'd fallen asleep so fast I hadn't had a chance to think about it at all.

Now, though, lying there in that half-sleep state, I *did* start thinking about it. I thought about all the stuff Jennifer had told me last night in the woods.

"*I heard their whispers. In the night. In the dark. In my room. I heard their footsteps. And I followed them.*"

It was the same old story, wasn't it? The whispers in the night. The demons out in her hall. Just the same old hallucinations. Just like before.

"*I followed them down the stairs and out the door. They went behind our house. They gathered there in the little shed. They whispered to each other.*"

Slowly I rolled over onto my back. I fought off sleep. I forced my eyes wider. I lay there staring up at the ceiling.

Is it? I thought. *Is it really the same old story?*

I mean, the stuff that Jennifer told me last night—it *could've* happened, couldn't it? If you left out the demon part, what she was telling me wasn't really that crazy at all. Let's say Jennifer was lying in her bed awake one night—well, she *could've* heard whispers out in the hall, couldn't she? Footsteps. She could've peeked out and seen something. And okay, so it wasn't demons, but it might've been . . .

I sat up. Oh, I was awake now. Yeah, I was wide awake.

Something had just occurred to me, something that had never occurred to me before. I thought back to what my dad had said when I asked him if Jennifer might be having visions of the future like one of the prophets in the Bible:

"The world is not a magical place. The things that happen are pretty predictable, and they can usually be explained in ordinary terms."

I knew that was right. There's always a practical explanation for the things that happen in the world.

But that doesn't mean that's the *whole* explanation, does it? That doesn't mean that things happen with no reason or rhyme.

"Who did you see, Jennifer?"

I remembered asking her that in the woods.

"Who did you see?"

"Demons. They had to be. They had to be."

But what if . . . ? I thought.

When I considered it, it was pretty obvious that Jennifer really *was* suffering from some kind of mental illness, like everybody said. Schizophrenia—or something—whatever . . . It was obvious she really *was* having hallucinations. But what if she was having hallucinations about something that was also real? Something that was in her mind, say, that she didn't want to think about, that she couldn't bear to think about in any other way. What if Jennifer had forced all these unhappy thoughts down to the bottom of her mind, but when the schizophrenia gave her hallucinations, the hallucinations were full of the things she didn't want to think about? That made sense. It wasn't "magical." It could really happen.

"I heard their whispers. In the night. In the dark. In my room. I heard their footsteps. And I followed them."

Mark, I thought.

His name came into my mind without me even thinking about it. Mark Sales, Jennifer's brother. I know, I know, it was ridiculous. Mark was a good guy, the track-star hero of the whole school, but who else could it have been? If Jennifer was asleep in her room . . . if she heard whispers in the hall . . . it either had to be her mom or Mark, didn't it?

And if it was Mark—if it was Mark whispering and planning with his friends to do something wrong—then that was something Jennifer wouldn't be able to think about. Because Mark was Jennifer's hero. He was her protector.

He always stood up for her whenever anyone teased her. If Jennifer found out something bad about him, something really bad, she might push it out of her mind . . . and with her being sick and all, it might come back to her in her hallucinations.

But Mark wouldn't do anything *that* bad. Would he?

"I'm kind of off Mark . . ."

I remembered Zoe writing that when we were chatting online.

"He can be kind of arrogant."

I remembered how shocked I was when she compared him to Jeff Winger.

And that made me think of Jeff . . .

"You think I'm scared of Mark? I'm sick of Mark. Mark's pushed me just as far as I'm gonna go."

Those were Jeff Winger's words, weren't they? I remembered he'd said them when he was bullying Jennifer that time—that time I stopped him—that time he and his goons beat me up.

"Mark's pushed me just as far as I'm gonna go."

What did he mean by that?

Now all these thoughts were tumbling through my mind at once. All these things I'd heard but hadn't really paid attention to, hadn't really understood.

"Harry Mac knew. He was going to tell the police. They decided to put him in a coffin. Under the tree. By the tarn. Send a warning to the others. Then they would be afraid."

That's what Jennifer told me last night.

And I thought she meant Jeff Winger and Ed P. had killed Harry Mac. I had asked her: *"Was this Jeff Winger? Jeff and Ed P.? Are they the demons?"*

And Jennifer answered: *"They would be afraid."*

I heard a noise come out of me, a sort of long, low moan as the breath escaped me.

The person who murdered Harry Mac wasn't Jeff. The murderer was trying to make Jeff afraid. That's what she was saying.

"You think I'm scared of Mark? I'm sick of Mark. Mark's pushed me just as far as I'm gonna go."

The jumbled ideas in my mind started to untangle themselves. I thought: *What if Jeff and Harry Mac and Ed P. knew something bad about Mark Sales? What if Mark had threatened Jeff, trying to get him to keep quiet . . . ?*

But then Mark found out that Harry Mac was acting as a police informer . . . So Mark killed Harry Mac to silence him—and to make sure Jeff and Ed P. really *would* be afraid of him from then on.

All right, all right, it sounded insane even to me. And it was all coming together so fast in my mind, I couldn't really lay it out logically. But I understood—I was beginning to understand—how the things Jennifer saw might be hallucinations and sort of visions at the same time . . .

And how it all might have something to do with Mark . . .

That was when the police showed up.

I could hear the knock at the door from all the way upstairs. There was something about that knock—I recognized it immediately. Most people rang the rectory doorbell, and even when they knocked, they didn't knock like *that*. I knew from the pounding, urgent sound of it that it had to be the police.

I jumped out of bed. Rushed to the window. Opened it. Stuck my head out into the bright, cold morning. I could just see around the edge of the house, and sure enough, the tail end of a police cruiser was visible, parked at the curb.

I pulled my head in. I swallowed hard. I tried to think. *What should I do? What should I do?*

Jennifer must have told them what happened at the hospital. She probably tried to keep it a secret but was too confused to hold out for long. So now they were going to take me back to the police station, question me, maybe arrest me.

And meanwhile, something terrible was coming. "*So many dead.*" Today. Any minute. It was all real.

I heard the knock at the door again.

I heard my mother sing out, "Coming! Coming!"

I rushed to the dresser. Started pulling out clothes and stuffing myself into them just as fast as I could.

I had just got my sneakers on when I heard my mother calling, "Sam! Could you come down here for a minute, please?"

I froze. Just stood there in the middle of the room.

All these thoughts were racing through my head and I just couldn't figure out what to do. Detective Sims told my father that if he saw me again, he was going to arrest me for being part of Jeff Winger's gang. Would he believe me if I explained to him about Jennifer's "vision"? If I told him my suspicions about Mark Sales, would he investigate?

I thought about Detective Sims. His round, snowman's face, his unwavering quirky smile that wasn't really a smile at all. I seriously didn't think he would believe a single word I said.

I didn't think anyone would. Not without proof. Not fast enough. Not in time.

Jennifer wasn't having visions. Her hallucinations were telling her what she knew but didn't want to know. Her brother had murdered Harry Mac. Her brother was planning something terrible that he was going to do today. Nobody knew or understood any of this except for me.

No one could stop it—except for me.

"Sam!" my mother called from downstairs. "Sam, do you hear me? Could you come down here, please? Detective Sims is here and he wants to speak with you right now."

I still didn't answer. It would probably be only a few more seconds before she—or my dad or my brother—came to get me.

So I grabbed my jacket and raced to the window.

The rainspout. There I was again, wrapped around it, shimmying down. Down to the grass alley beside my house. No point trying to get out the front way—not with the police parked right there. So I took off for the back, climbed over the fence, and was in the backyard of my dad's church.

Then I kept going, past the church, to the road.

I was on the run again.

The Shed

It was not a long way to Jennifer's house, even on foot, but it seemed to take forever. I ran—and at every step I expected to hear someone shout my name or to hear a siren sound as a policeman spotted me and chased after me in his cruiser. I cut past houses, through backyards, trying to stay off the roads and out of sight as much as possible. But even so, I worried that the word was out, that everyone in Sawnee knew I was a hunted kid, that anyone might look out his kitchen window and see me and call the cops.

It didn't happen. After ten minutes spent dodging between houses, I tumbled out of a backyard into a driveway and stepped onto the sidewalk of Arthur Street, where Jennifer lived.

It was a quiet lane of houses: two-story clapboards, most of them. Each with a porch out front. Each with a small square of lawn. There were no garages, so the cars were parked end to end on both sides of the street. A woman went past, walking her poodle. After that, it was quiet, empty.

Jennifer's house was right in the middle of the block. A two-story clapboard with a porch like the others. When I came out onto the sidewalk, I was directly across the street from it. What I needed to do was slip alongside the house into the backyard. That's where the shed would be. That was where Jennifer said she saw the "demons" meeting, where she overheard them discussing their plans. I had to get to it, and get into it, without anyone seeing me.

I came off the sidewalk, stepping between two parked cars, a minivan and a little Honda. I braced myself, gathering the courage to cross the street and make my run around the side of the Saleses' house.

I was just about to take the first step when the Saleses' front door opened. I caught my breath and froze, staring.

Mark pushed out of the house into the morning.

I jumped back quickly. Ducked behind the minivan. I knew if anyone saw me hiding there, it would look pretty strange, but I didn't know what else to do. The good thing was: from that position, I could peek through the van windows and watch Mark across the street.

He came out onto the porch and stood there looking around. He was dressed in the school's blue-and-orange tracksuit, long pants and hooded jersey, the hood pulled down behind him. He was carrying two large, heavy-looking duffel bags, the handle of one in each hand.

"They had bags. They opened the bags. The guns were in them."

Jennifer's words came back to me and I couldn't help it: I shuddered, looking at Mark's duffel bags. Was it possible—could it be possible—there were guns inside?

"I heard them whisper, 'We are the angels of death.'"

Even I didn't really believe it.

A second later a car came down the street and stopped in front of the house. It was an old car, really old, like from the eighties or something. Really flashy. Jet black with yellow racing stripes and fins like it was some kind of rocket. You could hear the muffler sputtering as the engine idled.

I'd never noticed the car around town before, but I recognized the driver sure enough: it was Mark's track buddy, Nathan Deutsch.

When the car arrived, Mark came toward it, carrying the duffel bags down the porch steps. As he approached, Justin Philips got out of the front passenger seat. Justin walked around to the back of the car and opened the trunk. Mark followed him. He tossed the duffel bags into the trunk, first one, then the other.

Justin shut the trunk and got in the backseat of the car. Mark slipped into the front seat, next to Nathan. A moment later, with a rattling roar, Nathan put the car in gear and the three of them drove off.

I breathed easier as I came out from behind the minivan. They hadn't seen me. What's more, looking up, I could see Mrs. Sales in the house, moving past an upstairs window on the left side. If I hurried down the right side of the house, she'd be unlikely to spot me.

I didn't wait any longer. I took off.

The space between the Saleses' house and the house next door was narrow. I went down it as fast as I could. Then I was in the backyard, a rectangle of sparse lawn. The only things back there were a couple of old garden chairs and the shed. It was a fairly big structure, taller than me and long enough to fit, say, a small car inside. It had double doors. They were held shut by a padlock.

Of course, the padlock wouldn't stop me. I was a trained thief, remember? I had the Buster in the pocket of my jacket, and I knew how to use it. I had spent a whole hour once with Ed P. schooling me on how to pick a padlock.

With a quick glance up at the Saleses' house to make sure Mrs. Sales wasn't looking out the back window, I ran to the shed and went to work. A real thief like Jeff Winger or one of his buddies would've probably had the lock open in five seconds. It took me almost half a minute before I got it to click. But then, I was nervous—really nervous—and that slowed me down. I kept looking over my shoulder to make sure Mrs. Sales didn't see me from the house.

When the lock dropped to the ground, I opened the shed door and slipped inside. I closed the door quickly, breathing a sigh of relief that I was out of sight. I brought my flashlight out of my pocket. I turned it on and panned the beam over the shed walls.

"O-o-oh," I said—a low groan coming out of me.

"They write evil symbols on the walls."

Boy, they sure did. The walls were covered with pictures and words just like the ones in the barn where I'd found Harry Mac. Only these were worse, uglier, meaner, sicker. And they covered every inch of the walls too, so it was like some kind of evil wallpaper. The scariest part was this huge picture of the devil's face, painted so that the eyes looked like they were on fire and the teeth were dripping blood. When the flashlight touched it, the thing almost seemed to come alive. The whole time I was in the shed, I felt that devil watching me—and it only added to my sense of gathering disaster.

I forced myself to look away from the walls and to pass the flashlight beam over the rest of the room. I saw a small window on one wall. It was dirty, but you could see through it. I imagined that's where Jennifer had posted herself as she'd spied on her brother and Nathan and Justin gathered here in the night.

There wasn't much else. The top of a round table sat in the center of the dirt floor—just the top; the legs had been sawed off. There were several half-burned candles on the table. And there were some cushions positioned around the edge of it—I guess so people would have a place to sit.

Then, against the back wall, there were two storage boxes, their lids held shut with padlocks.

I knew what I had to do.

I propped the flashlight on one of the cushions so the beam would point at the padlock while I worked. I was really nervous now, thinking about what would happen if I got caught in here—especially if Mark came back and found me. The image of Harry Mac dead in that crate was still very fresh in my mind. I could feel the devil on the wall watching me from the shed shadows. I could almost hear him chuckling at my fear.

Anyway, the point is, I was basically freaked. My hands were shaking really badly. I had to wipe the sweat off them twice before I could get a good solid grip on the Buster. But I finally got the padlock open. Then I lifted the lid. Grabbed the flashlight. Shone it inside the box.

Empty.

Which wasn't as reassuring as you might think, because I couldn't help wondering if maybe the stuff that had been in the storage box was now in the duffel bags Mark had been carrying.

"They had bags. They opened the bags. The guns were in them."

I re-padlocked the one storage box and then moved over to the other. Hard to work the Buster with the sweat pouring down my forehead into my eyes, but I did it. I opened the lid and grabbed the flashlight and looked in and thought: *Empty, just like the other one.*

But then I thought: *Wait a minute. No, it's not.*

Lying in one corner of the box was a small notebook. It was one of those old-style ones with a binding and hard cover that's sort of marbleized black and white. The cover worked like camouflage so that at first I didn't notice the book lying there. Only as I was getting ready to shut the lid again—only as I was turning away—did the flashlight's beam touch on the cover and give the notebook's presence away.

The minute I saw it, I felt my breath go short. I knew there'd be important stuff inside. I reached down and took the notebook out of the box. I set it on the dirt floor. I dragged my sleeves across my face to wipe the sweat off. Then, holding the flashlight on the notebook with one hand, I flipped it open with the other.

The notebook's pages were covered with writing and scribbles and doodles and drawings—sort of like the ones on the wall, except with more words in between the pictures. I turned the pages, squinting at the horrible images, reading the words as quickly as I could. It was all crazy, violent, nasty stuff—a lot of it too awful to quote. But my eyes picked out some sentences and phrases:

The little people have to learn to fear.

Worship me, worship me, worship me.

I kept turning the pages, kept reading.

The conspiracies against us will be paid for with death.

We are champions. We were cheated.

Death is my power, and through death my power will increase.

The words rose and twisted and curled around the pages like wisps of smoke. Filling the spaces in between the words were the drawings of snakes and skulls and demons and so on. And that was just the stuff I can tell you about. I wondered if Jennifer had been able to see any of this as she spied from the window. I wondered if these images had gotten into her head and become part of her hallucinations.

I continued to turn the pages—and then I stopped.

I had come to a page where there were no words at all. Just a very carefully drawn picture. It was a picture of a coffin. There was a man inside it. He was tied up and gagged. I knew it was supposed to be Harry Mac.

So they had planned the whole thing right here. And Jennifer had watched through the window. And even though she couldn't bear the thought that her brother was evil, the idea had worked its way into her schizophrenic hallucinations.

Then she had described the hallucinations to me, and I had run to the scene she described. I must've gotten there just at the wrong time. Mark and Nathan and Justin must have hidden while I came into the barn, while I discovered Harry Mac tied up in the box. Then I guess they had the bright idea that they could not only kill Harry Mac, they could frame me for the crime. And they would have gotten away with it too, if my dad wasn't smarter than they were, and smarter than Detective Sims.

I swallowed down something sour in my mouth and started turning the notebook pages faster.

More words. More images.

We have to do something really spectacular to make them acknowledge our superiority.

The die is cast.

We are the real champions!

Death is my power.

There's no turning back.

Now there were pictures of guns. Not hunting rifles or pistols. Machine guns like they use in wars. And hand grenades. And not just pictures. Lists of them: AK-47, M-6, Glock 9mm . . .

When we are done with this town, there will be nothing left but death and fear.

Finally, I came to the last page of the notebook. What I saw there was more horrible than anything. More horrible than pictures of skulls and demons and whatever filth had somehow polluted the mind of Mark Sales.

Because here there was a series of diagrams. Notes. A plan. It took me a couple of seconds before I figured out what it all meant, but then it became clear.

Mark and his friends had created a death trap.

The diagrams showed Sawnee Stadium. I caught my breath when I recognized it. The Empire and Cole meet—the big track meet—was today, this morning. After the whole crazy night with Jennifer at the mental hospital, and the police coming in the morning, I had forgotten all about it. But I sure enough remembered now. I remembered Justin saying how Empire and Cole needed to be taught a lesson. I remembered the team's bitterness at feeling they'd been cheated out of the championship. I remembered Mark saying, "*Come the big meet, we have to show them all who we are.*"

The diagrams detailed the whole plan. The road leading in through the trees. The parking lot outside. There were even scribbled figures meant to represent the crowds that showed up there for sporting events. There were labels under each drawing—"people"; "car"; "concession"—and there were arrows to show which way traffic moved, which way the people moved. It was all very detailed.

As my eyes went from diagram to diagram, I began to understand they were in a time sequence, one thing happening after another. In the first diagram there was just the stadium with lines of cars coming down the road. In the second diagram the cars were mostly parked and people were moving into the stadium itself, lining up and crowding around the main entrance the way they did.

The third diagram showed an explosion.

The explosion was represented by a violent scratchy splotch of ink near the front of the stadium. Underneath the splotch was the neatly written label: "Explosion: 9:15AM."

The next diagram showed the result: dead people all around. But more than that, there were also the people who weren't dead. According to the diagram, they would panic and run away from the explosion back into the woods. The arrows showed the directions they would go, the paths they would take.

And that's where Mark and Justin and Nathan planned to wait for them with their guns. The idea, I guess, was that the explosion would make people panic and run away from the stadium down the easiest path to reach: the walkways by the road and through the trees. And Mark and Justin and Nathan would be waiting for them there—waiting perched and hidden in the trees. And they would open fire, killing the people who survived the explosion.

Staring at the diagrams, I began to feel sick to my stomach. But there was no time for that. I looked at my watch. The explosion was supposed to take place at 9:15. It was already 8:50. The disaster was just twenty-five minutes away.

I had to call the police. There was no time for anything else. No time to get to the stadium on foot. Somehow I had to call the police and convince them that this was all happening, that it was all real . . . before the bomb went off. Before the shooting started.

I closed the notebook and stood. My stomach turned over, and for a second I really thought I would throw up. My vision went dark and I was afraid I would faint. I was never going to be able to do this. How could I?

I steadied myself. I took a deep breath. I remembered the statuette of the archangel Michael on my father's bookshelf.

Do right. Fear nothing.

Well, it was a plan, anyway.

I stuffed my flashlight and Buster back into the pockets of my jacket. I didn't bother to lock up the storage box. It didn't matter if anyone knew I was here. Nothing mattered but alerting the police.

I stepped to the door. Pushed it open. Stepped out of the shed.

Detective Sims and two patrolmen were striding toward me across the lawn.

"Explosion, 9:15"

I almost bolted. It was my first reaction to seeing the police coming toward me—marching toward me as if they were coming to arrest me for breaking into St. Agnes. Detective Sims was dressed in an overcoat, but it was unbuttoned so you could see the suit and tie beneath. You could also see his round, snowman-like shape. You could also see that little smile of his, as if he found this whole situation very amusing, in a not-very-pleasant kind of way. As for the two patrolmen—one striding along on each side of him—they didn't look amused at all.

"Why, if it isn't Master Sam Hopkins," said Detective Sims in a sarcastic drawl, "aka the magic friend."

I think I actually blushed. But I guess I knew Jennifer would blabber about all that eventually.

"Funny thing," Sims went on. "We were at your house

this morning, Magic." The three policemen—Sims and the two patrolmen—had now reached me. They were standing over me—towering over me—where I stood in front of the shed.

"Listen . . . ," I said.

But Sims didn't listen. "We figured there was a good chance you were home at that hour," he went on. "Especially because we know you had a kind of late night last night, didn't you?"

"Look, I'll tell you all about that, but . . ."

"And here's something odd. Your mom figured you were home too," said Sims. "But when we looked in your room—what do you know? You weren't there at all. There was nothing to be seen but an open window—almost as if someone had climbed out and shimmied down the waterspout in order to avoid talking to the police."

"Okay, okay, but you have to listen. You have to look at this, read this," I said, holding the notebook out to him.

"Luckily this is a small town," said Sims, ignoring the notebook completely. "One of our dispatchers was having her morning coffee when she looked out her kitchen window and, son of a gun, what should she behold?"

"Read the notebook. I'm telling you, this is an emergency," I said. I was practically jumping up and down with the urgency of it.

"She beholds young Sam Hopkins," Sims went on, "running through her backyard, heading toward Arthur Street."

"Please listen."

"Also luckily, as a trained detective," Sims went on sarcastically, "I was able to guess you'd be heading for Jennifer's house. After all, you're her magic friend."

"Mark Sales and his friends, Nathan and Justin—they're going to kill people. Lots of people. In, like"—I looked at my watch—"twenty minutes."

That—finally—stopped Detective Sims. He stared at me. The quirk at the corner of his mouth got even quirkier as his smile got wider. "What are you talking about?"

"Mark and Nathan and Justin . . ."

"Mark Sales," he said drily.

"Yes. He's got guns. Lots of guns. And a bomb."

"*The* Mark Sales? The track star?"

"Look at the notebook! They have this whole incredible plan. They're gonna set off a bomb at the stadium . . . They're going to hide in the woods . . . They've got rifles . . ." I was so desperate to make him understand, I could hardly finish my sentences.

I kept holding the notebook out to him. For another second, Detective Sims didn't take it. Then he took it, but he just held it and went on looking at me. Finally, he gave a sort of sniff—as if to say, *Oh well, all right, I'll have a look.* He glanced down at the book and started flipping through its pages.

"You see the diagrams?" I said. "Of the stadium.

They're about today. About the track meet. See where it says, 'Explosion, 9:15'? That's just twenty minutes from now. We need to get there!"

For a second my hopes rose as I saw the detective's expression grow serious. He could see what horrible stuff was on those pages as clearly as I could.

But then he looked up, held the notebook up. "Did you write this?"

"Me? No!" I cried. "No! I found it in there." I gestured at the shed. "It's Mark's. Jennifer saw him with his friends making plans. That's what she's been having hallucinations about. That's why her hallucinations showed the truth."

"This is pretty sick stuff, Hopkins," Sims said sternly. "What, did you come here to plant this on Mark, try to make him look bad?"

"*What?*" I practically screamed. "No! Why would I do that?"

"Maybe to get back at him for getting your friend Jeff Winger in trouble," said Sims.

I opened my mouth, about to answer, but nothing came out. I just stood there with my mouth open.

Because suddenly I understood: It didn't matter what I said to Sims. Nothing I could tell him was going to make any difference. It's not that the detective was a bad guy—or even a bad detective. Actually, I think he was a good guy and a good detective. I mean, I think he wanted to protect people and keep his town safe and get the bad guys off the streets and into jail and all that. It's just that I was trying to tell him something so different from what he already believed that it was going to take time to convince him. And I didn't have time. Dozens of people were about to be murdered. Hundreds maybe.

"All right," said Sims. "I might as well tell you, kid, you are in a super lot of trouble here. Your dad's not going to get you out of this so easily. You better come down to the department with us and we'll talk it all over, get to the bottom of it."

I could have shouted at him: "*There's no time!*" I could've shouted, "*We have to get to the stadium now, right now!*"

But I knew he wouldn't believe me. I knew he wouldn't understand. Not quickly enough. Not before the killing started.

Sims gestured to the patrolmen, and they both stepped forward to take me into custody. One came at me from the left and one from the right.

I bolted.

I dodged left. The patrolman on the left grabbed at me. I swerved and dashed to the right. The cop on the right reached out. I've never been so glad to be a little guy in all my life. I ducked and went right under his arm and took off across the backyard.

I raced to the edge of the house. I felt a little breath of air on my neck and knew that one of the cops was right behind me, reaching for me, his fingers just missing me. I put on a burst of extra speed.

"Where you gonna go?" I heard Sims yelling after me. "Where do you think you can hide?"

I didn't look back. I didn't want anything to slow me down. I just ran with all my might, with all my speed, down the side of the house, out into the front yard, across the street and down the side of the next house into the next backyard.

When I finally did glance back, I saw there was no one there. The cops weren't chasing me—not yet. But I knew Sims was right. There was nowhere to hide. I couldn't escape them forever.

But I didn't *have* to escape them forever. Just for—I glanced at my watch—just for seventeen minutes. Just long enough to get to the stadium and somehow warn the people there about the bomb, about Mark and the others waiting in the woods.

I stumbled out from behind the house. Onto the next sidewalk—Buchanan Street. More houses, more cars parked along the curb.

I stopped. I put my hands on my knees, breathing hard.

What now? The stadium was all the way across town. I knew I'd never make it in time. I thought of Jennifer's voice on the phone:

"So many dead. So many dead."

I had to do something to stop it. But what? How?

Then slowly, I raised my head, looked around me. I had an idea. It was a crazy idea. Dangerous. It would probably get me killed.

But it was the only thing I could think of.

Time Runs Out

Breathing hard, I scanned the cars parked along the curb. I saw the one I wanted right away. A blue Mustang. It looked new. It looked fast.

I took one furtive glance up and down the street. No one near. I stepped quickly to the car. By the time I reached the driver's door, I had the Buster in my hand. I pulled the car tool out. Worked it in the window the way Harry Mac had taught me.

A few seconds later I was inside the car. My heart was hammering in my chest. My eyes were wide—because I was shocked at what I was doing. I was stealing a car! But what else could I do? No one believed me. No one understood. The killing was going to start in minutes. I had to get there. I had to stop it.

I needed to use a second tool in the Buster to get

through the steering column and free up the wheel. That took a little longer than the door. I felt the time ticking away, felt every second go by as I worked. Then the column was broken; the wheel was free.

I went to work on the ignition. And as I did, I heard the sirens start. The cops. Sims and his patrolmen. Looking for me. Coming after me.

"Let's go, let's go," I told the Mustang as sweat poured down the sides of my face.

The next second, the engine coughed and the car came to life.

My heart was going nuts in my chest now. My head was reeling, the world spiraling around me. I tried not to think about what I was doing, what was going to happen next. I just said a prayer and did what I had to do.

I put the car in gear. I twisted the wheel. I edged out of the parking space onto the street.

I had my learner's permit, like I said. I knew how to drive. At least, I'd driven my dad's Passat a few times. My dad, as you would guess, was a careful driver and was teaching me to be the same. Always under the speed limit. Full stops at every sign. Look both ways. Then start again.

And so help me, after this, that was how I was going to drive every day for the rest of my life.

But for now—well, this was going to be different.

I stomped down on the gas pedal and the Mustang took off like a bullet.

A lightning bolt of pure fear went through me as the car shot forward, throwing me back against the driver's seat. I gripped the wheel with white-knuckled hands. The lane of houses rushed by the windows on either side of me, a surrounding blur. I watched openmouthed as the front fender rocketed toward the corner.

I didn't stop at the stop sign at all. I didn't touch the brakes. I just raced right through the intersection—and as I did, out of the corner of my eye, I saw the spinning red lights of a police cruiser charging toward me from the right.

Then I was through the intersection and gone. And as the Mustang kept hammering its way down the street, I glanced up in my rearview mirror. I saw the cop car come screeching to a halt at the corner behind me. It hesitated there. I think the cops weren't sure it was me in the speeding car.

I didn't wait around for them to come to a decision. I reached the next corner, hit the brakes, and wrenched the wheel to the left. The Mustang's tires screamed as the car went into a mad, looping turn.

Then I stomped the gas again and shot down the next street.

The highway. I had to get to the highway. That was the fastest way to reach the stadium. I knew where the on-ramp was and I headed that way. I was still on residential backroads. I saw one or two people getting their newspapers, walking their dogs, freezing to gape at me as I went flashing past. But I still hadn't seen another car. Then I did.

Up ahead . . . a great big lumbering SUV . . . just slowing for a stop sign at the next corner. It was looming in my windshield as I raced toward it at full speed.

"Get out of the way!" I screamed, my voice breaking.

I hit the horn with the heel of my palm. The Mustang let out a trumpeting blast. I saw the SUV jolt to a stop, rocking on its back tires. Terror seemed to freeze my brain. I didn't slow down at all. I just swung the wheel, and the Mustang pulled out into the oncoming traffic lane. I could've been hit head-on by anything coming that way—but nothing was there. I shot past the SUV and through the corner—risking a broadside collision now. I got lucky again: no traffic crossed me. And then I was gone, with the SUV's horn screaming angrily behind me and my mind only just beginning to work again, only just beginning to grasp how close I'd come to a blood-drenched disaster.

I drove on. Above the roar of the Mustang's engine, I heard the police sirens again. They were distant now. A small spark of hope lit up in me. Maybe I was getting away from them.

But still—still—how was I going to get to the stadium in time?

I turned a corner. Up ahead, I saw the highway ramp. A Volkswagen Beetle was just turning onto it. I cut him off, speeding up the ramp toward the highway as the Beetle beeped behind me.

"Oh no!" I said aloud.

Because I saw the traffic—the traffic on the highway. It was moving fast enough, but there sure was an awful lot of it. Of course there was—everyone was heading for the stadium. Everyone was going to the big meet.

I glanced at the clock on the dashboard: 9:06. Nine minutes to get there. To warn people. To stop the killing.

I'd never make it. Never.

But I had to try. I couldn't slow down.

My sweaty hands held the wheel. My wide eyes stared through the windshield as I raced through the traffic, dodging this way and that. I saw the rear fender of the car in front of me come slamming toward me like a fist to the face. A scream caught in my throat. At the last minute I saw an opening to my left. I jerked the steering wheel. I dodged through the open space—and instantly, another fender came shooting at the windshield full speed. Now the scream burst out of me. I wrenched the wheel to the right to get around.

Miraculously, I was through, still rolling, stitching through the traffic like the needle on a sewing machine—that fast. Horns started screaming all around me. I heard the sirens again, getting louder behind me now. I couldn't tell how close the police were. I didn't dare look up at the rearview mirror. I didn't dare take my eyes off the road ahead even for a second. I just kept dodging through the traffic, so scared I was practically choking on it, practically strangling on my own fear.

And every second that ticked away made the stranglehold grow tighter.

Then—there it was—the sign: Sawnee Stadium, Home of the Lions.

One more time I spun the wheel, cutting in front of a stately Cadillac. I heard the Caddy's tires screech. My own tires screeched back as the Mustang skidded sideways across the lane to the exit. The car plunged off the freeway without slowing.

And there in front of me, rushing toward me uncontrollably: a line of cars, stopped cold. The traffic for the stadium had thickened here, stopped by the stop sign at the end of the ramp. No way to get around. And the traffic on the cross street was too thick to get through. The rear end of the pickup at the end of the line was growing larger in the windshield, closer and closer. I had to stop before I smashed into it.

I hit the brakes as hard as I could.

The Mustang's tires let out a humongous screech. I let out a screech myself. Smoke—carrying the stench of burning rubber—went up around the windows. I was thrown forward and felt the rear end of the Mustang fishtail, swinging back and forth, as the car threatened to spin out. My blood seemed to freeze inside. I gripped the wheel for dear life. I saw the pickup grow huge in the windshield.

Inches from collision, the Mustang lurched to a stop. I gasped. Breathless, I looked at the dashboard clock: 9:10. Five minutes. Five short minutes. I threw the car into park, jumped out the door, and ran like a madman.

All around me, the traffic erupted with horns and shouts. I had left the Mustang blocking everyone.

But that, I realized, was good for me. Because the police were stuck back there on the highway. I heard the sirens screaming helplessly. I heard the police shouting over their loudspeakers: "Move out of the way! Move to the side!" Their voices nearly lost over the angry horns.

I didn't look back. I ran. As fast as I could. Faster.

I felt every second inside me as it ticked away.

28

Bomb

Here was the scene on Stadium Road: Cars lined up at the entrance to the parking lot. Traffic backed up along the road, closing one lane, making the other slow. Pedestrians were entering the surrounding park, moving through the trees along the pathway. I could see the stadium through the woods. I could see the riverwalk and the river beyond, the slow-moving water glittering in the morning sun, the far hills draped in haze.

I could hear the sirens behind me. More than one. I guessed the traffic had made a path for them because I could hear they were on the move again, making their way off the highway, coming closer, coming after me.

I ran, fear squeezing my throat like a strangling hand. I could hardly think. I could only move. I could barely hope. I just ran.

I ducked off the road into the trees. I dashed through the small forest park toward the parking lot. I guessed that Mark and Nathan and Justin were up above me somewhere, waiting in the trees like snipers. But wherever they were, they were well hidden. I couldn't see them. I didn't have time to try.

I came to the edge of the trees, the edge of the parking lot. I pulled up, my mouth hanging open. The crowd. So many. So many people. So many people I knew. Kids and teachers I knew. People from my dad's church and children from the Sunday school. Men and women who worked in the stores in town. Just about everyone in Sawnee and everyone in the nearby towns as well. I looked at them and I felt like there was a giant ball of fire in my chest, a ball of smothering smoke.

"So many dead."

It was all on me. Saving them. All on me. Like something out of a nightmare where you have to run but you can't run fast enough. How could I possibly run fast enough? How could I keep them from dying?

I forced myself to move. I came off the curb onto the parking lot pavement. I saw how the people were coming together at the entrance to the stadium. They had to show their tickets there, and the delay made the crowd bunch up and swell. Just the way they did in the diagram in Mark's notebook. Just as Mark had planned.

I watched them, breathing hard. I heard the police

sirens—very loud now. I glanced over and saw the whirling red lights through the trees—three cars, coming after me. If they arrested me now . . .

But what should I do? If I just started screaming, everyone would panic, everyone would run—just as Mark wanted, they would run down the exit paths where he was hiding, waiting with his friends to open fire on them.

I looked over the lot. Maybe I could find the bomb. Maybe I could move it somewhere. But I didn't see anything besides the people and the cars.

Wait. The cars.

Suddenly I understood.

Parked at the edge of the lot, just where the path to the stadium began, just where the crowd formed and gathered into a growing pool of human beings, was the flashy black 1980s sports car that Nathan had been driving when he'd picked up Mark this morning. The moment I saw it, the moment I saw how it was placed exactly where the explosion was supposed to go off, I knew that the car itself was packed with explosives. It was rigged to go off in—I glanced at my watch—three minutes from now.

The police cruisers came screaming around the corner into the stadium entrance. The cars lined up there blocked the cruisers' way. The police didn't wait for them to move. They stopped their cars and got out. They started running around the other cars toward me.

I started running too. Tears blurred my vision, flew

from my eyes as I ran. They were tears of desperation and terror. So little time. I had to move that car away from the people before it blew. I couldn't let the police stop me. So little time . . .

I reached the sports car, running so fast I slammed up against the driver's door, hard. I already had the Buster in my hands. I fumbled out the blade and went to work, forcing it into the car's window.

My hand was shaking—my whole body was shaking—but I forced the blade to the lock. How much time was left before the explosion? Two minutes? Two and a half? I didn't know.

"Do right; fear nothing. Do right; fear nothing," I kept muttering through my teeth, my voice cracking, the tears blurring my vision. I was so afraid. So afraid.

I popped the lock.

"Yes!"

I yanked the door open.

"Hold it right there!"

The police. Shouting at me:

"Freeze!"

"Put your hands up!"

I looked up and saw the patrolmen charging toward me from the entrance. There were at least five of them now—and Sims too. All of them running at top speed, all with their hands on their gun holsters, ready to draw and fire.

And then, without warning: a gunshot. A loud, piercing

crack. A sickening thud. A hole opened in the side of the sports car right in front of me.

My heart seemed to stop beating. My mouth fell open in shock. Someone was shooting at me!

The police saw it too. They halted and dropped down fast, scrambling to get behind cars for cover. They looked to the woods. One of them shouted: "Gun!"

The police started yelling at everyone, "Get down! Get down! Take cover!"

Even in my confusion and terror, I realized what was happening. Mark Sales or one of his friends was trying to stop me from moving the car away from the people, trying to stop me from ruining their plans. They'd only just missed me too.

Well, I didn't give them time for a second shot.

I jumped into the sports car. I turned the wheel in my hand. It wasn't locked. I didn't have to cut the steering column. I went right for the ignition, working as fast as I could, babbling a prayer as I worked.

Another gunshot cracked. The car's rear window exploded, glass flying over the backseat.

I shouted out in fear.

I ducked down and kept working the ignition wires. The car started.

"Please!" I prayed, tears streaming down my cheeks.

I sat up behind the wheel.

More gunshots. I glanced over my shoulder and saw the

police. They were ducked down behind cars in the parking lot, firing back into the trees, firing at Mark and the others. People were screaming, dropping to the ground, grabbing their kids and running to hide behind cars.

I glanced at the dashboard clock: 9:14.

One minute left.

I hit the gas.

The sports car roared to life. It jumped over the curb, heading straight for the stadium. I wrenched the wheel and the car turned, its tires throwing up turf. I pointed the front around the side of the stadium, toward the riverwalk, toward the river. I knew it was going to blow any second.

"Go!" I screamed in an agony of fear. I expected to be blown to bits any second.

The car shot across the grass. It bounced and jolted as it hit the pavement of the riverwalk. I never let my foot off the gas, not for a second. The car kept flying forward. Over the walk. To the riverbank. And then . . .

Then the car and the bomb and I were all airborne, flying through nothingness toward the water beyond. For an endless second the windshield was full of nothing but the blue, blue sky. My mind was full of nothing but red, red fear. I didn't breathe. It seemed there was no more air in the world and no more time. And I so didn't want to die.

Then the car hit the river. Instantly the water began pouring in through the back window, the one shattered by the gunshot. I knew I had only a second before losing the electrics so I buzzed down the front window, hoping to escape. No way. More water came rushing in. I tried to push through it, to get out of the car. But it was rushing in too fast, too hard. I couldn't fight my way to the window.

I let out a roar of despair, fighting against the tide. The car filled up and started sinking. The water poured in—a solid torrent that overwhelmed me. The car pitched forward and sideways. The water filled it, covering me. The last bit of air in the car was up in the rear. Even knowing the car was about to blow, waiting for it, expecting it as each second ticked by, I had no choice. I swam up and stuck my head into the air pocket, gasping for air. The pocket got smaller and smaller. It was disappearing quickly. I had to get out.

So much was in my head just then. My dad—my poor mom and dad—burying what was left of my body. Zoe. Her sweet face. Jennifer—poor Jennifer. All alone without her magic friend . . . Who would explain to her how I'd died?

The air pocket was shrunk nearly to nothing now, just about to disappear. The car was almost full. That meant the water wouldn't be rushing in so hard anymore. I grabbed one last breath and plunged down into the water that filled the car.

I twisted around in the tight space, searching through the muddy river water to find the window. I could see the silt rushing past outside as the car sank down to the bottom. I found the windows and swam toward them.

I reached through, feeling broken glass scratching at my hands. I grabbed the edge of the car and hauled myself out through the window.

I craned my neck, looking for the light of the surface. There it was, falling in yellow-gold rays through the water. I swam for it, pushing against the river as hard as I could, trying, trying with everything in me, to get away from that car before it blew.

My heart thundered in my ears. My lungs strained in my chest. I wondered if I would hear the eruption, if I would feel the pain as it tore me apart . . .

And then, with a splash, I broke, gasping, out into the clear, cold light of day.

I didn't wait. I swam for shore. The river's slow but steady flow pushed me downstream, but it wasn't far. A few strokes and I gripped the riverbank. My fingers clawed at the earth. I dragged myself out of the water. I stood up and stumbled onto the strip of grass beside the riverwalk.

"Stop right there, Hopkins!"

"Put your hands up!"

Dazed, drenched, I looked toward the voices. I saw Detective Sims and one of the patrolmen coming toward me, their guns drawn, the bores leveled at me, hollow and deadly.

Behind them, I could see other policemen in the parking

lot. They had their guns leveled too—but they were pointed at the woods. And I could see Mark and Nathan and Justin coming out of the trees, their hands held high in the air.

There were sirens everywhere. Flashing lights. More police cars arriving on the scene. Mark and his friends were under arrest.

"I said put your hands up!" Sims screamed at me.

I started to laugh and cry at once. It was over. Over. I put my hands in the air, laughing and crying.

And the car in the river exploded.

There was a great gurgling roar—it sounded as if some monster were rising out of the riverbed. I ducked down, spinning to look behind me, and saw the surface of the river rise in a great flashing silver dome. And then the dome burst and the water flew out through the sunshine, the droplets sparkling like shattered glass.

Sims grabbed me and put his arms around me, shielding my body with his own. But it was only water that hit us. It slapped against us hard, a single cold wave of it. Then it was gone. Harmlessly, painlessly. Gone.

Sims slowly let go of me. I saw him staring at the water as its roiling waves settled back into a steady flow. Then he stared at me. I saw understanding come into his eyes. He saw what had happened. He knew.

He turned to the water again. I turned to it too. There were still tears streaming down my cheeks.

"Was anyone hurt?" I managed to ask.

I heard Detective Sims make a noise. I turned and looked at him. I saw that his eyes were filled with tears too.

He looked down at me, amazed. "No one," he said in wonder. Then, for once, he smiled with both sides of his mouth. "Not a single soul."

Epilogue

That's pretty much the end of my story. There's just one more thing I ought to tell.

It happened in late May, full spring, the afternoon. I was running. The trees were blooming with light-green leaves and the hills were green and grassy. The sky was blue with big, slow white clouds moving across it. And the air—I don't know how to describe it exactly—it had that strange cool spring feeling in it, that feeling as if you remember something wonderful but you're not quite sure what it is.

Anyway, like I said, I was running, training for track next year. It was going to have to be next year because the principal had canceled all the rest of the meets this year. He and the teachers and a lot of the parents figured that the kids in school were too traumatized about what had happened at the big meet to go on having track. They figured we were so traumatized that they kept sending therapists and doctors to talk to us. They kept making us have assemblies in the auditorium to discuss our feelings. Politicians gave speeches to us. And even some people on television yelled at one another about us. That's how traumatized everyone figured we were.

In real life? In real life, mostly, it was obviously they, the grown-ups, who were the traumatized ones. We kids just figured we had to put up with our parents and teachers therapizing and talking and arguing until they all calmed down. They just needed time, that's all.

Still, with track canceled, I kept running as much as I could so I'd be ready for next year when the meets started again. Sometimes I ran at the school track and sometimes over in the eastern part of town.

But this day, this beautiful spring day, I went running back up into the western hills, back up that dirt road that led to Jeff Winger's barn, the road where I had seen Jennifer that time and where Winger and his pals had found us and beaten me up while Jennifer escaped.

I had stayed away from this place for several weeks. Somehow, for a while, I just didn't feel like going back there. But then, this day, it being spring and so beautiful and all, I guess I just figured the time had come. It was just a place after all. Just a place where things had happened. It wasn't haunted or anything. So back I went.

Running along there with the hills on either side of me—knowing the barn where Jeff had held his stolen cars was up ahead—knowing that the other barn, too, where Harry Mac had died was right nearby—I couldn't help thinking about the whole thing again. All those kids were in some kind of detention now. Jeff and Ed P. had pleaded guilty to charges of grand theft auto. Nathan and Justin had pleaded guilty to attempted murder and all sorts of other stuff. They were all going to spend a lot of time locked away.

But it was Mark Sales who got the worst of it. He was going to be charged as an adult for a whole bunch of things surrounding the attack on the school: several counts of attempted murder, attempted use of an incendiary device—all kinds of things. If he was convicted—and he was sure to be convicted—he was probably going to go to prison for the rest of his life.

One of the therapists who visited the school said she didn't think that was fair. She said Mark was just mentally ill like Jennifer was. She said sometimes schizophrenia runs in families that way. It was a genetic condition, she said.

I didn't believe that. Or at least I didn't believe that was the whole story.

Sure, Mark and Jennifer were both mentally ill—but Mark was something else too. Because even when she was hallucinating, Jennifer was a good person. All she wanted was to help and protect people. She was confused and sick and it was painful for her. But there was no cruelty in her, and no violence.

But Mark—Mark was different. He had all these horrible ideas in his head—about how the people in Sawnee didn't understand his greatness and his power, how the little people had cheated him out of his championship, how they needed to be taught to be afraid, and how he was going to teach them by killing them, and on and on. So, okay, maybe Mark was mentally ill. But he was also evil. And those aren't the same things at all.

Whatever he was, Mark had somehow managed to talk Justin and Nathan into following him. I guess they were the following type and didn't bother to think things through for themselves. The three of them had been buying supplies for their big plan—guns and explosives and the car they used—from Jeff Winger, who'd been getting all that stuff from his criminal friends in Albany. When Jeff started asking questions about what Mark was up to, Mark threatened him, told him to shut up or he'd kill him. That's why when Jeff found out Harry Mac was talking to the police, he told Mark because he was afraid Mark would think it was him doing the talking. Mark and Nathan and Justin killed Harry Mac—which made Jeff so scared, he didn't tell the cops about Mark, even after they'd arrested him.

I was thinking about all that as I ran up the long, slow hill. And I guess I was lost in those thoughts because, all of a sudden, I got this weird feeling, like someone was watching me. I glanced back over my shoulder—and I was really startled to see there was a green pickup trundling along right behind me. Somehow it had come up on me without my even knowing it was there.

The next moment, the pickup pulled up alongside me and slowed to a stop. I stopped too and looked in through the window, breathing hard from my run.

At first I didn't remember the old man sitting behind the wheel, but then the scrunched, round, wrinkled face and the dark, sparkly eyes came back to me. This was the same farmer who had come along this road before, when Jeff and his thugs were beating me up. He was the reason the thugs ran off. In fact, without him, they might have really done some serious damage to me.

The farmer's shriveled old hands held on to the wheel as he leaned over and looked out the window at me. He chewed thoughtfully on his wrinkled lip.

"I know you," he said after a moment.

"Yeah," I said through my panting breath. "We met once before."

"That's right. That's right. I see you around too," he said. "Walking to the school sometimes. With that girl, that pretty little black-haired girl . . ."

"Zoe," I said.

"Zoe Miller, that's right." He nodded slowly. "Nice girl, seems like."

"Yes, sir. She sure is."

The old man chewed on his grizzled cheek some more, as if he had a very dry joke stuck in there, wanting to be told. "You're the preacher's kid, ain't you? The one who stopped those fellas with all their guns."

"Well . . . the police stopped them."

"But you drove that bomb car into the river. That was nice going."

I shrugged. "Thanks."

"Bet your dad must've been proud of you."

I laughed. "He said I must be the only kid in the world who could break into a mental hospital, steal a car, run from the police—and have it turn out to be the right thing to do."

The old man in the pickup laughed too, a hoarse, wheezy laugh. "That's good, that's good. I like that. I like a man of God with a sense of humor. If God don't have a sense of humor, we're all in big trouble."

"Yes, sir. I guess that's right."

The old man looked out through the pickup's windshield at the road as if he were considering something far away. I thought he was going to drive off then. But he didn't. He glanced over at me again and he said, "So tell me something."

"Sure."

"The way I heard it, there was some girl—some crazy girl in the mental hospital. Way I heard it, this girl was having visions about it all. She saw the things that would happen before they did."

"Jennifer," I told him. "And she's not crazy. Anyway, I don't like to call her that. She's just . . . well, she's just got a sickness, that's all. And she doesn't exactly have visions . . ."

"No?"

"No. She overheard her brother's plans and that became part of her hallucinations."

"Ah. Is that right?"

"Yeah," I said. "There's always some kind of explanation for things like that. It's not a magical world or anything."

"No?"

"That's what my dad says."

"Well, your dad sounds like a good fellow."

"Yes, sir, he is."

"And how's she doing now? The girl in the hospital, I mean. This Jennifer."

"She's not in the hospital anymore," I told him. "They gave her some medicine and she's back home now. The medicine seems to help her a lot. She's even started coming back to school sometimes."

"Has she? Well, well. The things they've got these days. That's good to hear. Must be tough for a girl like that to fit in, though. Tough for her to make friends and all."

"She has friends," I told the old man. "I'm her friend. Zoe's her friend too."

He made a sort of smacking sound with his lips. "Good deal then," he said. "Good deal."

"Yes, sir."

"Well," he said, "you take care of yourself, son."

"You too."

"And keep on training. You're gonna run a good race when the time comes. I'm sure of it."

"Thanks."

He put the truck in gear, and it made a loud grinding noise. And once again, so softly I could hardly hear him under that sound, the old man said, "Do right. Fear nothing."

And the green pickup started to pull away at the same slow pace as always.

I stood there watching the truck pull away—and wondering if I'd heard the old man correctly. Because his words reminded me of something else now. I remembered how, after everything was over, after the police had questioned me and brought me home, after the newspapers and radio and TV had interviewed me, after the mayor had held a celebration and given me an award, I sat down alone with my dad in his study and told him everything that had happened from the beginning to the end. He wanted to hear it all, he said, step-by-step, from the very start of it. And so I told him, beginning with the day I played chicken with that oncoming freight. I told it to him pretty much as I've told it here.

And while I was telling him, a funny thing happened. I got to the part about the angel statue—the statuette of the archangel Michael on his shelf. And when I reached that part, my dad kind of blinked at me from behind his round glasses.

And he said, "What statue?"

And I said, "The one right over . . ." And I began to point at where the little statue was. Only it wasn't there anymore. "It was right there," I told my dad. "The archangel Michael. With his sword. It had this Latin writing on it: *Recte age nil time*."

My dad shook his head. "No, I don't . . . I don't have a statue like that. I've never even heard that phrase before."

"It means, 'Do right; fear nothing,'" I told him.

"Yeah, I know what it means. But I've never had a statue like that. You must've seen it somewhere else."

I started to say no—no, I knew it was here, it was right here. I was sure of it. And I was sure I hadn't imagined it, because I didn't know any Latin, and I couldn't have made the phrase up myself.

But my dad was just as sure that he'd never had a statue like that.

And somehow, I've never been able to find the thing again.

As I watched the green pickup drive away, for some reason I found myself wishing I had asked the old farmer about the statue. For some reason—I'm not sure why—I thought he would have been able to help me understand it. I've never been able to make any sense of it myself.

But it was too late now. So I just stood there watching the pickup get smaller and smaller in the distance, trailing a cloud of dust behind it. Finally, it trundled out of sight over the rim of the hill.

And after a while, I started running again.

Acknowledgments

My thanks to Alan J. Fridlund, Ph.D., a clinical psychologist and Associate Professor of Psychological and Brain Sciences at the University of California, Santa Barbara; and to George Bifano, D.O., a psychiatrist: both were tremendously patient and helpful with my questions about schizophrenia and mental illness.

I'm also grateful to champion runner Bob Lunn for helping me describe high school track events.

Of all the books and articles I read on mental illness, two books stand out for their harrowing firsthand accounts of what it's like to suffer from these painful diseases: *The Center Cannot Hold: My Journey Through Madness*, by Elyn R. Saks; and *A Shining Affliction: A Story of Harm and Healing in Psychotherapy*, by Annie G. Rogers.

My thanks, too, to my wonderful editor at Thomas

Nelson, Amanda Bostic, who is a joy to work with and to know. Likewise, my agent at Trident Media, Alyssa Eisner Henkin, who has been more helpful than I can say.

Finally, and always, my thanks to Ellen Treacy Klavan, who remains, after all these years, my muse, my song, my only ever love.

Reading Group Guide

> Warning: Reading Group Guide contains spoilers!
> Do not read until you have completed the novel.

1. Sam acknowledges that he didn't always make the right decisions early on in the novel. What do you think would have happened had he not made those bad decisions? How would events have played out later in the novel? Have you ever had any bad decisions that might have led to something good? Was it worth the error in judgment?
2. What do you think is the true nature of Jennifer's visions? Why do you think she chose to tell Sam about them? What do you think her brother thought of the visions?
3. Why do you think Sam was so certain that Jennifer's warnings were true? Why do you think no one believed her even after her first one proved true?
4. Sam longs to be on the track team—to be a part of the popular group. How did that affect his decisions in the beginning of the novel? How did it change toward the end?

5. Who do you think the old man in the truck is? What is his significance?
6. Name the times when Sam had to remind himself to "Do right. Fear nothing." How difficult was it for him to follow that mantra? What were some times in your life when you've had to remind yourself to "Do right. Fear Nothing."?
7. When Joe advises Sam to tell his father everything that is going on with Jeff, Sam agrees that he should. But then he doesn't because his father is distracted. What do you think would have happened had he been able to talk to his father that night? Have you ever dreaded having to tell your parents something? What made you face your fear and tell them? What were their reactions?
8. Do you have a mantra similar to Sam's that you rely on when you have to make a tough decision?
9. Sam's dad didn't know what statue he was talking about. Do you think Sam imagined it? What other explanation could there be?
10. Do you think that the fact that Sam is a preacher's kid has any effect on how he responds to Jennifer? How would you have responded to her?
11. There are a few times in the novel when the timing on an event is perfect, such as when the old man in the truck shows up when Sam is being beaten up. Do you think that was a coincidence?

About the Author

Author photo by Meredith W. Walter

Andrew Klavan was hailed by Stephen King as "the most original novelist of crime and suspense since Cornell Woolrich." He is the recipient of two Edgar Awards and the author of such bestsellers as *True Crime* and *Don't Say a Word.*